Death Among
the Doilies

Books by Mollie Cox Bryan

The Cora Crafts Mystery series

DEATH AMONG THE DOILIES

The Cumberland Creek Mystery series

SCRAPBOOK OF SECRETS

SCRAPPED

SCRAPPY SUMMER E-Novella

DEATH OF AN IRISH DIVA

A CRAFTY CHRISTMAS

SCRAPPILY EVER AFTER E-Novella

SCRAPBOOK OF THE DEAD

Death Among the Doilies

Mollie Cox Bryan

KENSINGTON PUBLISHING CORP.
http://www.kensingtonbooks.com

KENSINGTON BOOKS are published by

Kensington Publishing Corp.
119 West 40th Street
New York, NY 10018

All Kensington Titles, Imprints, and Distributed Lines are available at special quantity discounts for bulk purchases for sales promotions, premiums, fund-raising, and educational or institutional use. Special book excerpts or customized printings can also be created to fit specific needs. For details, write or phone the office of the Kensington special sales manager: Kensington Publishing Corp., 119 West 40th Street, New York, NY 10018, attn: Special Sales Department, Phone: 1-800-221-2647.

Kensington and the K logo Reg. U.S. Pat & TM Off.

ISBN-13: 978-1-4967-0464-1
ISBN-10: 1-4967-0464-9
First Kensington Mass Market Edition: September 2016

eISBN-13: 978-1-4967-0465-8
eISBN-10: 1-4967-0465-7
First Kensington Electronic Edition: September 2016

10 9 8 7 6 5 4 3 2 1

Printed in the United States of America

Dedicated to the helpers and the crafters,
most especially to those who are both.

Acknowledgments

When the character of Cora Chevalier came to me, her voice was demanding to be heard. I fought the urge to place her in Cumberland Creek with my beloved scrapbookers. It would be easier and certainly less risky. But, after a good bit of soul searching, I thought she'd be better suited for her own series. I hope you do, as well.

I'd like to thank my readers who've come along from the Cumberland Creek Mysteries. Thanks and welcome to new readers, as well.

Also, thanks to the Waynesboro Police Department for the fingerprint inspiration and for answering my questions. I have yet to pass a fingerprint test. Sigh.

A special thanks goes to my very hardworking editor, Martin Biro, who let me speak two or three sentences about Cora before he said: "I love it. Let's run with it." Editors who know the correct of use semicolons and commas are a dime a dozen. But editors with imagination and vision (along with all that other stuff) are a bit harder to come by. Thanks, Martin.

And speaking of vision, I must thank Sharon Bowers, who did not bat an eye at this newbie cookbook author who wanted to try her hand at fiction. She merely said,

"Let's see what you can do and how we can help."
Thank you, Sharon.

A great big hug goes to my beta readers: Amber
Benson, Jennifer Feller, and Rosemary Stevens. I don't
know what I'd do without you! Thank you so much!

Writing can be a lonely endeavor, but I've found the
mystery-writing community to be open and very supportive. I won't list everybody's names (because I'm
sure to forget someone), but you know who you are.
Some of you have driven miles with me, some have
stolen away with me at conferences to offer a shoulder
and advice, been my "lucky" roommates, and others
comment on my Facebook feed nearly every day. Heart-
felt gratitude to you all—as well as the countless bloggers
and reviewers who give their time and energy freely.

Last, but not least, I want to thank my family, though
I'm sure I could never thank them enough. Emma,
Tess, and Eric, I love you madly. I appreciate the time
and space you give me to follow my dreams.

In gratitude,
Mollie

Chapter 1

Did Jane just say "police station?"

"What did you say?" Cora Chevalier said, then typed on her laptop: *Every detail—from the mundane cleaning of the chestnut floors and ordering of broom straw and beeswax, to crafting centerpieces and designing class curriculums—has been attended to.*

No wait—attended to? Was that right?

."Cora!" Jane said, bringing her attention back to the voice on the phone.

"I'm sorry, Jane," Cora said, turning away from her computer. "Writing about our first craft retreat takes more focus than blogging about crafting paper lanterns or making bird feeders out of old teacups and saucers. I'm in the zone. But you have my full attention now. Did you say you're at the police station?"

"Yes. Please pick up London from school. We'll talk about this later," Jane said, with exasperation in her voice. Cora's best friend throughout childhood, and now her partner in a new business, Jane and her daughter lived in the carriage house on the property.

"But wait—" Cora said, but Jane was already gone.

Cora pictured her sophisticated-looking, long-legged friend sitting at the police station, surrounded by Barney Fife types. A totally unfounded image, of course; she'd never even seen a police officer in her new hometown. They now lived in North Carolina, which was also where the fictional Mayberry was located, but Indigo Gap was no Mayberry.

Why was Jane at the police station? What was going on? It was odd that she couldn't get away to pick up her daughter from school. Why wouldn't the police allow her to pick up London?

Cora pressed SAVE on her blog post, glanced at the clock on her computer, and realized she'd need to hurry if she was going to fetch London. She dreaded going inside the school. Because she wasn't an actual parent, she wasn't allowed to collect her from the car. For being in such a small town, the school was extremely concerned about security. Maybe it had something to do with the recent suspicious death of the school librarian.

Cora left her attic apartment, which also housed her makeshift office, and walked down the narrow half flight of stairs to the third story. The door opened to a wide hallway. Four bedrooms, already prepared for the guests, were located here. The lemon scent of polish tickled Cora's nose as she took in the gleaming chestnut floors before descending the next flight to the second floor, also shiny and smelling clean and fresh. She moseyed down the half flight to the landing before the main story, where she always paused to take in the stained-glass window, its colors vibrant or soft depending on the time of day. Crimson, gold, and shades of blue glass pieces formed an image of Brigid, goddess or saint.

After moving into her new home, Cora had done some research on both the history of the house and St. Brigid and discovered that Brigid was a goddess in ancient Ireland. She was the goddess of poetry, fire, the hearth, and crafts, an appropriate deity for a craft retreat. Through the centuries in Ireland, the myth later became tangled with stories of the abbess and much later, the saint. These stories became so enmeshed that it was difficult to tell the Brigids apart.

Cora loved to muse about Brigid and thought of her as her patron goddess. The original owners of the house must also have had a strong connection to Brigid, as they had immigrated from Kildare, Ireland, where St. Brigid's Cathedral still sat.

Cora ambled down the rest of the stairs to face a mess in the foyer. She was knee-deep in a shipment of broom straw, which she navigated her way around. Their first guest teacher, Jude Sawyer, an award-winning broom maker, hand selected and ordered the straw for the upcoming weekend retreat.

Now, where had she left her purse? Cora worked her way around the boxes and moved toward the kitchen, which was in the back of the house and where she usually left her purse.

Ah-ha! She spotted it on the kitchen counter. She grabbed her crocheted bag and turned to leave, running smack into Ruby, the woman who came with the house. Literally. She was grandfathered into the mortgage. She'd lived in the gardener's cottage for years and wanted to stay. Luckily for Cora and Jane, she was a gifted herbalist and fit right in with their plans for the old place.

"Oops!" Cora said, dropping her purse and bending over to get it.

"Where are you off to in such a hurry?" Ruby said, sounding accusatory.

"I'm off to pick up London. Something's come up with Jane." Cora was again thinking of Jane at the police station—she wanted to laugh the image off, but ominous feelings tugged at her.

What the heck was Jane doing there? Where was the police station, anyway? Cora had witnessed much of Jane's troubled past and hoped this incident was not a harbinger of more trouble heading her way.

"Okay. I need to talk with you," Ruby said, following Cora to the door.

"Sure," Cora said. "But can it wait until I get back?"

"I suppose. It's about the beeswax shipment. They sent me the wrong stuff."

"Great." Cora sighed as she slid in her car. "Just what we need. We'll take care of it later."

Ruby stood with hands on her hips, shaking her head as she watched Cora drive off.

"Take a deep breath, girl," Cora told herself. She'd smooth things over with Ruby after she picked up London. Ruby, a slightly stooped white-haired woman of a certain age, used specific suppliers for her herbal crafts. But if Cora was going to pay for them, she thought she should get a say in it. Simply one of the little hiccups in establishing a new business, Cora told herself. There had been plenty—and she expected more.

Getting the place in shape and up to code had been

a challenge, but things were finally coming together. The paper-craft room was almost finished. The fiber-arts room still needed a lot more work. And her first three-day retreat was scheduled to start Thursday night with a welcome reception. Classes were to be led by Cora herself, a guest teacher, and Ruby. Nine women registered to stay, plus three locals signed up for the classes. Cora couldn't have been more pleased with the number. Oh sure, they could take more crafters, but for their first retreat, nine was manageable.

Cora parked the car in the school lot, and noted the snaking line of cars full of harried parents. She was impressed with herself, as she'd reached the school a few minutes early. Cora had been to the school before and knew the earlier she arrived, the better. She walked into the office and was met by a well-coiffed reception-ist. "Can I help you?" the woman asked.

"I'm here to pick up London Starr."

"Are you on her approved list?" She gazed at Cora over the top of her glasses.

"I think so," Cora said. Something about the woman's tone made her self-conscious. Her perfectly made-up face and hot-pink nails tapping impatiently on the desk didn't help matters.

Cora tried to remember if she'd even brushed her hair today. At least she had gotten dressed earlier than usual because of the expected deliveries. She wore her favorite 1970s vintage blue baby-doll dress with leggings and red tennis shoes. Nothing wrong with what she was wearing, yet this woman spewed bad vibes. Was it Cora's unruly red hair? She ran her fingers through her bangs and tucked a few strands behind her ear.

"Name?" said the receptionist.

"Cora Chevalier."

"Yes, Ms. Chevalier. You are on the list," the receptionist said, after checking her computer files.

Cora stood a little straighter, now that she'd met with official approval.

"Ms. Teal?" the receptionist said into the phone. "Please send London Starr to the front office. She'll be right down," she said to Cora and went back to her work on the computer.

Cora shifted her weight, looked at the clock, and folded her hands together in front of her. The office behind the receptionist buzzed with end-of-school-day activity. Phones were blaring, backpacks were handed over, and weary office workers glanced at the clock.

Soon the door flung open and there stood London, holding Ms. Teal's hand. When she spotted Cora, the girl ran toward her.

"Cora!" she said and hugged her, but then immediately asked, "Where's Mommy?"

Cora was just about to blurt out the news when she realized that everybody in the little school office was within hearing range. Best not to say, *Your mom's at the police station.*

She reached for London's hand. "Let's go, sweetie. We'll talk in the car."

Chapter 2

Indigo Gap was exactly the kind of small town Cora dreamed about moving to when she envisioned a major change in her life. Time had almost forgotten Indigo Gap. Located in the mountains of western North Carolina, it had been bypassed by major transportation systems—like railways, highways, and so on. While the town had moved forward with some things—like electricity and plumbing, thank goodness—many of the original streets and much architecture from its founding days in the early 1800s still existed. Even a few of the stone streets had been left alone—now closed off to cars, but not to pedestrians. As Cora drove toward her new home on the other side of town from the school, she reminded herself that though this place was perfect for her new life, it was a small town and she certainly didn't want the rumor mill cranking about Jane being at the police station. That's all she needed.

One bad incident could mean disaster for her new business—and for those who took a chance with her.

London had forgotten her earlier question about

her mother and did nothing but sing to the Stevie Nicks track playing in the car. Cora smiled, approving of the child's good taste in music. Cora adored London's singing—the unbridled, off-key gusto that only a five-year-old offered.

Jane was still not home when Cora and London arrived. London hopped out of the car with her *Frozen* backpack sliding off her shoulders, the blue of the bag almost matching the girl's eyes.

"Why don't we go into the kitchen and get you a snack?" Cora said.

"Do you have any of those peanut butter cookies?" London glanced at Cora, and then she twirled down the back sidewalk.

The cookies London wanted were not cookies at all but rather Cora's special peanut butter-oatmeal protein balls. The protein balls offered no added sugar and were full of vitamins and protein. What London didn't know wouldn't hurt her, Cora mused. The two of them walked around to the back of the large Victorian home. Cora pushed open the iron gate, which was original to the property, and sauntered down the flagstone sidewalk and up the stairs to the back door of the screened-in porch. London led the way—or rather skipped and danced the way, singing her own tune.

"What did you learn in school today?" Cora said, opening the back door.

"I met the new librarian. The old one died, you know, so we had to get a new one," London said, flinging her backpack onto a kitchen chair.

"What's the new one like?" Cora asked, reaching into the fridge to get the "cookies."

London started to reply, but was interrupted by the doorbell.

"I'll be back," Cora said. Was she expecting another delivery? She didn't remember. She thought she had everything she needed by this point.

She headed down the chestnut-floored hallway to the front door. The floors alone had almost convinced her to buy the house when she had first toured the place. The inspector said that because of all the chestnut used in the house, it would be the last place standing in town if a disaster ever occurred.

She opened the door to find the caterer for the retreat. *Uh-oh.* She had forgotten about their meeting. "Hi, Ms. Day, come in. Please excuse the boxes. I just got in a shipment of broom straw."

"No problem, Cora. It won't take long to go over and finalize these menus," Darla Day said. She was a young woman with a crisp and clean look, with a personality to suit. She wore a light blue oxford shirt, tiny pearl earrings, and a gold chain with a heart-shaped locket.

"I was hoping Jane would be here, but I'm afraid she's indisposed," Cora said. *At the police station.* "In fact, her five-year-old is in the kitchen. I need to check in on her and I'll be right with you. Please take a seat in the sitting room," she said, gesturing to the room she had taken such pride in furnishing with overstuffed chairs and couches, big pillows on the floor and around the fireplace, and the arts and crafts made by herself or other generous crafters. The Moroccan-tiled mosaic table was a gift from one of the women in the shelter. A lush chocolate-colored macramé wall hanging hung over the fireplace. Hand-loomed earth-toned rugs were scattered through the room. When Cora mentioned her dream of opening a craft retreat, crafters donated their work—she never asked. Somehow, the room came together as a sort of upscale shabby-chic space that beckoned with warmth and cozy ambience.

"London?" Cora called as she entered the kitchen.

London peeked up over her picture book. "It's a good story, Cora." The child didn't want to be bothered.

"I'll read it later but now I have a meeting in the sitting room. Do you want to come in there with me?"

London's eyebrows lifted as if to say, "I'm reading, why don't you leave me alone?" This was a child who had never been treated like a child. As much as Cora loved Jane, she felt Jane had always expected a bit too much from her daughter.

"Or will you be okay here?" Cora asked.

"I'm good," London said, and popped another protein ball into her mouth.

Well, okay, then.

Cora left her alone, went into the other room, and sat down next to the caterer on the big velvet sofa. "Now, what do you have for me to review?"

"Local wine and cheese for the opening reception," Darla said, and presented her with an itemized list and a contract to sign.

After reading everything over, Cora signed her name, trying not to let the cost give her heart palpitations. They were not set up to cook and serve food to large groups of people—yet. The kitchen left a lot to be desired. The retreat fee included a welcome reception, plus three lavish brunches. On the last night, they scheduled a dessert party. Cora hoped this arrangement placed her in good stead with some other local cafés and restaurants. Her guests would be venturing out for their own meals from time to time, even though she planned enough food for the brunches that they could possibly snack on the rest of the day. Snacks were important to creativity.

"We're getting as much local produce in for your brunches as we can. But what about the dessert party? Do you want to go with a chocolate theme or a seasonal theme—apple pie, pumpkin pie, and so on?" she asked. When Darla said *chocolate,* a youthful expression came over her face. Cora then wondered if Darla was younger than her first impression implied.

Cora thought a moment about her dessert choices. Her first inclination was always chocolate. But the retreat was advertised as a fall harvest and Halloween retreat. "Will we have plenty of apple and pumpkin food otherwise?"

Darla nodded. "Chocolate then?"

Cora couldn't resist. Her French roots made chocolate a necessity to her life. At least that's what she told herself.

A commotion erupted in the kitchen, and Jane's voice came trailing down the hall.

"You didn't need to worry about me, sweetie, I was just at the police station being fingerprinted," Jane said as she entered the room, with London in tow.

Darla lifted an eyebrow as she caught Cora's eye.

"Jane," Cora said. "I'm so glad you were able to make it. This is Ms. Day, the caterer for our retreat."

Jane held out her hand. "Nice to meet you," she stammered.

Darla nodded. "Well, actually, I think we are about done here." She stood, shook Jane's hand, never making eye contact, then immediately began gathering her things and shoving them into her bags. "We'll see you Thursday. Call me if there's anything you need before then," she said.

"Okay," Cora managed to say before Darla hightailed it out the door.

A flummoxed Cora turned toward an equally confused Jane.

"Was it something I said?"

Chapter 3

Later, after London was asleep, Cora and Jane sat in the studio of the carriage house, shared some wine, and chatted about the day. Eager to know the details about Jane's visit with the local law officers, Cora accepted Jane's invitation without argument.

"You've done so much work on your place. It's coming along," Cora said, taking in the old house that had been almost uninhabitable when the two of them found the property. London and Jane made their home upstairs, which had been refurbished into a two-bedroom apartment with a small kitchen and bathroom.

"It's perfect for us," Jane had said. "You know I love you, but I don't want to live in the same space with you," she had joked.

Which was fine with Cora. She cherished her attic apartment in the big house. It offered plenty of room for her and her cat, Luna. The property came with several outbuildings, and Jane was enamored with the carriage house from the start. The place oozed charm, with its sloping, pointy roof, and window seat on the top floor. The upper level jutted out, which provided a quaint overhang, enough for a bit of a front patio, with columns on each side and gingerbread railings posted into the ground. The large front double doors were solid wood and easily fitted with modern locks. With the carriage house freshly painted in colors approved by the historical commission, it resembled a fairy-tale cottage.

"So, why were you at the station?" Cora asked.

"It was not a big deal, really," Jane said. "My fingerprints were taken because of my volunteer work at the school. They want all substitutes and volunteers to be fingerprinted now. As a parent, I think it's a good idea."

"But I thought you already had that done," Cora said.

Jane sipped her wine, then nodded. "Yes, but there was a problem with them. They smeared or something. So this time I had them done on the computer. They came out much better. But according to the computer I still failed. Something about the ridges in my fingers being too smooth? But the officer said he'd explain it to the head honcho at school. So I should be cleared to keep volunteering, even with my lack of a clear fingerprint."

"Whew," Cora said.

"You didn't think I was in trouble, did you?" Jane leaned forward, her long dark hair falling across her shoulder.

"Not like that," Cora said. "I was worried about . . ."

"Neil," she finished for Cora.

Cora nodded reluctantly. Neil was Jane's ex-husband and London's father. He was a violent man whom Jane and London had been lucky to escape.

"Don't worry about him," Jane said. "Seriously." Her almond-shaped dark blue eyes looked sincere. "He's out of our lives for good."

But she had said that at least twice before. Once, when she first came to Cora for a place to stay. Then, last year after she had gone back to him—for the last time. Cora understood it as textbook behavior, but that didn't make it easier to witness in anybody, but especially her best friend.

And people wondered why Cora was reluctant to date. As a counselor at a women's shelter, she had seen it all. And what she saw was not good.

"You know what you have to worry about?" Jane said. "Besides the fact that we are going to have a bunch of people traipsing around here in a few days?"

"What's that?" Cora leaned back into the couch cushions, glancing at the pottery placed methodically throughout the room. The first floor of the house would be a shop someday soon, with the kiln and studio in the back. She was beginning to see it. Who knew an old carriage house could hold such possibilities?

"The new librarian at the school," Jane said with a wide grin on her face.

"What? Why?"

"He's hot and exactly your type."

"What's that supposed to mean? I have a type?"

"Eh, you know, bookish. He wears these nerdy glasses, has dimples to die for, and these eyes that are like, um, I don't know, jade green, or something. I thought about you immediately," Jane said.

Cora couldn't help but grin. As if she had time to date. "That's hilarious. You know what my life is like." Blogging, crafting, getting the house ready, organizing retreats, and so on—Cora barely had time to sleep, let alone have a social life.

"Yeah, you're busy right now. But once things get going and you can hire more people, you can make time for a guy. C'mon. You're thirty-two years old. Live a little, girl. It's time to move on."

Cora knew exactly what Jane was leading up to—or rather *who* she was leading up to. But Cora certainly didn't want to talk about Dante. It didn't help. Not now.

"Let's hope the shop is up by Christmas," Cora said after a few seconds, deliberately changing the subject. "You could sell a lot of pottery. Maybe I'll have something to sell by then, too."

"I know you're changing the subject. But whatever. I'm telling you there's a librarian with your name all over his book-loving, luscious body. It's up to you what you do with that information," Jane said with a twisted grin.

"With that, I'm going to call it a night," Cora replied. "Now that you've got my love life figured out, what else is there?"

Jane laughed—a rippling, musical, girlish laugh. Jane was a woman who only laughed when she meant it.

"Let's get to those boxes first thing in the morning. We can unpack and get the room set up. How's that sound?" Cora asked.

But Jane's answer was interrupted by a knock at the door. "Who could that be?" she said.

Cora opened the door to see Ruby, standing with her hands on her hips.

"Did you forget about me?" Ruby said. Her jaw was clenched.

"No, I thought we'd chat in the morning. I was just

leaving. I'm so tired," Cora said. "Would you like to come over for breakfast? Both of you? I'll make a big breakfast, we can go over some details, and get those boxes unpacked."

Ruby's stance softened a bit. "That sounds good. I'll see you in the morning, then."

As Ruby and Cora started to leave, two police officers walked down the path toward the carriage house.

"Is this where Jane Starr lives?" one of the officers asked as they approached.

"Of course," Cora said. Ruby stood back, silent.

Jane poked her head out of her house. "Can I help you?" she said to the officers.

"We need you to come to the station with us," one of them said.

"What? There must be some mistake. I was just there this afternoon," Jane said.

The other officer stepped forward. "I'm sorry, Ms. Starr. We've been sent to bring you in for questioning for the murder of Sarah Waters."

"The school librarian?" Ruby blurted out.

"What?" Cora said. "There must be some mistake."

"No, ma'am," the officer said, and he turned to Jane.

"Jane?" Cora said, as if she might have an explanation.

"I don't know what's going on here!" Jane said, quietly, but forcefully.

"I'll come with you," Cora said.

"No, stay with London," Jane ordered, her dark eyes wide.

Cora reached out and grabbed Jane's hand. "I won't leave you."

Jane's face tightened with terror. How could she let Jane go alone to the police station?

Ruby stepped in and rescued them. "I'll stay with London. And I'll call my son."

"Your son?" Cora said. "Why?"

"He'll meet you at the station. He's a lawyer. Don't say a word to these guys until you've talked to my Cashel," Ruby commanded.

Chapter 4

Cora had driven by the police station every day and had not even realized it. The station's facade fit in with the rest of Indigo Gap, with its strict rules about the businesses and homes in its historic district. So the outside of the building was an elegant eggplant, trimmed in soft yellow, and the main waiting area reflected the outer decor.

Cora thought it the prettiest station she'd ever seen—and she'd seen quite a few, unfortunately. When she worked as a counselor in the women's shelter, she used to say that the police station was her second home. The first, of course, being the shelter itself. She rarely even slept at her own apartment—she bunked on a cot in the storage room of the shelter, which she cleaned off before she could lie down and catch a few hours of sleep. Rarely even four hours, let alone the full eight her doctor prescribed.

This began the somewhat crooked path to her starting a new life. Or starting *a* life, actually. Before, she never had the time to read a whole book, see a complete movie, or sometimes even to eat an entire meal. Which set her up perfectly for a severe panic disorder. Her condition had gotten so bad by the end of her counseling career that her doctors practically ordered her to quit.

Now, Cora and Jane sat in the sparse but comfortable room in the police station, waiting on Cashel O'Malley.

"I don't understand this," Jane said. "What have I done to make them think I killed someone?" Her voice quivered and her blue eyes widened.

"I'm sure there's been some kind of mistake," Cora said with confidence. Of course this was all a terrible mistake.

"But what if—" Jane began.

"Shhh," Cora said. "Don't even think it."

Cora could hardly bear to look her in the eye—Jane's fear was so raw that it was difficult to witness. She'd seen dread in her eyes before—and with good reason. Jane had a record. Cora had been by her side in court several times.

Cora looked around the room. One table. Four chairs, two of which they were sitting on. Nothing on the gray walls. Plain but clean. It wouldn't hurt them to spruce up the place with some prints or other framed art.

When the door opened, both Cora and Jane jumped. Cashel O'Malley entered the room with a confident stride and a bit of a swagger. Handsome, downright hot; he could have stepped off the pages of *GQ* magazine, with those piercing, intense blue eyes, a strong jawline, and a dimple in his chin.

This man was Ruby's son? He was so sophisticated and well-groomed—exactly the opposite of earthy Ruby. Cora admired her lack of pretense; she was a woman who probably never even wore lipstick, let alone got a manicure.

"Which one of you lovely ladies is Jane?" he asked.

Jane blushed at the mention of her name, and Cora's tongue would not move, but she managed to point at Jane.

"I'm Cashel O'Malley." He held out his hand to Jane. "Your attorney." She reached out her hand and they shook, and then he took Cora's hand as well.

Cora's eyes wandered along the ridges of his perfectly sculpted face and then to his eyes. *Zing!* The prettiest blue eyes she'd ever seen. In fact, he may have been the prettiest man she'd ever seen. *Focus,* she told herself, *Jane may be in serious trouble here.*

"So let's get right to it, shall we?" Cashel said. "The police will send someone in to take your official statement, but we have a few minutes to chat." He pulled out his laptop and set it on the table.

"I need to know what you were doing the night of Sarah Waters' death," he said point-blank, as he clicked on his computer.

"I, uh . . ." Jane stammered.

"It's very important I know where you were and what you were doing on August 23."

"I think I was at home," she said.

"You think?"

Cora's thoughts raced. The twenty-third? Where had she been? Could she answer that question if it were asked of her? She'd have to check in her journal or on her phone. Who knew off the top of her head where she was on any given day? Jane apparently felt the same.

"I can't remember," she said. "I assume it was like any

day. I was probably working at my home. I was probably still unpacking. We'd just moved here."

Cora mentally sifted through dates and times. They'd moved to Indigo Gap about a month before the librarian's death two weeks ago. Cora, Jane, and London spent months in the Lucky Bee hotel, on the outskirts of town, while they worked on getting the house ready. So it was likely Jane had been unpacking then—in truth, Cora was *still* unpacking.

"Can you prove it?" Cashel asked.

Jane shrugged. "I don't know. How would I do that?" Her fingers twitched on the table in front of her.

"Did someone see you?"

"Not if I was in my house. Well, there is London, my little girl," Jane replied. Fingers still twitching, she folded her hands together.

Cashel nodded. "So your alibi is you were home with your daughter and your daughter is the only one who knows that?" He talked with a succinct, fast cadence. He wasted no time.

"I'm sure I would have known if they were gone— as would your mother," Cora offered, but she was uncertain about the exact date. "The houses are all close together and we keep close track of one another."

"Yes, but can you say that you saw her that night, specifically?" he asked.

Cora clamped her own hands tightly on her lap, and they started to ache from the clenching. "I need to check my journal and my blog and so on to see if there's a mention of what we did that day. But I'm fairly certain I could testify as to her whereabouts."

Cashel gave Cora an appreciative sweep with his eyes.

He grinned. "You won't need to testify. At least I hope not. I hope there won't be any charges at all."

"Why do they suspect me?" Jane asked.

"When they entered your fingerprints in the system, they matched some of the prints that they found at the murder scene."

"How can that be?" Cora asked, indignant, frightened, and confused all at once. She felt sweat pricking at her forehead. *Great.*

"Don't panic," Cashel said. "The prints are only half prints and Jane's prints are slight. So they will be calling in fingerprint experts. If you're not guilty, you've nothing to worry about."

"There's a problem with my prints," Jane said, her eyes shifting back and forth. "I know that. That's why they called me back for a second round of fingerprinting so I could volunteer at the school."

"You're a potter, correct?" Cashel said, glancing at Jane's hands. Cora loved Jane's hands; they were a working woman's hands, with clean, short nails and long fingers, the sinews and tendons visible.

Jane's gaze steadied as her eyes met his, and she nodded.

"That's why they will never be able to convict you on your prints alone. Your prints are, in all likelihood, just not that deep from all the clay work you do."

Cora started to feel relieved.

"But let me be clear," Cashel continued. "This could get serious if you can't come up with a sound alibi. The town is crying for a conviction. I've seen people get convicted on less evidence."

Cora felt her breath stop.

"With your background and this wee bit of evidence . . .

it could get bad. So our work is cut out for us," Cashel concluded.

"You know about—" Jane began to say.

"Of course," he said. "My assistant pulled up your files when I received the call."

"That was self-defense," Cora said with a note of belligerence in her voice.

"Of course it was. But she was charged with attempted murder. I know the charges were dropped and she had a sound alibi, with the history of abuse so well-documented," he said.

"Then they can't use that against her," Cora said.

"They sure as hell can try," Cashel replied. He glanced at Cora and then back to Jane and softened his expression. "But that's what I'm here for."

Chapter 5

"I'm so sorry about all this," Jane said to Cora in the car on the way back to the house. Her voice was strained with weariness and fear.

"It's not your fault," Cora said.

"I know, but my background complicates things. Starting over wasn't a good idea for me. I'll never be able to put it all behind me," Jane said, her voice cracking.

Cora's stomached fluttered. "But you already have," she said. "This is a minor blip." Cora had worked to persuade Jane into this venture. A gifted potter, Jane added plenty to the craft retreat's offerings.

They sat silently, with the hum of the car engine and the radio station blaring the news of the day.

"Let's hope word doesn't get out about all this. You know what small towns are like," Jane said. "We have a business now and reputation is everything."

Cora had been thinking similar thoughts. "Well, let's keep it on the down low. Nobody needs to know anything, right? You weren't charged."

"Yes, but I'm still a person of interest."

Cora pulled the car into the drive and parked it. "Let's keep doing our best with the retreat. Let's just focus on what's in front of us and not get carried away."

They both were still slammed with preparing for Thursday's opening. At least the menu was settled. The cleaning seemingly never ended. Boxes of broom straw still needed to be unpacked and put away, and the paper-crafting room still needed sorting. Crafters would be here in three days.

If she managed to pull it all off in time, this business would be a dream come true for Cora.

She watched Jane walk down the garden path to the carriage house. Jane's normally proud, confident gait had turned into a wilting trudge.

"Good night," Jane turned and said.

"Good night."

Cora stopped before entering the main house and gazed at the autumn night sky. She made a wish that nobody would find out her friend was a person of interest for the murder of the school librarian. Even as she thought about it, she marveled at the absurdity of the situation. Jane had come a long way since she had tried to kill Neil.

Cora remembered the first day Jane walked into the Sunny Street Women's Shelter. They were friends as girls, growing up together in Pittsburgh, then lost track of one another when Cora went to college. But out of the blue, her drop-dead gorgeous long-lost friend appeared at the shelter. But she was dejected, standing in the lobby, seeking help.

That look of dejection and shame was a familiar one

to Cora by then, and it tore her up to see Jane in such a condition.

That was the beginning of the end of Cora's counseling career. By that point, she had started her blog—"Cora Crafts a Life." Not a moneymaker back then, but the blog was a creative and therapeutic outlet for her. She blogged about her life as a counselor and a crafter. She wrote stories about the women in her shelter life. The abused women who found solace in a craft, whether it was knitting, needlepoint, or scrapbooking, inspired her. Soon, her blog was earning more money than her counseling. She realized her doctors were right—writing and crafting helped to prevent her panic attacks. But not quite enough.

So she began to envision a craft retreat.

She searched several months to find the right place and the right investors. But here she was, now, climbing a flight of stairs in an old Victorian almost mansion, where she lived in the attic with Luna. In a few days, a group of crafters would be filling the place. A broom maker would be teaching a class, Ruby would be teaching candle making, and, the way Cora envisioned it, some women would be drawn into the paper-crafting room, others into the almost-finished fiber-arts room. They were still working on the alcove that had been marked for upcycling—a "craft" that Cora adored. She loved this craft of turning ordinary objects into pieces of art, or into something new and useful. She'd found a box of burlap sacks in the basement and planned to use them in her class, making decorative pumpkins out of them.

Cora made plans upon plans and made a wish as she

slid into her bed that night, with Luna curled up beside her, that this small town would be unlike the stereotypical ones where gossip spread quickly, and tomorrow nobody would know about Jane's adventure at the police station. So much hinged on this first retreat. Cora had sunk every bit of her savings into it, plus got a few investors, like her great-uncle Jon and his new wife Beatrice. She didn't want to disappoint him—nor did she herself want to go broke. In truth, she already teetered on the edge of financial ruin.

The next morning, Ruby, Jane, and London all gathered in Cora's kitchen.

"Who wants chocolate chips in their pancakes?" Cora asked.

"I do!" London squealed.

"Me, too," Jane said.

"Well, of course, I do, too," Ruby grumbled and poured herself a cup of coffee.

Ruby was a bit moody at times, but she fit right in with the craft-retreat plans. She had been earning a living as an herbalist and was hired by the previous owners of Kildare House to tend to the gardens. Her agreement with them, made about twenty-five years ago, was that she lived rent-free while working there, which was important since her husband had died and left her penniless—with a child to raise—which is something Jane could certainly relate to, as a single mother.

"So the plan of attack this morning is to get those boxes unpacked and—" Cora began before Ruby cut her off.

"I need you to check out this wax. It's not what I ordered. Is there time for us to return it?" Ruby asked.

"I'll confirm their return policy," Cora said. "But we can figure out something."

"I wanted sheets of beeswax for one of the projects. Some very simple rolling up of the sheets with a wick inside will give you a fun, easy candle. Some folks don't want to get involved in the more complex candle making," Ruby said.

"I love the ones you made with the herbs and wild-flowers in them," Jane said.

"Thank you. Those are my biggest sellers. But only three people signed up for that class. But that's okay with me. I like a small class," Ruby replied.

Soon the room smelled of coffee, chocolate, and pancakes. The conversation was light and business oriented. As long as London fluttered about, it was as if all the women had made an unspoken agreement to not talk about last night's events with the police.

Jane's cell phone rang and she answered it, getting up from the table and moving to another part of the room. Jane returned to the table with an air of annoyance.

"Finish up, London, we need to get going. Don't want to be late," she said.

"Everything okay?" Cora asked.

"Oh yeah, sure," Jane said with a forced, fake lightness in her voice. She was fuming and trying to hide it. Cora knew her friend too well. "The school found another volunteer for tomorrow. They knew I'd be busy here with the opening and so on."

"Yes, I'm sure that's it," Ruby said, with a note of sarcasm.

London's head tilted in curiosity.

"Let's go," her mother said, grabbing London's hand and leaving the room.

After Jane and London abruptly exited, Ruby helped Cora clear the dishes. "So how did it go last night?" she asked.

Cora shrugged. "It's hard to say. She's not charged with anything, thanks to Cashel."

At the mention of her son's name, Ruby beamed. *That doesn't happen too often,* Cora thought.

She didn't quite get Ruby. Not yet.

"He's a good boy," Ruby said, stacking dishes in the sink.

He didn't look like a boy to me, Cora thought. No, Cashel O'Malley may have still had a boyish, impish grin, but she bet the rest of him was all man.

"And he's got good perspective. I raised him right, you know. He knows the score," Ruby continued, pulling Cora away from her thoughts.

"The score?" Cora said.

"Yeah. Never trust a cop. Especially the ones in Indigo Gap," Ruby said.

At first Cora thought she was teasing, and started to laugh. But when she noticed the expression in Ruby's eyes, she knew the woman was dead serious.

Chapter 6

"What's wrong, Mommy?" London said, after Jane buckled her into her car seat.

"Nothing, other than it's seven-thirty am and you know I how feel about that," Jane said, trying to keep it light. She didn't want to worry London. The child had had enough worries in her five years of life.

"I know," London said. "I know you hate being up this early."

Jane leaned in and kissed her daughter—one of the few people who mattered to her in this world. She was bound and determined to give her a good life—inasmuch as any mother could.

Last night, she had been hopeful that Cashel had tamped out any negative effects from this murder suspect business. But the phone call from the school principal led her to believe otherwise.

She pulled out of the driveway and turned onto the street, then flipped the radio on and London started to sing. Jane only half listened.

"I like this song, Mommy," London said.

"I do, too, sweetie." Light and breezy. When she

arrived back at the carriage house, she'd have a good cry and then head to the main house to help unpack the boxes.

She felt in her gut that the principal didn't want her help this week because somehow word had already spread. But how?

Schools had to be careful these days, and as a parent, Jane appreciated that. But as a person working in the schools, she thought it might be overkill.

But she wasn't even working—she was volunteering. Still, they did not want a murder suspect volunteering in the schools. They were leaping to conclusions and not even giving her a chance to defend herself. Was anybody even asking why she would want to kill Sarah Waters?

She sifted through her memories of the late school librarian. She had been sixty-ish and seemed nice enough, but was not someone Jane warmed up to. In fact, if she were to be honest, Jane didn't warm up to many people. But Sarah had been a bit stand-offish. Or maybe she was just quiet. Jane hadn't bothered to find out. As a volunteer in the school, she was kept busy cleaning desks and floors, sorting activities, and lining children up for bathroom breaks, which didn't leave much time to socialize.

"Miss Teal is so pretty," London said from the backseat, as they pulled up into the line of cars at the school. "Today, we're going to talk about the pilgrims and Native Americans."

"That sounds like fun," Jane said, wondering exactly what they would be teaching London about Native Americans. Jane had been told her biological mother was part Cherokee. She'd always had this romantic notion she might have been a potter, like Jane. But her adoption records were sealed. Even if they weren't, she wasn't certain she could bring herself to open that door. Her mother had given her up for a reason.

The car in front of her pulled up in the line, and she followed.

"You'll have to tell me all about it when you get home," Jane said. She loved this part of parenting, the talking about new things together. Her daughter's mind fascinated her. That she had created this kid with Neil floored her. He was such a loser, but their kid was amazing.

"Tell me the story about my name, Mommy," London said.

"It's almost our turn, London. I'll tell you later," Jane said, trying to concentrate on not hitting one of the many teacher's aides and teachers flitting around from car to car to fetch the children. No matter how orderly, the drop-off always made Jane nervous. So much could go wrong.

London wanted the story of her name repeated every day. A few times every day. Repetition seemed to comfort her. Jane would do anything for her daughter, of course, but the repetition of the same stories sometimes made her want to scream. She could recite them backward and forward now.

The story of London's name was also not something Jane necessarily wanted to think about. London was named after the city she had been conceived and born in. The city where Jane and Neil lived for a few years until everything turned sour. London had been the happiest place on earth, but then it became a nightmare of a city, as Neil began to show signs of unhappiness and violent tendencies. Jane thought it was depression and maybe a change of scenery might help. The first few months in New York City were blissful before his drug habit took over. He became violent and almost unrecognizable. She tried so hard to find him help. The few times he was clean gave her and London hope. They had some good times, but they always spun into dark times. Unfortunately, her own little London carried memories of both the good and bad times within her.

They were next in line, and Jane pulled up to the curb, put the car in park, and slid out. She opened the back door and unhooked London from her car seat.

"Do you have everything?" she asked.

London nodded. Jane quickly kissed her as an aide came to fetch the child and take her into the school.

"Good morning," Jane said to the same woman she'd seen every day for weeks. She said it automatically, politely; it was what you did when an aide collected your daughter.

Jane listened for the response, which usually came quickly and with a smile.

This time the woman only turned and glared at her before walking off, holding London's hand.

A chill came over Jane. Time seemed to hold her in place. Somehow, word must have leaked that she was a person of interest in the murder of Sarah Waters. She knew it.

The person in the car behind her gently tooted their horn, bringing her back to earth.

"Sorry," she mouthed, waving before she got into the car.

As she pulled away from the school, she no longer

wanted to go home and cry; she wanted to scream at someone. But who?

She thought about Cora and the craft retreat, their months of hard work getting the house up to code and beyond, and Cora sinking her retirement funds and her savings into the business, plus her investors' money. It was a good plan. A solid foundation. Craft retreats were popular. Cora's blog earned money and had a growing following. Jane's pottery sold well. Everything was coming together.

Now this. Could this be the unraveling of all of it?

What to do? Should she go to Cora with her worries? Or wait until she knew for sure what was going on?

She rarely kept things from Cora. But Cora was such a nervous wreck these days with the first retreat on the horizon. Jane hated to add to her woes until she knew exactly what was happening.

Her mind settled. She decided there was no point in going to Cora with nothing but a strong inkling that word had leaked out in their new small town. At least not yet.

Chapter 7

When all was said and done, the boxes were twice the size of the broom straw, all wrapped neatly in rows underneath a ridiculous amount of packing peanuts.

"Check this out!" Jane gasped, holding up some crimson broom straw. "Isn't it gorgeous?"

Cora grinned. Fresh crafting materials, plus the happy note in Jane's voice, added to her air of excitement.

Jane had been brooding since she received the phone call that morning, and she and Cora hadn't been left alone long enough for them to discuss it. What was it about the call Jane found so disturbing that it sent her into a funk for the rest of the morning?

"I like the eggplant color," Ruby said, waving straw from the box she was unpacking. "Stunning. Oh, and the crimson. Gone are the days of plain broom straw, I suppose."

"The brooms will be amazing," Cora said. She began to set baskets in a row along the wall of the main crafting hall, a wing added on to the house in 1912 and filled with floor-to-ceiling windows. Twelve women had signed up for the broom-making class—not including the three of them. Each person would get broom straw, a handle, and the tools to make their brooms. It would all be given to them in baskets made by a local basket maker. Cora had been thrilled to find out that this region of North Carolina offered a multitude of crafters.

This part of the state had a rich heritage of Appalachian craft traditions, and the quality of techniques had stayed the same throughout the years. They were handed down from elder to younger crafter, which was the best way to learn. Some of these crafters launched art careers by taking their crafting to the next level. Many of them could be found in galleries in Asheville.

The hills around Indigo Gap appeared to be scattered with older women, like Ruby, who were "wildcrafters," or herbalists. Many of these women quilted, sewed, and crocheted just as a matter of course. But they had as much pride in their workmanship as the professional artist-crafters.

"You know," Ruby said. "There's nothing like a well-made broom." She flipped her fingers through the colorful broom straw. "I inherited one of my mother's. It's in good shape, too. I'm not sure they make brooms that well anymore."

"Well, Jude Sawyer does," Cora said, starting to place straw in each of the baskets.

"Oh yes, don't I know it. So does his daddy," Ruby said.

"I hate housekeeping," Jane said, after a moment.

"But I don't mind sweeping. There's something, I don't know, meditative, about it."

"I agree. But for me, it's more than that, really," Ruby said, pulling out more straw from her box. "You can sweep away negative energy with them."

"Metaphorically speaking, of course," Cora said.

Ruby harrumphed. "You can call it whatever you want, honey."

"In any case, it's a great craft for our fall retreat, with Halloween right around the corner," Cora said.

"And the candles will be just the right touch," Jane added. "Oh damn, paper cut. Where are the Band-Aids?" She held up her bloody finger.

"In the downstairs bathroom medicine cabinet," Cora said.

"Come by my cottage later. My homemade herbal salve will soothe it," Ruby said as Jane walked off to find a Band-Aid.

Cora stood back and surveyed the filled baskets. "They should be a bit more festive," she muttered. "What else can we do to them? Ribbons? Paper flowers?"

"I don't know," Ruby said, coming up beside her, her hands on her hips. "I like them the way they are. Earthy and simple."

"Good point," Cora said, as her cell phone rang. She took a step away from Ruby as she answered the call. "Cora here, how can I help you?"

"This is Isabel Collins. Is it too late for me to cancel my registration for the broom-making class?"

"Cancel?"

"Yes. Is it too late? I'd like a refund."

Cora looked around at her baskets and sighed. "Certainly, I'll issue a refund. May I ask why you're canceling?"

"I have better things to do with my money," the other woman said in a clipped tone. And she hung up.

"What was that about?" Cora said more to herself than to Ruby, who was busy breaking down the boxes the broom straw had come in.

"What's that?" Ruby asked.

"A cancelation. Isabel Collins," Cora said, searching her cell phone for the app that would issue the refund immediately. She loved the convenience of running certain parts of her business from her phone. No clunky cash registers or receipts. It was as green and as convenient as it could get.

"Humph," Ruby said. "Good riddance to bad trash."

"What? She seemed nice enough to me. That is until . . ."

"Until what?"

"She said she has better things to do with her money. She was kind of, I don't know, cocky about it." Normally Cora hated to make snap judgments and tried not to. "Odd. She was so lovely the other day. And so enthusiastic."

Ruby made a singsong sigh sounding like "oh well." But then she said, "Maybe she was drunk."

"Who?" Jane said as she walked in. "Who is drunk?"

"Isabel Collins canceled and she was kind of rude about it," Cora said, ignoring Jane's question for the moment.

"What? That sweet lady?" Jane said.

"That sweet lady you're talking about is a drunk and I've seen her trash-talking a grown man to tears," Ruby said and smacked her hands together to brush off whatever dirt or dust the broom straw had left behind.

Jane's eyes widened as she looked at Ruby in surprise. "Really?"

Jane and Cora giggled at the thought of Isabel Collins being drunk, let alone trash-talking anybody.

"I just can't believe it," Cora said, still giggling. "I guess this town is full of surprises."

"Stick with me, kid, and I'll fill you in on everything," Ruby said.

Cora knew this was true. Ruby was a valuable asset to them, once you got past the gruff exterior. Cora and Jane glanced at one another, and Cora refrained from rolling her eyes.

"The baskets look great," Jane said, changing the subject. Jane did not like to gossip. She'd been the butt of mean-spirited gossip far too often. "Do you think they need a little something? How about some little shiny bags full of candy? Halloween is right around the corner."

Ruby shook her head and laughed.

"What's so funny?" Jane asked.

"We just discussed the baskets," Cora said. "Wondering about ribbons and paper flowers. Ruby likes them just the way they are. I agreed."

"What?" Jane looked incredulous.

Cora nodded. "It's more elegant this way. So simple, you know?"

"Whatever happened to glitter girl?" Jane grinned.

Cora started to answer. It was a stage she had gone through—every bit of her paper crafts used glitter for a few months. She was admittedly taken by glitter and all things sparkly.

"Let's hope glitter girl is gone and buried," Ruby said and then left the room.

"What's the big deal?" Cora said to Jane. "A little glitter never killed anybody."

Chapter 8

Later that same day, Jude called to check on his broom-straw shipment. The caterer then called with a few changes to the menu—again. And all of the registered locals called to cancel. Cora had no choice but to refund them. What was going on? One cancelation wasn't suspicious, but three of them? Was there another event going on that weekend in town? Cora didn't think so, but she went to her computer and searched until she found the local paper online. She had thoughtfully planned what weekend to start the retreat so local crafters would have the opportunity to take classes. The annual fall arts and crafts festival was scheduled in a few weeks. Last week the annual fall heritage tour took place. She hadn't participated, but hoped to next year.

As she searched, the name "Sarah Waters" jumped out at her. New Lead in Sarah Waters Murder. Good news. People were certainly on edge since the woman had died under suspicious circumstances, the details of which the police were keeping to themselves.

Cora clicked the article.

She skimmed the text. She blinked. No. That could not be! Jane's name appeared in the article as a person of interest! How did the reporter find out? Who had given them permission to use Jane's name?

Cora's heart thundered and her stomach tightened. Cora and Jane had chosen to move to Indigo Gap because it was so far off the radar from most of the people they had known. It was deep in the mountains and as secluded as a town could get, without being too backward. A town of artisans. A town of historians and antique collectors. They both felt comforted there, surrounded by the quaint cobblestone streets, the hills, the springs and rivers. All of it felt welcoming. Until now. Cora now felt trapped, as if everybody in town was suspecting her friend of murder.

She took a deep belly breath, trying to will off a panic attack. She could do this. She hadn't had a panic attack in over a year. No pills, not now. Air. She needed air.

Cora rose from her desk and cracked open a window. She inhaled the autumn air. The scent of earth and crisp autumn leaves filled her nose, and her lungs expanded. She closed her eyes and breathed.

One mystery was solved: the reason for the cancelations. People learned Jane was suspected of murder.

Calm down, she told herself. It was perfectly normal for her heart to race. *Breathe in, breathe out.* Normal people had racing hearts when something like this happened, right? It didn't mean it was going to escalate into the chest-crushing sensation of a panic attack.

What to do? Had Jane seen the article?

That thought filled Cora with more dread. But,

she reminded herself, Jane was no fragile flower. Not anymore.

But this could set her back. If Jane knew her name was in the paper as a person of interest, it would alarm her. Worse, it may make her want to leave town. Leave Cora and the business. Jane was integral to the plan. Cora didn't want to do it without her—in fact, she considered Jane her partner, even though she had no finances to invest. Her energy, creativity, and heart had gone into every detail of the retreat.

"Get a grip, Cora," she said out loud to herself. Most likely, Jane had not seen the article. She was not a reader. Hell, Cora loved to read, but even she barely read the local paper.

Although, obviously, the local crafters did read it.

Cora sighed, wilting into herself as she sat back down in front of her computer. What to do?

Should she call the paper? Call Cashel? Call her Uncle Jon? No, he mustn't know what a mess things were becoming. Her careful plans were becoming undone. All because Jane was ridiculously being accused of murder.

She decided to dial Cashel.

"O'Malley and DiPalma, can I help you?" a female voice said. A clipped, efficient voice.

"Um, yes, is Mr. O'Malley in?" This was a mistake. What would she even say to him? She fought the urge to hang up.

"Who may I ask is calling?"

Would he even know her by her name? They had only met briefly yesterday.

"Who may I ask is calling?" the woman on the other line asked again.

"Oh, I'm sorry. This is Cora Chevalier."

"Just a moment please," the voice said.

"Yes, Cora?" Cashel's voice came over the line. His voice was like sweet Southern honey. She imagined him sitting behind a big shiny desk. *Don't go there, Cora.* "Can I help you?"

"Have you seen today's paper?" she blurted out.

"Which paper?"

Why was he being so calm? Cora heard the shuffling of papers in the background.

"The local paper! Jane's name is in it as a person of interest in the murder case." Her voice started to quiver. *Where did that come from? Her voice never quivered!*

"Damn," he said. "I didn't see it. I've been in court all morning."

"Is there something we can do about this?"

"Do? What do you want me to do?" he asked. Again, the calmness. It was annoying.

"Get the paper to print a retraction? An apology? I don't know. You're the lawyer!" Cora tried to tamp down her hysteria. She wasn't doing a very good job of it.

She was met with silence on the other end of the phone.

"Hello?" she finally said.

"I'm here. I'm sorry. I'm trying to figure out how this reporter got a hold of the information so quickly. It is a high-profile case. Sarah Waters was a beloved citizen in this town. We've not had a murder here in at least twenty years. People are jumping the gun. The situation might be escalating," he said.

"Escalating? Our first retreat is this weekend and every one of the locals who signed up has now canceled. I'd say it's escalated. Past tense."

"It's worse than I thought," he said. "I'll be there within the hour. Please ask Jane to be there."

"Jane? I don't want her to find out." Cora said, her heartbeat starting to quicken again. If she didn't have a panic attack, it would be a minor miracle.

There was silence on the other end of the phone.

"Seriously," she said. "She doesn't need to know, does she?"

"Not precisely," Cashel said reluctantly. "But she is my client. And this is about her. Why would you want to keep it a secret?"

He might have been the hottest guy she'd laid her eyes on since moving to Indigo Gap, but he was also the most irritating.

"Can I hire you on my own? I mean, like, for my business? Like, to sue the paper for printing this ridiculous story?" Cora asked.

"No," he said flatly.

She was really beginning to dislike him.

"First of all, that's a conflict of interest for me," he said. "Secondly, Jane doesn't need that kind of protection from you or anybody. She's a capable grown woman. I know about her background, remember, I know you might want to protect her. But take it from me, she has the best protection available. She hired me."

Well, at least *he* was confident. She had to hand it to him.

"Don't forget, besides all that," Cora said, "she is innocent."

"There's that, too. Please let her know I'm coming. We'll talk then."

The phone line went dead. Now all Cora had to do was walk over to the carriage house and tell her best friend the bad news.

Chapter 9

Jane saw Cora coming and instantly recognized that something was wrong. You didn't know someone for most of your life and not know when they were upset—even when they tried to hide it. Normally Cora moved like a butterfly; she was lithe and graceful and flitted about. But when she was upset, she stiffened and her shoulders hunched, just a bit.

Jane watched Cora walk across the yard from the big house toward the carriage house. She must also now be aware that everybody in town knew Jane was a person of interest in a murder case.

The justice system, even with all its flaws, had done well by her in the past. She needed to muster faith that it would again. She inhaled the air as she opened the door.

"Jane, I have bad news," Cora said.

"I know."

"You know what?"

"People in town know about last night," she said.

Cora pushed by her friend as she entered the house.

"It's not that simple," she said. "It's not as simple as a few rumors."

Jane felt her pulse start to quicken. "What do you mean?"

"It's in the newspaper," Cora said, her shoulders hunching even more.

Jane felt the hot tears prick at her eyes. She gasped. "I didn't kill anybody."

"I know that," Cora said and wrapped her arm across her shoulders, leading her to the couch and gently sitting her down. "Cashel is coming over and we're going to meet about it."

"But what could I possibly do about this now?" Jane said, with some effort. Her thoughts were jumbled. "What can we do about it?"

"I don't know. Hopefully Cashel will have some advice for us. I wanted to sue the paper for printing it, but I guess since it's the truth, well, I wouldn't have much of a case. What did you mean about the rumors?"

Jane told her about the school and what happened with the aide who helped London that morning.

"Maybe she was just having a bad day?" Cora said, with hope.

"No, I don't think so," Jane said. Sweat prickled at her forehead, which always happened when she was upset. "Word does get around in a small town."

"That quickly? It's almost as if someone couldn't wait for something like this to happen, you know? Like someone was watching us, waiting for one bad move," Cora said. Her eyebrows gathered into a V.

"That sounds kind of paranoid," Jane said, but found herself grinning. Even in the most heated situation, Cora tickled her. "But it's typical of you."

"I'm sure this will blow over," Cora said. "It's just bad timing. All the local registrants have canceled."

"What?"

Cora nodded. This first weekend retreat meant so much for them both. "How about the others?" she managed to ask.

"I've not heard anything from them yet," Cora said. "I doubt it will affect them at all. And it's going to be fine. We'll be fine with the other crafters. Having locals at the classes was just a bonus."

She sounded more like she was trying to convince herself than Jane.

"But our reputation is everything. I'm afraid this is going to spiral out of control," Jane said. What had made her think her new life would be easier than her old one? What made her think anything in her life would be smooth and go right? Nothing up to this point should have led her to believe it.

A life of art. That is all she had ever wanted. To make pottery. It made her happy; more than happy. This life was what Cora wanted, too. She wanted Jane to continue making her pottery. Teaching it to others.

The business was the cornerstone of it all. A way forward, where she'd not be pulled back with regret and sink into the mistakes of the past. A way forward for her, London, and Cora.

How had this happened?

"Jane? You've got that one-hundred-yard stare going on."

"Hmm," she said. "I was just thinking."

"And?"

"I was thinking this situation has got to blow over and we're going to be okay," Jane said, meeting Cora's worried eyes. "It's going to be fine. We've come so far already, right?"

"Well, that's true enough," Cora said. Her shoulders were still slightly hunched, but less so than when she first walked across the yard. "Are you ready for the meeting?"

Jane wiped the tears that had formed under her eye with her finger. "Yeah, sure."

Cora stood. "At least we can gaze upon the beauty of Cashel O'Malley."

"What?" Jane exclaimed. "You are not serious. If you want a man, I told you about that librarian guy. That's your man. Don't be messing with Ruby's son. What's wrong with you?"

Cora laughed. "You know, I hadn't thought about it like that. But you're right. Talk about possible complications! That's too bad because, wow, Cashel is hot."

Cora opened the door and there he stood. Cashel O'Malley in all his glory.

"Um," Cora said, her face reddening. Had he heard what she said? He didn't appear flummoxed. He was cool, calm, and collected. Unlike herself and Jane. If he had heard her, he was not affected by it—as if it were something he'd taken as a matter of course.

"I thought the meeting might be better here," he responded, peeking around Cora to Jane, who was standing behind her. "Is that okay?"

"Of course," Jane said, a polite smile on her face.

Jane's own face flushed as she fought the impulse to run into the bathroom, or upstairs, or anywhere far from Cashel. Cora's frankness had sometimes placed her in embarrassing situations. Like this one.

"Come in. Don't mind Cora. She's a little upset. Well, we both are," she said, leading him toward the couch.

Cora sat in a nearby chair and would not look at Jane, now. And Jane knew if she looked in Cora's direction, it would be over. No eye contact. Sometimes they acted just like they had in high school. Which is what happened when you grew up too fast. In some ways, you never got over it.

Chapter 10

"Damage control is different than providing a good defense for you," Cashel said, after they settled in. "I'm no expert in public relations. I'm a lawyer. Believe me, you have no case against the paper. I have asked the judge for a gag order though. We'll see how that flies. The paper, of course, has first-amendment rights to protect it. Even with the gag order, it can print information about the case, just not interviews and follow-up and so on."

"I haven't heard from the media—have you, Jane?" Cora asked.

"No."

"My advice is if they call, don't speak to them," Cashel said.

"Unless . . ." Jane said. Her eyes narrowed.

"Do not speak with them," Cashel said again with sternness in his voice.

"What if we give our side of the story?" Cora asked.

"We have no side of the story. I didn't do it. Period," Jane said.

"That's right," Cashel responded, with an approving glance. "And frankly, that should be your attitude in all things. Go about your business, as if this never happened."

"How can we do that when almost everybody who signed up for classes just asked for refunds?" Cora said. Go about their business? What kind of advice was that?

"Look," Cashel said. "You're going to take a hit. You've already taken a hit. But if you keep face, it will all turn out in the end because Jane is innocent."

He was talking about doing nothing. And doing nothing didn't sit well with Cora. Doing nothing was not something she could manage. She never had been able to.

"Unless we somehow can prove Jane is innocent," Cora said.

Jane and Cashel eyed her, both incredulous.

"That's what we're doing here," the lawyer said.

"Yes, but it's going to take the police way too long. What if we found proof that Jane had nothing to do with the murder on our own?" Cora said.

"What do you mean?" Jane said, her voice rising. "How could we prove that?"

"Maybe there's something the police are over-looking," Cora said.

"I suggest you drop that idea," Cashel said. "Leave the police work to the professionals."

Silence filled the room as Cora considered her options. Perhaps Cashel didn't need to be informed about everything.

"What can you tell us about Sarah Waters?" Jane asked.

"I can only tell you what is on the public record.

Which is that she was killed in her home on the night of August 23."

"How was she killed?" Cora asked.

"Look, I know where you're going with this and I have to warn you the local police won't take too kindly to you poking your nose in this case," he said. Suddenly, his good looks seemed to fade. He looked pinched and inflexible, two attributes Cora found unattractive.

"Very well, I'll go to the court and ask for the record myself, if you won't answer me," Cora said.

Jane was picking some imaginary lint off her jeans.

"She was strangled and then her fingers were cut off and strewn about the house," Cashel said. "It was a bloody mess. With bloody fingerprints everywhere."

Cora felt a wave of nausea and gaped at Jane, whose eyes were wide with fear.

"And people think *I* did that?" Jane said.

"Who knows what people think?" Cashel said. "They want answers. They want justice. Sarah was well loved. You are new in town. Part of your prints might have turned up there. That's all people know. They are jumping to conclusions. But if you take my advice and lay low, go about your business as if nothing happened, it will be fine."

Easy for him to say.

Cashel gathered his papers, then his briefcase, cueing them that their time together was almost finished.

"I need to know where you were that day. You haven't gotten back to me about it," he said to Cora.

"Oh yes, that's easy. I was babysitting London," she said. "We went to the movies and then came home and made brownies."

His face fell. "You were with London that night?"

She nodded.

He glanced at Jane. His jaw muscles clenched. "Jane, please stop by my office later today."

"Okay," she said, attempting a smile.

A bolt of fear pinged through Cora as she watched him leave. Why did he glower at Jane like that? Had she lied to him? Why would she do that?

"Jane, what's going on?" Cora turned toward her friend once Cashel had closed the front door behind him.

But Jane's face was in her hands and her shoulders were shaking.

Cora rushed to her side. "Shhh," she said, placing her arm around her. "It's going be all right. One way or the other. We're going to be fine."

After Jane calmed down and gained her composure, she began to talk. "I didn't mean to lie. I mixed up the dates. I told him I was here with London. I forgot about that Friday night when I was out of town. I'm sure he thinks I'm lying."

"Calm down," Cora said. "Just tell him what you told me and it will be fine." But Cora wasn't so sure. This was weighing on Jane, as it would anybody. But Jane's hefty baggage made it worse.

"Tell him where you were and he will corroborate it and voilà," Cora said.

But when Jane looked back up at her, there was something in her eyes—something that made Cora shiver. What was going on with Jane?

"You're right. I'm just being silly and I'm starting to panic."

"I get that," Cora said. "But we've got to keep our cool about this."

Jane glanced at the clock on the mantel. "It's almost

time to pick up London from school. Can I ask you to get her for me?"

"Why?"

"I don't want to face all of those people."

"You'll need to face them eventually."

"I know. Just not today."

Chapter 11

On the drive to the school, Cora thought about Jane and Sarah and how she was going to prove Jane's innocence.

She knew her way around the court system, unfortunately, from years of working as a counselor for battered women. But only to a point, and most importantly, she had no idea how to go about investigating a murder.

The first thing she planned was to find out more about Sarah. That seemed to be the place to start. She intended to Google her when she returned home from picking up London.

Cora parked the car and walked into the school, the same way she had the day before. This time, the woman behind the counter stiffened when she spotted her, and two other women came up behind her. No welcoming smiles met her. They stood like cardigan-wearing soldiers, flanking either side of the receptionist.

"Hi," Cora began, "I'm—"

"I know who you are," the receptionist said. A clipped tone and an icy eye sweep let Cora know exactly what the woman thought of her. "I'll get London for you."

"It such a pretty day outside," Cora said, nervously trying to make small talk.

Silence.

A few moments later, London came traipsing into the office.

"Hey," she said. "Is Mom at the police station again?"

Did she really just say that?

"No, sweetie," Cora said, drawing in smooth and steady breaths. "She's a bit tired today so I decided to help her out."

The room felt like it was closing in on her, so she grabbed London's hand and walked toward the door. She needed to get away from there; away from the prying eyes. Jane was right. Cora had thought maybe she was exaggerating. But Jane was definitely right.

She tried not to show her anger or embarrassment to London. She inhaled air deeply before she slipped into the driver's seat and started the car.

Her hands gripped the steering wheel all the way home.

London hummed her own tune in the backseat. Cora thanked the gods that the child wasn't in one of her questioning moods.

When they arrived at the carriage house, they were greeted by a note from Jane pinned to the door:

I need some time away. Be back soon.

She needed time away? For what?

"Where's Mommy?" London asked.

"She wanted a little time to herself," Cora said, after a minute. Trying to calm herself, she was reminded of how typical this was of Jane. The fight-or-flight response was developed by years of abuse. But to leave Cora to deal with this pressure alone? Anger thrummed through her body.

"When will she be back?" London said, crossing her arms.

Cora fished around in her bag for the carriage-house keys. She didn't want to alert London that anything was amiss, but at the same time, she wanted to drive her fist through something, anything.

"I don't know, sweetie," she said, her voice an octave higher than usual. "She didn't say. But you and me . . . we'll have a good time. How about pizza tonight?"

It was the only thing she could think of to cheer the girl up, plus Cora didn't have time to cook. She had a blog post to write and a few more phone calls to return.

She finally found the key and slipped it into the door. It opened to the downstairs studio, which was full of Jane's pottery, stacked on shelves, on tables, and on the floor. At this moment, Cora's hands itched to throw one of Jane's goddess-shaped cups across the room.

In the meantime, London's hand reached for hers, and the child looked up at her with questioning eyes. Cora's rage began to slip away.

"Let's go upstairs and get your pj's and whatever else you think you'll need tonight," Cora said.

"Are we having a sleepover?" London asked.

"I don't know. Best to be prepared."

London stopped in her tracks, her face crumpling. "I want my mommy!" she wailed.

Sometimes Cora forgot that such a bright and mature child was still just a child.

Cora scooped her up into her arms, with her heart turning to mush.

"C'mon, we're going to have a blast, right? And who knows? Your mom might be back tonight." She kept her voice light and breezy.

"Okay," London said, calming down and rubbing her eyes. "I'll get my Princess Anna pj's and my favorite books."

"Don't forget your toothbrush."

As London scampered about the tidy apartment, Cora peeked in the closet where Jane kept her suitcase—still there. Reassurance swept through her. Jane must be planning to come back. Perhaps she just needed a few hours to collect herself, away from her daughter. Cora hoped Jane just needed a little time. She trusted Jane wouldn't buckle under the pressure.

Cora had known Jane a long time. She knew that deep down Jane was strong. But sometimes Jane didn't realize her own strength, and her first inclination was always to run away.

But the retreat started in two days. Surely Jane realized the stress Cora was under and would be back soon. Cora choked back her fear and anger. Jane was being accused of murder—which had to be terrifying—but running away never solved anything. Jane should know that by now.

"I'm ready." London interrupted Cora's thoughts. She had a little suitcase in one hand and a few books in the other.

Cora couldn't help but smile. It reminded her of the first time she had met Jane. Jane had just moved into her neighborhood in Pittsburgh and decided she didn't like it there and ran away. Cora happened upon her, with her suitcase and books, behind the garage between their families' properties.

That garage between the properties became a haven for both Cora and Jane as they grew up, dated, had spats with their parents and grandparents, studied for tests, and practiced the latest dance moves.

On the day they met, Cora didn't know Jane was running away. She only knew she had found a friend.

"What are you smiling about?" London asked her.

"I'm thinking about how you remind me of your mommy. And about how much fun we're going to have," Cora said.

London reached for Cora's hand once more. "Do you have more of those cookies?"

Chapter 12

Later, after London was sound asleep, a rapping came at Cora's apartment door. Fully expecting Jane, she opened it without asking who was there. She was surprised and disappointed by the person who stood before her—Ruby.

"Cashel has been looking for Jane. He says it's important. I went over to her place and she's gone. What's going on?" Ruby asked. "Besides all that, I've been hearing rumors and they are doozies. I need to talk to you."

Rumors? Jane was right. The news was spreading through the little town quickly.

"Please calm down," Cora said to Ruby—and to herself in her head, yet again. "Come in. London is in the guest room sleeping."

Most of the attic apartment was an open floor plan, except for the bedrooms. Tonight, she was glad London was tucked away in one of them.

"So, it's true, then," Ruby said, following Cora into the kitchen, then sitting at the kitchen table.

"Can I get you something? Tea? Juice?" Cora said.

"No, thanks," Ruby said with a flat tone. She clearly just wanted Cora to get on with it.

Cora put the kettle on, anyway. She might need a little herbal tea to help her get to sleep tonight—and to handle Ruby's interrogation. Ruby was difficult to figure out. At first, Cora didn't think they could work together, but as she got to know her, she realized she was just brutally honest and impatient. Even now she was sitting at the table, tapping her fingers, watching Cora. Waiting for answers.

"So where is Jane?" Ruby asked, more forcefully.

"She went for a drive."

"A drive?" she said, with her eyebrows drawn-in. "The day before the guests start to arrive? She takes a drive? Honestly!"

"She's just upset because of this fingerprint business," Cora said, sitting down in the chair across from Ruby.

"When will she be back?"

Cora blinked and glanced at the clock. Her fingers found the edges of a placemat and picked at a frayed thread.

"You don't know," Ruby said.

Cora didn't know what else to say. She couldn't lie to Ruby. After all, she had a vested interest in the craft retreat as well.

Cora sighed. "She will be back for her daughter, if for nothing else. I'm sure." She would, wouldn't she? But she'd not heard from Jane, and it was getting late. Could it be Jane was more fragile and more damaged than what Cora knew? Was Jane just not going to be able to handle this situation?

"It's so hard for single mothers. I know that. If it wasn't for the previous owners of this place taking me in, I don't know what would've happened to Cashel and I when his father died. But I never ran away."

"Jane just needs a little time to think." She said it with more conviction than she felt. In truth, she was more worried about Jane, at this point, than the retreat. Possibly it was all too much for Jane. Maybe she was cracking.

"They say she tried to kill her husband," Ruby said. "Is that true?"

There it was. The very thing Jane didn't want people to know about her. She'd worked so hard at starting over, yet it just kept following her around like a bad penny.

"Ruby—"

"Please do me the honor of telling me the truth. You wouldn't believe the wild rumors. I can't fight back if I don't know what the heck is going on," Ruby said.

Cora hesitated—she felt this was Jane's business and hated spreading around her personal history. But then again, Ruby had a point. She was a part of their new life, of their business, and she was vital to its success.

"Jane did shoot her ex-husband. It was in self-defense, after many years of her husband . . . hurting her, she took matters into her own hands," Cora said. "She didn't kill him. But she perhaps would have if she wasn't such a lousy shot. He was trying to kill her. Make no mistake about that."

Ruby grimaced. "Poor girl," she said. Her voice softened, revealing what Cora had known all along: Ruby was a big softy beneath her gruff exterior. "What a terrible thing to live with." She blinked slowly as if remembering or thinking deeply.

"So you can see why the incident with the fingerprints and Sarah's murder and all that is freaking her out a bit," Cora said.

"I can see that, but running away?" Ruby said, sitting back against her chair now.

"I'm not sure that she's run away. I think she'll be back tonight or tomorrow. I think she just needs some alone time," Cora said. Was she trying to convince Ruby, or herself, as well?

The tea kettle whistled. Cora made her way over to the counter. "Are you certain you don't want some tea?"

"On second thought, I will have a spot of tea. That looks like quality stuff," Ruby said. "I love chamomile."

After they had made their tea, they sat back down at the table with their steaming cups.

"You have more faith in Jane than I do," Ruby said, after stirring some honey into her tea. "I just keep thinking about what we will do if she doesn't come back."

Cora didn't want to think about that. Her best friend would not leave her in the lurch this weekend—would she? She took a sip of her tea, ignoring the queasiness coming over her, and inhaled the mist of the chamomile tea.

"You know, my mother just took off once, sorting herself out about something. I never did know why. She was gone a few weeks. I stayed with my granny. Oh, I loved staying with her, way back in the hollows. She knew her herbs," said Ruby.

"Is that where you learned it all?" Cora seized the opportunity to change the subject.

Ruby nodded. "That was the start of it. I learned a lot from her. She was one of these old wise women, you know? Midwife. Herbalist. I wanted to be just like her."

Cora smiled. "We all need people like that in our lives, didn't we? Especially when we're kids."

"She had the sight, too," Ruby said, brightening.

"The sight?" Cora asked.

"You know, she had dreams and visions. Things that would come true," Ruby said.

Cora didn't know what to say to that.

"There's a lot more to life than what we can see with our eyes, you know? Some of us are gifted, some cursed, with a second sight."

Was Ruby trying to tell her something? Did she think she was psychic or something? Cora had seen a lot of people who claimed they were psychic. She wanted to believe it could exist, but it had never been proven to her.

"I've been worried about Jane," Ruby said. "I have a weird vibe about her, like she's not quite as together as she appears. She's hiding something."

"I just told you about her past."

"No," Ruby said. "It's not that. I'm not quite sure what it is. I've been keeping my eye on her."

"She's a grown woman, Ruby. She doesn't need you fussing over her," Cora said.

"I know that. That's not at all what I mean. I think she's fragile and full of fears and secrets."

That actually was a pretty good description of Jane. But then again, thought Cora, to believe fears, secrets, and fragility were Jane's only qualities would be selling her short.

Later, after Ruby left, and London was still asleep with Luna the cat curled up next to her, Cora texted Jane. There was no reply. Was Ruby correct in thinking she wouldn't return?

Jolts of panic and worry zoomed through her. Jane was not going to leave her hanging all weekend, was she? This, of all weekends, she wouldn't abandon her—right? *Right?*

Cora sat at her computer, trying to focus on her blog post. She ran a spell check and set it up so the post would publish in the morning.

She needed to occupy her mind with something other than the missing Jane. So, she turned to Google—and Sarah Waters.

She keyed in her name. A whole slew of links came up: newspaper articles and the obituary. And an auction. An auction?

She clicked the link.

Sarah's family had held an auction of her things last week. She had been quite the collector. The auction ad listed first-edition books, Victorian sunglasses, antique opium kits, and a priceless broom collection. Priceless broom collection? Antique opium kits? Whoa! There was more to Little Miss Librarian than met the eye. There usually was when it came to people, Cora reminded herself.

Why would anybody collect opium kits? Cora did some more Googling and immediately saw the reason. The silver-plated tools were encased in intricate etched and carved cases. Elegant designs on enamel cases flicked on her screen. One was a necklace, and tucked inside its huge locket were little sharp instruments. She had a vision of opulent opium dens, flappers dressed in sheer sparkling dresses, lounging on overstuffed velvet couches with jazz music playing softly in the background.

Cora had been around the drug culture long enough to be aware that the romance of any drug was short-lived—no matter the era. She hated the fact that she herself had had to rely on drugs to help control her panic attacks at one point. Now she only took a pill when absolutely necessary.

Cora mulled over the whole "collector" thing in her mind. She didn't understand the desire to own a lot of objects. She did gather objects she could use in her upcycled crafts. Old tea cups and saucers and silver-ware, mostly. She fashioned them into all sorts of things—garden markers, chandeliers, candleholders, and so on. But to collect "things" for the sake of it? She just didn't have that disposition.

Evidently, Sarah Waters did. Cora looked over the list of Sarah's collections once more. She clicked on a link about the priceless broom collection.

A beep announced a text message from Jane, at last:

I'm on my way home. More later. Is London asleep?

Cora's neck and shoulder muscles unraveled. Had she been holding all that in?

Yes, she texted back. Everything is under control.
I'll take her to school in the morning. Get some
rest. XO.

Her phone beeped again, indicating a new message from Jane:

Thank you, my friend.

Cora was more than relieved. She chided herself: Did she really think Jane was going to run away? She had come so far. Their bonds of friendship were deep. Why this glimmer of mistrust when it came to Jane? She was ashamed of herself. Back to the brooms.

One of Sarah's brooms was from Italy and was gorgeous, with a colorful, intricate basket weaving on the top of it rather than metal or wire. Evidently, it was an altar broom from a church in Rome during the eighteenth century.

Another was an old Shaker broom, which delighted Cora. She loved the Shaker brooms with their stark simplicity. It was utilitarian art. She knew the Shakers invented the flat bottom broom—until then, brooms were round, with mostly ragged bottoms. Sarah's broom dated back to the 1800s.

Another broom, called "Morganna's Broom," was Welsh. Ragged and undated, the broom belonged to a woman who was burned at the stake for witchcraft. Cora felt a chill along her spine. Who'd want a broom like that? She read on. The broom was said to have special magical qualities. It was made by a powerful broom maker in Wales who used particular twigs and grass gathered during auspicious times—a full moon during May.

There was one last broom in Sarah's collection to read about, a Native American broom that dated from twenty thousand years ago.

Cora blinked. That must be a typo. No broom on this planet could be twenty thousand years old. She read on.

The broom had been found in a cave between Indigo Gap and Asheville, North Carolina, and truly did date back twenty thousand years. It was basically a stick with grass at the end of it, but apparently made to last.

Why and how would Sarah be in possession of what was basically a museum piece? Just how much money do school librarians earn, anyway?

Chapter 13

Jane downed the last bit of coffee in her paper cup and slid it into the cup holder of her car. She turned up the radio and cracked the window—the crisp air helped keep her alert. She needed to get home. The drive worked its magic; it gave her time to sort through it all, emotionally. Now, she was able to think.

If this business failed, it was on her. There was no getting around that.

She had almost killed her ex-husband. True, it had been in self-defense. But people were going to twist this around, as they often did. Even if she was proclaimed innocent, the damage had been done. They could not deny this.

The idea of cops, courts, and judges freaked her out. It brought up memories she'd rather not think about. It was hard to start fresh with all these painful memories tugging at you—and then just when you think you've done it, bam. Your life circles back around on you.

How many times did this have to happen to one person? How many times did one life need to be forced into reinvention? How much of a price did she have to pay to be happy?

Was Cora right when she said it would be okay? The woman had a lot of faith in the justice system—even after she'd seen it fail time and time again. Even though they both had lost several friends to it.

It's not perfect, Cora's voice rang in her head. *But it does more good than harm.*

"Do more good than harm" seemed to be her friend's mantra. Most of the time, Jane agreed. She tried to live by it as well. But sometimes, she wasn't as strong as Cora.

She drove toward Indigo Gap in her Volkswagen bug, then entered the small town. The speed limit slowed and the quaint storefronts and businesses welcomed her. The florist. The pub. The café. The Christmas Store. The Nature Store. The bookstore. Despite what she was going through, she felt herself loving this place and allowed herself a glimmer of hope that it would work out.

Jane had hated leaving that afternoon. She knew it would upset Cora and London, and she hated that. But her taking off was self-preservation. She needed to do it. She'd learned over the years that sometimes you needed to walk away, gain some distance.

That space and time served her well. She dug down deep, as she drove, and decided it was all worth fighting for—every piece of this new life of hers. This is exactly what she would do with the help of Cora, Cashel, and Ruby. They were counting on her. As was London. She couldn't let them down. Not this time. Not these people.

The moon shone brightly on Kildare House. She

pulled into the driveway, exited her car, and stood in the light of the moon, whispering a little prayer that her new secret wouldn't destroy everything.

The secret that had been hers to keep could also be the secret that destroyed a friendship. She had to be careful about this, because it was also her alibi. Every secret found its way out, eventually. She grimaced. She had just been hoping to keep it a little while longer.

Jane, Cora, and Ruby met in the kitchen the next morning to go over some last-minute details about the retreat. What time was Jude getting in? When would their first crafter arrive? Did they have enough coffee, tea, and munchies? While the meeting was going on, Cora whipped up yet another batch of blueberry muffins.

"You can never have enough muffins on hand," Cora said. She pulled out the last batch.

"I agree wholeheartedly," Ruby said, barely looking up from the scarf she was knitting.

"Let's go over the list one more time, just to make sure we are covered," Cora said as she set the muffins on her cooling rack, their smell taunting her. With her emotions running on high, she could eat about a dozen or so.

As Jane read items off the list, Cora made another pot of coffee.

"You can't have enough coffee, either," Ruby said.

"Or chocolate," Cora said.

"Or sex," Jane added, then burst out laughing.

The doorbell rang. Could it be? Could their famous

broom maker be arriving? All three women headed for the front door.

When Jude Sawyer, the broom maker, walked into Kildare House, it was as if he filled it. Not that he was such a huge man, though he was tall and well built, with wide shoulders, narrow hips, and long legs. It was more his sheer presence. Charisma radiated from him. Cora, Jane, and Ruby greeted him and flitted around him like a group of chickadees.

"I'm so glad you could make it. It's good you're here a bit early, too," Cora said.

"Can I get you anything?" Ruby, normally a bit dour, suddenly perked up. Her face was a little pink and her eyes brightened as she smiled. Her happy face complemented the rainbow sweater she wore—handmade with hand-dyed wool, of course. "Cora just made blueberry muffins and a fresh pot of coffee."

Jude looked at her a bit bashfully. The younger man knew he was appreciated by women, including this woman, old enough to be his mother. Was he embarrassed? Cora wondered. Or was it false humility?

"How about some coffee?" he asked Ruby.

"We've got the coffeepot on most of the time," Ruby replied. "How do you like it?"

"Black," he said.

"I'll show you to your room while Ruby gets your coffee," Jane said. "You can put your things away and get a feel for the place."

Cora watched Jude take Jane in. He apparently liked what he saw. Her long black hair was pulled up into a messy bun. She had just smeared red lipstick onto her upturned lips before he entered the house. It brought out those deep blue eyes of hers. Soulful, just like Jane.

Cora and Jane hadn't had a chance to catch up yet, between getting London off to school, breakfast, and attending to last-minute details.

"Gorgeous woodwork," Jude said, his hands grazing the banister as he and Jane made their way up the stairs.

"The house was built in 1892," Jane said. "There are so many wonderful details. The woodwork. The floors. Wait until you see the main fireplace. I live in the carriage house out back. Even there, the workmanship is exquisite."

"This is a Tiffany window," Jane said as they stopped on the landing. "You wouldn't think to see it in a small town like this, but the family were admirers of fine art and craftsmanship."

"It's a Celtic goddess, Brigid," Jane said. "Goddess of poetry and crafts."

"Very appropriate," Jude said.

As Jane and Jude walked farther up the stairs and out of listening distance, Ruby appeared with Jude's coffee.

"He'll be back down," Cora said. "He's a bit entranced with the place."

"He's entranced with something," Ruby snorted.

"Most men are."

"You ain't so bad yourself," Ruby said. "Why don't you have a guy?"

Cora shrugged. *Go out and get a guy, like you were picking apples.* As if it were that easy. She thought of Cashel, momentarily, but then immediately erased him from her mind, while his mother stood in front of her.

"I just . . . haven't met the right guy, I suppose." She thought she had once—but Dante was history.

"You're young and pretty," Ruby said. "You should be out experimenting. You know, getting laid."

Cora felt her cheeks flush—and hated herself for it. It was one of the many scourges of being a fair-skinned redhead.

Ruby cackled, noticing her flush. "I'm sorry—didn't mean to embarrass you. I've got some sorting to do in the cottage," she said after a moment of uncomfortable silence had passed. "I do hate to leave and miss that eye candy. But I'll catch you later."

With that, she was gone. Ruby knew how to disappear out of a room.

Jane came back down the stairs. "Jude asked for his coffee in his room. Says he needs some time to get organized. He'll be down for lunch."

Cora handed Jane the mug of coffee, and Jane headed back up the stairs.

"I had no idea he was so, um, hot," Jane said over her shoulder with a grin.

"Behave yourself," Cora called back. That was all she needed—a love-struck Jane. They had talked about how it was not a good idea for Jane to get involved with anyone quite yet. How she needed to give herself some time alone. But a voluptuous woman like Jane had to beat back the men sometimes.

When the doorbell rang, Cora thought it might be Mary-Laura Johnson, who was bringing gourds over for the gift baskets. But when she opened the door, she was distressed to see two police officers, different ones than had visited the carriage house earlier.

"Can I help you?" Cora asked.

"I'm Officer Glass and this is Officer Shimer. We're looking for Jude Sawyer. Is he staying here?"

"Mr. Sawyer is a guest here, yes," Cora responded, wondering what this could be about. How did they even know Jude? He was from Tennessee. "He'll be teaching a class here this weekend."

"That's what we thought," Officer Glass said. "We need to talk with him. Where is he?"

"In his room."

"And where is that?"

"I don't think it's appropriate for you to bother him in his room, Officers. I will be happy to bring him to you," Cora said.

"No problem, Cora," Jude said as he came down the stairs. "I'm here."

"Is there someplace private we could talk?" Officer Shimer asked.

Cora sent them all into the paper-crafting room. Before she shut the door, she stood back and took in the contrasting sight of the big uniformed police officers surrounded by beautiful paper, ribbons, and sparkly embellishments.

She couldn't resist standing outside the closed door and eavesdropping. Why were the local police here to see her guest teacher? She sort of had a right to know, didn't she? Two visits from the police in two days? She hoped this wasn't going to be a habit.

She pressed her ear up to the solid chestnut door but couldn't hear a word.

"What are you doing?" Jane said from behind her.

"Shhh!" Cora pointed toward the door.

A bewildered Jane pulled Cora off to the kitchen.

"What's going on?" she asked once they were alone.

"Jude's in there with two police officers," Cora answered.

"What the—"

"Exactly," Cora said, crossing her arms. "I had a bad feeling about having a man at our first retreat."

"I know, I know, but this could be something fairly mundane."

"Like what? A parking ticket? They've been in there a while. It doesn't make sense," Cora said.

"Did you do a background check on him?" Jane asked after a moment.

"He's Jude freakin' Sawyer," Cora said.

"Does that mean no? You didn't do a background check? Honestly, Cora!"

Cora always assumed folks were innocent until proven guilty and didn't see the need for background checks. She preferred to judge after getting to know someone. But the longer Jude's meeting with the local police went on, the more she started to see the wisdom of background checks.

Chapter 14

Jane needed to go back to the carriage house. But Ruby had entered in the back kitchen door and stood in her way. Like a stone. Or more like a mountain. She was immovable.

"I don't think you should go back there," Ruby said, with a quick glance at the back door that opened to the screened porch.

"Why?" Jane said. Cora came up behind her.

"Just trust me on this," Ruby said. Her eyes were rimmed in red. Had she been crying?

"What's wrong?" Cora said.

"I saw the cops are here. Are they still here? What are they doing here?" Ruby said, her bottom lip twitching.

Why isn't Ruby answering the question?

Jane knew how paranoid Ruby was about the police. She was definitely part of the generation of aging hippie-flower children who thought cops were all out to get them. Jane had some issues with the cops, as well, but not like this.

"Do you mind?" Jane said. "I need to go back to my

place. I've got some things to take care of before I need to go get London."

"Let's go back in the kitchen for a minute," Ruby said, pushing both Jane and Cora back inside. She was agitated—or was she frightened?

"What's going on? For God's sakes, Ruby. We don't have time for this . . . ," Jane said.

"Where are the cops?" Ruby demanded.

"Are you worried about them?" Jane said. "They're in the paper-crafting room with Jude." She headed for the paper-crafting room, with Cora and Ruby trailing behind her.

"Look, I bought the brooms fair and square. I can't help it if her family doesn't like it. They took my money, didn't they?" Jude said, with a booming voice.

"I'm sorry to interrupt," Ruby said. "But we've got a situation."

"You're damn right we do," Jude said. "I've been accused of theft and I don't like it."

"What?" Cora said. "That's absurd."

Officer Shimer eyeballed the three women. "What do you want?" he said.

"I'd like to report a crime," Ruby said.

"What kind of crime?" he asked her.

"I was walking around back, walking from my place to the main house. And I walked by the carriage house—"

"You live here?" Officer Glass interrupted.

"Yes, on the property, in the gardener's cottage," Ruby explained impatiently. "And Jane lives in the carriage house."

"How many people live here in total?" Officer Glass asked, scratching his head.

"Three adults and one child," Cora answered. "Ruby, what's going on?"

"As I was walking by, well, I noticed something strange," she said.

"Strange? A strange person?" Glass said, standing up.

"No, I wish. I didn't see him," she replied. Her hands were on her hips, now, and her voice was forceful.

"Him?" Jane said. "Him who?" Jane's voice rose a few decibels.

"Calm down," Shimer said, standing up. "Let her finish."

Jane stood close to Cora, wondering what Ruby was blathering on about. She tended to be a little dramatic at times.

"Someone spray-painted a message on Jane's door," Ruby said.

"Huh? My door?" Jane said.

"What does it say?" Cora asked.

Ruby shook her head back and forth.

"Let's go out there and check it out," Shimer said.

They all followed Ruby out, through the back kitchen door, past the rows of marigolds and mums, and down to the quaint carriage house Jane called home. The place was newly painted in sky blue and cranberry trim around the windows—with the approval of the historical commission. They had hung shutters and flower boxes to match last week.

A gasp escaped from Jane's mouth as she read the message. GO HOME, KILLER was spray-painted in orange across her door.

Cora stood beside her and wrapped her arm around her.

Ruby cleared her throat. "There was an intruder on

this property, Officers, one who vandalized this house. What are you going to do about it—stand there, looking stupid?"

The cops eyed each other. Shimer pulled out his cell phone and called the station. "We'll need to search the area. It couldn't have happened very long ago. What time did you leave your house this morning?" he asked Jane.

Jane couldn't speak. Her mouth wouldn't move. Why was her tongue so dry?

"She came to a breakfast meeting at eight-thirty," Cora said. "I'm sorry, Officers, I think she's had quite a shock. I should really get her inside."

"I agree," Shimer said. He slipped his cell phone in his pocket. "We're going to search the area. It's eleven-thirty, so the person could be anywhere by now. But we'll ask around. Maybe a neighbor saw something. You never know."

"Thanks, so much, Officer," Cora said, leading Jane away and into the house, past Ruby and Jude, who stood by, befuddled.

Jane forced a smile as they passed Jude and went back into the kitchen, where Cora sat her down and put a glass of water in front of her. Jane held the water in her hand—it was so nice and cool against her sweaty skin. She took a drink and then pressed the glass to her face.

"Are you okay?" Cora asked.

"I don't know," Jane said, after a minute. Light was streaming through the kitchen window and shining right on Cora, her best friend in the world, standing there with an air of concern pasted on her face, but sheer fear was just beneath the facade. Jane knew this because she knew Cora so well. "Stop biting your lip."

"Okay. It's going to be okay," Cora said. "Cashel is going to get you completely off, of course, because you are innocent and then . . ."

"But someone believes I'm guilty," she said.

Cora sighed. "It looks that way, doesn't it? Okay, let them believe what they want."

"But in the meantime—"

"In the meantime, we do as Cashel suggests."

"You mean we just . . . act like nothing has happened?"

"Yes," Cora said after a minute, but she looked away.

"Really?" Jane said. There was something about the way Cora turned from her and started wiping off the kitchen counter. She was hiding something. "For some reason, I don't quite believe you."

Cora turned to face her. "Well, as far as Cashel and the rest of the town know, we are going to do what we do best. Crafting. Retreating. Being nice and friendly."

"But?"

"But we also need to find a murderer."

Jane took a long drink of water and set the glass down. "You aren't suggesting, again, what I think you are? That we somehow investigate Sarah's murder on our own?"

"That's exactly what I mean."

"Girl, you have lost your ever-loving mind."

"No, I haven't. It doesn't look like the police are getting anywhere. Why shouldn't we poke around a bit?"

"Because, um, murder? If we piss the killer off, they might come after us. Besides, we could make the police mad. I don't need that."

"No, you don't," Cora said after a minute. "Which is why we need to be careful."

Jane knew then that Cora had her mind set. There was no turning back. Not now. And it scared Jane to death. Only Cora would attempt something like this, so blinded by her absolute need to help.

"I don't think this is a good idea," Jane said.

"Relax," Cora said, crossing her arms and leaning on the counter. "It will be fine. Trust me."

She did trust Cora. But she was talking about investigating a murder case. It wasn't the same thing as starting a new business together—or even working with abused women, tough as it was. This was life and death, and they had no idea what they were doing. She'd have to keep a close eye on Cora, who often went into situations purely on instinct, without much thought. This could get downright messy.

Chapter 15

"I'm sorry, ladies," Officer Shimer said, walking toward them as they came out the back door. "We haven't been able to find anybody. None of your neighbors witnessed anything, other than the usual UPS delivery, catering van, a florist, and so on. In fact, most of the neighbors are not even home. It's the middle of the day. Everybody must be away at work."

"The grass over that way was bent in such a way that we could follow the trail for a few minutes. We even got a dog involved. We checked down by the river as well," the officer explained.

The river was a couple of miles from Kildare House, down a rocky landscape. If someone had run in that direction, he or she would have had an unpleasant time of it, unless they were familiar with the area.

"What are the chances we can get the door painted over before Jane's daughter comes home from school?" Cora asked.

"Depends on if you have paint. We've taken photos and gathered all the evidence," Officer Glass replied.

"Evidence?" Cora said.

"We took a sample of the paint, which will tell us what kind it is and then we might be able to figure out where it was purchased," he said.

The officers of Indigo Gap wore indigo blue. Officer Glass's uniform seemed to almost blend in to the sky as he stood in the garden between the big house and the two smaller houses on the property.

"Can you get back to me and let me know?" Cora said.

"That's police business."

"It's just that this is my property," she replied. "It would make me feel more secure to be kept informed. Besides which, I was thinking maybe the vandal is also the person who killed Sarah Waters."

"Whoa," he said.

"Whoa indeed," Jane said.

"That's quite a leap of logic," Glass said.

"Not really. Who else would want to make it look like Jane is guilty, but the guilty person?" Cora said, as if he should know.

Officer Glass shook his head. "It's never that simple with cases like this. I get what you're saying. But it's probably a local kid looking for mischief."

Glass was called away by another officer.

"A local kid looking for mischief that the cops can't find," Cora said to Jane. "Makes me feel all warm and cozy."

Jude, who had been hanging around on the periphery, walked up to Cora and Jane.

"I couldn't help but overhear what you were saying," he said. "I didn't want to bring up Jane's predicament . . ."

"You know, of course, that she's innocent," Cora said, perhaps a bit too fast.

Jane stood by silently, brooding. Her were arms crossed, and the nearby mums and marigolds framed her long curvy figure.

"Of course," Jude said, smiling at Jane. "But I wanted to say I think you're on to something. I think someone wants people to believe she killed Sarah. That's how it appears."

Cora warmed. She already liked this guy a lot, and now, she liked him even more.

He hitched his fingers in his jeans. "Sarah Waters, man, what a pain in the ass."

"Excuse me," Jane said. "Did you know her?"

"Yes, that's one of the things the cops were talking with me about."

"I'm all ears, Jude," Cora said.

"I bought her broom collection at this auction the family had," he said. "Evidently one of the daughters is protesting and wants the brooms back."

"Broom collection?" Jane said, raising her eyebrows.

"I read about it online," Cora said.

"Who collects brooms?" Jane said, incredulous.

"I do," Jude replied and chuckled.

"You're a broom maker," Jane replied. "That makes sense. But why would Sarah?"

"Who knows why anybody collects anything?" Cora said, realizing the police were still scattered about the backyard. "Maybe we should take our conversation inside."

"Nah, you go ahead," Jane said. "I need to find some paint and get that door fixed before London gets home."

* * *

Cora poured Jude a glass of sweet tea. He sat at her kitchen table eating an egg-salad sandwich. While Cora loved her new home, she despised the small, somewhat dingy kitchen. One of these days, the kitchen would also be remodeled. Eventually, she wanted to offer baking classes. But, first things first.

"So, you knew Sarah?" she asked Jude.

"I did. Not well," he said, then took a drink of his tea. "I knew her ex-husband better. We worked at the mill together for a few years before my business took off. He actually worked more with my dad."

Cora knew the "mill" everybody talked about was the local textile mill, now closed, just another blow in the local economy. It was famous for its fine indigo-blue cotton.

"Her ex lives in Pennsylvania now," he added.

"What was she like? Why did they get a divorce?" Divorce wasn't such an odd occurrence these days, but Cora made a mental note to check into the court records to see exactly what kind of divorce occurred. Cora knew enough about murder to know that usually the victim knew her killer. Husbands and ex-husbands were usually at the top of the suspect list—for good reason.

"You know, I never knew why. Nobody did. But she changed. I think she became a health freak or something and lost a lot of weight at one point and the next thing you knew, they were getting a divorce," he said and bit into his sandwich.

"Someone said she was a typical librarian," Cora prompted.

"I suppose," he said. "Whatever that means. But I guess she was bookish. She had quite the book collection. Still does, from what I hear. The family didn't sell her books."

"How odd that they want the brooms back," Cora said.

"There's one daughter who wasn't around when all of this went down," he said. "She wanted the brooms for herself. But I paid for them fair and square." He hesitated. He seemed to be considering his situation. "I love those brooms."

"But?"

"I kind of feel bad that the daughter wants them."

Cora felt her heart flutter. What a nice man.

"What are you going to do?" she said.

"I'm not sure. What are you going to do?"

"About what?"

"About Jane."

"I know she's innocent. I have faith in our judicial system. It will be fine," Cora said with finality. She placed the lid back on the plastic bowl containing the egg salad.

"I hope you're right," he said. "This is a fine place. I love what you've done with it. I love the whole idea of it."

Cora beamed. "It's a dream come true for me."

"Sometimes I teach at a prison. And I tell you what, it makes a difference. Giving people something to do with their hands . . . it's healthy and healing," he said, then took his last bite of sandwich.

Cora could hardly believe what she was hearing. This handsome man sat across the table from her, spouting her own beliefs. Her eyes met his and her faced heated. She glanced away. She thought Jane might be interested in Jude—and no matter how good-looking or nice, that meant hands-off for Cora.

Chapter 16

Cora's pencil pointed at each item on her list again. Everything seemed to be in order. The food would come tomorrow. Fresh clean linens were on the beds. New bars of rosemary-mint handcrafted soap and clean towels filled each of the bathrooms. The craft rooms were spotless and well organized. The place had been dusted and preened over until it shined. And it was a shining, gleaming jewel, this house of hers. Well, not hers, technically speaking. It still belonged to the bank and her investors. One guest was scheduled to arrive that evening, but the others were all getting in the next day. Tomorrow was the day. Grand opening.

She wondered how far Jane had come with removing the graffiti from the front door of the carriage house. She didn't want London to see the monstrosity, nor did she want any of her guests to see it.

Now, on to her next project: proving Jane's innocence. Jude gave her a little more information to mull over. Sarah was divorced. She had two daughters—one of whom had been living who knows where, and was not happy the family had sold her mother's collections.

Cora wanted to talk with her. It might lead her to learn more about who would have wanted to kill Sarah.

Of course, the other daughter would help, as well. Where did these women live? And how about the ex-husband? Did Jude say he was in Pennsylvania? What about Sarah's house? Was it sold? Was there someone living there?

Given what Cora knew about murdered women—way too much for any person to know—she thought she'd start with the divorce and the husband. What was that statistic she'd read about recently? That 30 percent of murdered women were killed by their spouse—or boyfriend. Did Sarah have a boyfriend? How would she find out?

After researching everybody online, she came up with a list of people to question:

Husband: Josh Waters (living in Pennsylvania)
Daughter: Dee Waters (the one who was at large)
Daughter: Rebecca Saunders (must be married and where was she living?)
Boyfriend? (Perhaps Jude would know?)

She wrote down Sarah's address. She decided to take a walk through the town by Sarah's house to check it out, just out of curiosity. She stood and stretched out her arms, and the tightness in her shoulders gave way.

Her cell phone buzzed.

"Yes," she said.

"It's Jane. I've lost track of time and I'm covered in paint. Do you mind picking up London?"

"Sure, I can do that," Cora said. *So much for the walk.* "Did you get the door painted?"

"Yes, but I'm a mess and need to get in the shower. A guest is expected in a couple of hours, right?"

"Yes," Cora said. "I was getting ready to Google more names. Mostly family of Sarah's."

"For what?"

"I think we need to talk with them about their mother. We need to find out more about her if we're going to find out who killed her."

There was silence on the other end of the phone.

"Jane?"

"Yes," Jane said.

"What's wrong?" Cora asked.

"Other than the fact that I'm a murder suspect?"

"Well, not officially a suspect. But yes, other than that." Cora paused, wanting to change the subject. "I thought we should look into her ex-husband. Where was he on the night of the murder?"

"He'd be the number one suspect, wouldn't he?" Jane said. "I'm sure the police have already talked with him. What we need is a cop to tell us what they know and go from there. Some cop likes to talk or that newspaper article wouldn't have gotten published. Well, I have to get in the shower. Can you bring London to your place and I'll meet you there?"

"Sure," Cora said. It was a great idea to chat with the police, just like it was a good idea to go for a walk. But first, London.

Cora grabbed her purse and headed for the back door just as the doorbell rang for the front door. When she opened the door, a huge basket full of fall flowers greeted her.

"Oh!" Cora gasped. "How stunning!"

"Glad you like them," the delivery man said. Blond,

slight, and with a pleasant smile, he stepped forward. "I'm Matthew Reardon, one of the owners of Cattail Florists. We haven't met yet." He extended his hand, and Cora wanted to cry as she shook his hand. Here was a local who either didn't read the paper or didn't care what the paper said and was willing to give them a chance. She hadn't realized until that moment how stressed she had been about it all.

"Good to meet you," she said. "I'd ask you to come in, but I'm on my way to pick up a child from school."

"I'll take a rain check," he said. "I've been so curious to see what you've done with the place."

"Why don't you come by Sunday afternoon? We're having a dessert reception. We'd love to have you."

"I'll check my schedule," he said. "I might see you then."

He left, leaving Cora to read the card attached to the flowers:

So proud of you and can't wait to see you. With much love, Uncle Jon.

Overcome, Cora held back tears. Uncle Jon—what an old softy. She was blessed to have him in her life. He wasn't her grand-père, but he was close enough to be a comfort. Uncle Jon was her grandfather's brother. Her grandfather had emigrated from France to the States when he was a student, then he stayed because he married an American. Her grandmother was the woman who basically raised her because Cora's parents traveled so much with their work, up until their accident. Jon and her grandfather kept in touch and remained close through the years.

She remembered her grandfather and grandmother with such clarity, it almost felt as if they were with her here. She knew they would be happy for her and proud of her and Kildare House and what she was building. She caught a faint whiff of her grandmother's favorite scent, L'Air du Temps, so slight that she told herself she imagined it.

Cora mustn't forget how far she'd come. She mustn't forget to stop and celebrate this dream come true.

Like all dreams, it had come with a price. And it wasn't turning out to be the smooth road she'd wanted.

The bouquet included salmon-colored roses, deep orange calla lilies, and miniature sunflowers and black-eyed Susans. She sat it on the foyer table, where it would be the first thing to greet her guests.

Chapter 17

After Cora picked up London and delivered her to Jane, her mission was to take a walk before dinner. She planned to treat the whole crew to dinner tonight—sort of a calm-before-the-storm dinner. Their first guest would be coming in late that night.

She walked down Azure Lane toward the center of town, where Sarah had lived. Cora loved that many of streets in Indigo Gap were named after shades of blue. The town had several different legends about how it had gotten its name. The most believable one was that it had been a crossroads gap in the mountains where people came together and traded fur, pottery, and cloth. Because the locals grew the plants that gave indigo dye its color, the town became known as Indigo Gap.

Another interesting theory was about a group from India who settled in the region and became friends with and married into the local Native American tribe. The Indians were expert in the art of dying fabric and taught the locals their craft and trade. Over the years, the intermixing of the Indians and Native American gave the locals much to ponder, providing fodder for some interesting legends—like the belief there was a whole tribe of them deep in the mountains somewhere, practicing a mix of Native American beliefs and Hinduism. Cora doubted any of this ever happened. But still, there were interesting, somewhat unexplained relics around—like a Ganesha temple deep in the woods. For years, this group of people were just known as the "Indigos." History had yet to prove their existence, but it was fun to ponder.

Cora gazed into the distance—dusky skies, the sun setting low against the mountains that gave off a blue hue, which could also be described as indigo. The shops were starting to close and the lantern-shaped streetlights to glow.

Leaves scattered across the sidewalk as Cora made her way down the street. One more block and she would be able to see Sarah's house, which was one of the historical houses in the village. It was stationed on a corner, with its main door facing a side street.

She spotted Sarah's house, painted in a terra-cotta shade and trimmed in teal. It had a gabled roof, which was quite steep, and was a bit taller than the surrounding houses and businesses. Cora wrapped her sweater closer around her as she approached. Oddly enough, smoke puffed out from the chimney. Someone must be inside.

As she walked closer, Cora saw a yard-sale sign. Hadn't they sold everything at the auction that was in the paper?

A car sat in the off-street driveway. Should she knock at the door? In addition to the smoke, there were lights on inside the house. Someone walked around inside, maybe preparing for the upcoming yard sale.

She fought the urge to turn and go home. This was awkward. But it might be a good break for her—a way to help prove that Jane was innocent. She thought of everything that was on the line—Jane's case, their new business—and she mustered her courage. *Awkwardness be damned.*

She opened the gate, which gave off a loud creaking noise, shut it, and walked up the stone path to the front door.

Settling her nerves, she knocked.

"Just a minute," came a male voice. She heard some scuffling and movement behind the door, which finally opened.

"Can I help you?" the man said. He looked as if he were in his late fifties, perhaps early sixties. Pale. Shadows circled his eyes. He wore glasses and a Steelers baseball cap, along with a UNC sweatshirt. He frowned at Cora.

"Um, hi," Cora said. "I was walking by and I saw the sign. I'll be busy tomorrow and wondered if . . ."

"Yeah, yeah, you can come in and take a look around. You're not the first early bird," he said. He moved his head, and Cora noticed he was shaking slightly. He was perhaps older than Cora had first thought. "This stuff didn't sell in the auction we had a few weeks ago and we need to get rid of it."

He ushered her inside. The place smelled of burning wood, cats, and something else that she couldn't quite place. Something floral and a bit spicy. Incense-like.

Sarah's things were scattered on tables throughout

the house. Even though Cora didn't know her, an overwhelming sense of sadness overcame her.

"Are you okay?" the man asked.

"Oh yes, yes," she said. "I just, you know, feel so terrible about Sarah."

"Bloody awful business," he said. He had apparently been in the middle of organizing a group of items down at the end of a long card table.

Cora briefly glanced at the items in front of her. Tupperware containers, a few plates, and a big box full of doilies and handkerchiefs. Five dollars for the whole box. It was the kind of thing she liked to find at sales; she was certain she could make use of the items. She picked the box up and carried it along with her, until she reached the end of the table, near where the man was organizing old vinyl record albums.

There, at the end of the table, was part of Sarah's collection of opium antiques, which shone and glittered like jewels.

"These didn't sell?" Cora said to the man with surprise.

"Not these pieces. I'm afraid not," he said. "It takes a collector, I think, to appreciate their value."

"They are just beautiful."

"Yes, I was with her when she purchased the first one. We were on our honeymoon in Turkey," he said.

"You're—"

"I'm Josh Waters, the ex-husband," he said and coughed a bit.

What was he doing here? They'd been divorced for years.

"She left it all to me," he said, with an odd, beleaguered grin.

Cora took an eyeful of Josh Waters. He was now standing in much better light. His demeanor was off—almost as if he were stoned.

"Did she think she was doing me a favor? Pfft," he said. "Like I don't have anything better to do than get rid of all this junk."

Cora sat the box down, fighting the sudden urge to leave this place and this man. "Turkey," she said, changing the subject. "That must have been wonderful." It was the best she could do.

She ran her fingers along the cool surface of the opium kit. She opened the lid—that same sweet, floral scent that had greeted her when she first walked in came pouring out. Was the smell opium? Had Josh been smoking opium before she had come inside? Or could the smell be the lingering scent from the paraphernalia? There was more here than what was pictured on the Web site. There was quite a collection of pipes, which were also stunning, with jewel-tone colors and delicate accents.

"You wanting to buy?"

"Excuse me?" she said, turning back toward him.

He coughed a little, again. His eyes were red and watery. He was definitely stoned. Or drunk? Something was off.

"Did you want to buy some of that stuff?" he said.

"No, what would I do with it?" She tried to laugh. But as she examined the dangle tools used for opium cutting and so on, she could imagine a lovely mobile. It would be quite the conversation piece. "I'll tell you what." She reached into her bag and handed him a card. "If you don't sell this stuff, give me a call. I might be interested."

"Really? You don't look the type."

"What type? A collector or an opium smoker?" she joked.

"Neither," he said.

"Well, I'm not. But I like to repurpose things. I'm into crafts. I will take this box of doilies."

Josh rubbed his nose and he sniffed. He took the card and her money. "My allergies are so bad when I come back here," he grumbled.

Allergies, my ass, Cora thought.

"I better go," she said. "It's getting late. You have my card."

She carried her box to the front door and opened it to find a frantic woman rushing up the path.

"What you doing?" she screamed at Cora.

Cora peeked behind her. Surely this woman wasn't talking to her.

"You!" the crazed woman said and shoved Cora. Startled, Cora dropped the box of doilies. She took the stance she'd been taught over and over again in self-defense class. "Get back!" she said and raised her hands.

The woman jumped back and then reached for the box on the ground. "These are my mother's things. Who do you think you are?"

"I just bought them," Cora said, her hands still up, heart pounding and adrenaline coursing.

"Well, la-di-da," the woman said and fished out the doilies and hankies and flung them all over the yard, skipping through the grass.

"Becca! Good God, what are you doing?" came Josh's voice from behind Cora.

Cora stilled. What was going on here?

"I'm so sorry, Ms. Chevalier," the man said. "It's my daughter. She's having such a hard time with all of this."

Cora relaxed a bit. "I can see that," she said after a minute, a wave of sympathy swept through her for the woman who was still throwing doilies all over the front yard. At least she had stopped skipping.

"Rebecca, this just isn't helping," Josh pleaded.

Rebecca looked up at him, as if it was the first time she'd seen him. He walked up to her slowly, as if approaching an animal, or a stranger half crazed with grief, not a daughter. He held his arms out to her.

"You've got to be kidding," she said to him.

I should go, Cora thought. *Why are my feet not moving?* She was no longer a counselor, she told herself, and yet she couldn't help reaching out.

"Can I help?" she asked. "Are you okay?"

"Look, lady, I don't know who you are, but I think you should mind your own damn business," the woman said.

That was all Cora needed to hear to be on her way. When some half-crazed, grief-stricken woman tells you to leave, you march.

Chapter 18

Jane, Cora, Ruby, and Jude were on to dessert and coffee before they discussed Cora's visit to Sarah Waters' house. London was finally asleep, leaning on her mother in the corner of the restaurant booth.

After Cora relayed what had happened, Jane sat stunned. "She really threw the doilies all over the front yard?" Jane said.

Cora nodded.

Ruby and Jude exchanged knowing glances.

"What?" Cora said.

"That family has had more than its share of troubles," Jude said, stretching his arm across the seat.

"Rebecca?" Ruby said.

"Yes, I think that was her name," Cora said.

"Troubled doesn't begin to cover that one," Ruby said.

"So the whole family is messed up?" Jane said.

"Who knows what goes on behind closed doors?" Jude replied. "But I always thought there was something a little off about them. I never met the one daughter, the one they said was in England."

"I suspect the ex-husband was on drugs tonight," Cora said.

"That's hard to imagine," Jude said. "He seemed to be the most normal of all of them."

Ruby harrumphed. "That's not what I heard."

"I don't like to gossip," Jane said in a clipped tone. "Let's not go there."

"I agree," Cora said. "But it interests me because of Sarah's case. Do either of you think anybody in the family is capable of murder?" she said with a lowered voice.

The waitress came by and filled up their coffee cups, smiling. The conversation stopped until she left.

"I don't know them well enough to say yes or no to something like that," Jude said. "But I always thought that any of us might be capable, given the right circumstances."

Jane blinked and blushed, and stared off toward the window. But Cora knew that her friend had softened toward Jude. The two of them together? They would make a gorgeous couple. But she wasn't certain Jane was ready for a real relationship. But what the heck— did every relationship have to lead to something serious? Why couldn't Jane and Jude casually date and just have a good time?

"I know I could kill someone. It's not something I like to think about or something I'm proud of. Hell, I'm a pacifist. But if someone came at me or my kids, I have no idea what I'd be capable of," Ruby said.

Cora and Jane exchanged glances.

"But within a family, the mother is the nurturer. Usually kids don't kill their mothers. When kids kill their parents, usually it's their father," Cora went on. "So, statistically speaking, the odds are if someone within the family killed Sarah, it would have been her husband."

"But you're talking about a relatively normal family," Jude said. "And I never thought they were normal."

"What do you mean, specifically?" Cora asked.

"One of the daughters was arrested in college for prostitution. I don't know which one. But if that doesn't tell you something, I don't know what does," Jude said. "The other one had a baby when she was like, I don't know, fifteen? Fourteen?"

"It keeps getting deeper," Jane said.

"The more we find out about this family, the more it leads me to believe the police have a lot to investigate with Sarah's murder. That gives me hope," said Cora after a moment.

"You are such an optimist," Jane said, and lifted her coffee cup in a toast. "To Cora, the Queen of Optimism."

"Hear, hear," Ruby and Jude chimed in.

Fog had settled over the hills by the time the group was finished with dinner and walking back to the house. Fog unsettled Cora—perhaps it was too many cheesy horror flicks she had watched.

"I've always thought this town was one of the prettiest I've ever seen," Jude said when they arrived at the top of the hill where Kildare House was situated, and surveyed the town, despite the fog. At first, Cora had thought the house was simply named for the family who built it. But Kildare was actually the name of their hometown in Ireland, where they had made a

small fortune with horses. So they changed their name
when they came to America to honor their hometown.
When they first bought the piece of land in the gap
between two mountain ranges, they pretty much owned
the town. The house was situated in such a way that it
looked out over the town and valley. The view remained
spectacular.

"It is pretty," Cora agreed.

"And the damned historic preservation folks will
keep it that way. No matter what," Ruby mumbled.

"I'm impressed with what you've done to the place. I
love your mission. I hope it all works out for you," Jude
said.

"Thanks, Jude," Cora said and opened the front
door.

"Mind if I take a look around?" he asked.

"Go right ahead," she said.

"God, if I were twenty years younger," Ruby said as he
left the foyer. "I'd go for it."

Jane laughed. "Really?"

"He's hot! Come on, what's wrong with you young
women? Live a little!" Ruby said and added a little
flourish with her hands.

"Not my type," Jane said.

Cora didn't reply. She was busy fussing over the floral
arrangement.

"Is he your type?" Ruby said, elbowing her.

"Who?" Cora said, still distracted by the flowers.

"Jude!"

"Jude, my type? I don't know. He is charismatic," Cora
said, thinking she would keep her true thoughts on
the luscious man to herself. "But he is here on business.

I make it a policy to not sleep with colleagues." Was that her policy? Since when? Since now, she decided.

"Usually a pretty easy policy to enforce since most of our colleagues are women," Ruby said. "But Jude is all man . . . and also not your type?"

"Her type is the new librarian who works at the school. Nerdy," Jane interjected.

Cora preened over the flowers and didn't react to Jane's jabs. Jane knew that just the word "nerdy" made her heart skip a few beats. Visions of being "taken" among the stacks at a library or bookstore played in her mind. Or perhaps a science lab.

"By the way," Jane said, nonchalantly, "I invited him to the chocolate reception. I hope you don't mind."

"What? Who?" Cora's voice rose.

Just then, a woman walked in the still-open front door, carrying a suitcase. "Hi there," she said. "I'm Ivy Renquist, checking in."

Cora had always imagined this moment. Her first guest. She paused to take it in for a moment before saying:

"Welcome, Ivy. I'm Cora."

"Oh, Cora! I've been such a fan of your blog! I'm thrilled to meet you!" Ivy squealed.

The woman was short, a little plump, and in her forties—right in the market they had targeted. "Look at the gorgeous house!"

The others introduced themselves.

Jude suddenly appeared in the foyer. "Can I take your bags?"

Ivy's face reddened. "Jude Sawyer!"

Ivy ate the man up with her leering eyes. Cora thought

she might growl, pass out, or attack Jude at any moment. Instead, she giggled and bounced on her feet when she saw Jude. What a broom-making rock star!

"Ivy's room is on the second floor. Second room on the right," Cora said, thinking that Ivy might prove to be a handful.

Chapter 19

A little past midnight, Cora heard a noise at her front door. Her window seat was right above the front door. She had just fallen asleep—or had she? Had she just been dreaming? But then she heard it again.

She slid out of her quilt-covered bed and gazed out the window. It was so dark. One of the town's ordinances was that streetlights could only be placed every other block, and Kildare House was without them. But the moon was bright and almost full. Cora blinked. Should she go downstairs? Call the police?

The noise came again. She reached for her cell phone, and right at that moment she saw him. A lone figure starting to walk toward her gate. He had a familiar air. He wore a baseball cap. Josh Waters! Why was he here so late at night?

Her fingers hit the *9*, and then she saw another figure. A shadow. A woman. And what was that? She had a gun!

She dialed the *1*, then *1* again.

"9-1-1. What's your emergency?" a woman said promptly on the other end of the line.

"There's an intruder in my front yard. And someone with a gun." Cora's voice shook. The air in her lungs dwindled. She should be used to this kind of thing by now. But she'd never get used to it.

"What is your address?"

What *was* her address? For a moment, Cora's mind went blank. She had almost given the address of her old place in Pittsburgh.

"Um . . . I live at Kildare House at 566 Kildare," she said, still watching the scene out of her window.

The man's hands were up, as if in surrender. He gestured back toward the house, and tried to get the woman with a gun to go in the same direction. What the heck?

The woman moved forward, but she kept her gun pointed at the man. Sirens rang out. And then both the man and the woman froze in their tracks.

Cora saw the lights first, then the car. Where was her robe? She searched around on the pile of clothes on her chair. Clothes she had placed there to sort and put away, but had never gotten around to. Her robe was at the bottom of the pile. She slid it on over her T-shirt and fuzzy pj bottoms and raced downstairs.

Luna looked up at her and meowed a decidedly disgruntled meow, then laid her head back down. She knew it wasn't morning yet. Smart cat.

As Cora descended the stairs, she heard a door open—could it be Ivy, awakened by all the noise out front? She turned her head to inspect, but she kept walking. No, it was Jude—but wasn't that Ivy's room he was exiting? No, it couldn't be. Had there been some kind of mix-up with the rooms?

"Everything okay?" Jude said to her as she flew by

him. Oh Lord, the man was rumpled and sexy and looked as cute and dangerous as the Cheshire Cat.

"I'm not sure," Cora managed to say. "I'm on my way to investigate."

"I'll come with."

"Suit yourself," she replied and kept going. *He wasn't sleeping in Ivy's room, was he?* The idea was preposterous.

She turned on the porch light and opened the front door. There stood two uniformed police officers with Josh Waters. He was cuffed. Ruby stood on the porch talking with the officers.

"Yes, of course, I have a permit," she said, indignant.

"Ruby?" Cora said, looking at the gun in her hand. "What are you doing?"

"I saw this man out walking around on the property. Didn't recognize him at first. Sorry, Josh. But what the hell are you doing out this time of night on someone else's property?" Ruby said.

Her pacifist, ex-hippie herbalist packed heat? Cora made a mental note about scheduling a long conversation with Ruby.

"Are you the owner of this house?" An officer approached her. Was he one of the same officers from the graffiti incident? Of course he was—how many cops could a small town employ?

"Yes," she said.

"Do you know this man?"

"We met earlier in the day. I stopped by his house for the yard sale," she said.

"I told you that," Josh said to Shimer.

Shimer nodded. "Still doesn't explain what you were doing here."

"I was delivering something. It's over there on the

front porch," Josh stated, bright eyed and alert. Not how he looked earlier in the day.

Cora turned and faced the box, which she suspected contained the doilies she'd purchased earlier. She walked back up the steps and bent over and lifted the box. It was full of the doilies and handkerchiefs, plus more—he added in other bits and pieces of lace and cloth. How delightful.

But also how strange. Why would he drop it by at this time of night?

A note was attached:

Sorry about earlier today. You purchased these. I want you to have them.
                                    Josh Waters

"Thank you," Cora said to Josh. "Officers, I think you can let him go."

"Just a darn minute. He was trespassing," Ruby said. "Ain't no man up to any good at this time of night."

"Explanation?" asked the other officer, who Cora now realized was Officer Glass.

Josh hung his head a bit, then scanned the gathered crowd.

"You bought them. I wanted you to have them. I don't know," he said and shrugged his shoulders. "I sometimes lose track of time. I'm not sleeping these days. So I thought I'd sit them on your porch and you'd find them first thing in the morning. Thought it would be a nice surprise. I'm sorry. I didn't mean to scare you."

"Scare me? It takes more than the likes of you to scare me, Josh Waters," Ruby said indignantly.

"Ruby!" Cora said.

"Okay," Glass said. "We'll let you go with a warning, Waters. This all seems to check out. This is Indigo Gap, not Philadelphia. Folks don't roam the streets after certain hours. Got that?"

Josh nodded sheepishly.

But he used to live here. Doesn't he know all about Indigo Gap? Cora thought.

Cora shivered in the October night—but it wasn't because of the chill in the air.

Chapter 20

A full, bright moon beamed through Cora's lacy sheer curtains. How was she supposed to sleep after the incident that happened right in her front yard? She turned over one more time, then decided to get some blog writing done.

Instead, she found herself searching on the Internet for information about Josh Waters. He was a retired school teacher in Philadelphia, Pennsylvania. He had remarried—to a Charlotte Bow—and had two children with her.

His family must love him being here, tending to his ex-wife's estate, Cora mused.

More probing revealed an article about drug addiction in which he was quoted as saying, "It rules your life until you rule it."

That is true enough, Cora thought.

A huge follower of Al-Anon, Waters had apparently lost his first marriage because of drug addiction. He stated in the article that he didn't want to go into detail, but that those years were rough and he'd rather put them behind him.

Hmm. So was it him or his wife that had the addiction?

Most nondomestic murders in the United States were drug related. But it was hard to imagine that Sarah Waters—the school librarian—had a drug problem, especially when Cora knew about the tight security at the schools. They would not let a woman with a record work there, let alone a woman involved with drugs.

She had suspected Josh was on something when she was with him in his ex-wife's house. Was Sarah killed because she or Josh owed money to a drug lord somewhere?

Drug lord? This was not her old borderline neighborhood in Pittsburgh, Cora reminded herself. Did they have drug lords in Indigo Gap? The unusually low crime rate was one reason she picked this place to relocate to. She'd had enough criminal excitement to last her a lifetime—which was partly why she had developed the panic disorder. She was not built for daily hard-core stress.

The possibility of drug involvement in Sarah's case was extremely high—at least in Cora's estimation. She Googled Sarah Waters again, and the same list of links appeared.

But there was a new one—it was about the historical commission in Indigo Gap, a tough bunch of people who kept a watchful eye on the main few streets of the town to make certain everybody was abiding by the rules. Some of those rules included things like what you could plant in your garden, what color you could paint your house, and what kind of curtains you could hang in the windows. Cora thought it was a bit much, but she had to admit the historical integrity of the town had endured as a result.

She clicked on the article. It was about a new proposed color for Sarah's house. She had wanted to paint it, and the board struck her down. It wasn't the first time Sarah had gone head-to-head with them. A certain man, Edgar Thorncraft, always seemed to reject her proposals. The article listed the several things she'd tried to change over the years, and sometimes the commission would be split almost right down the middle, with Edgar delivering the final blow of rejection.

Cora had actually met Edgar Thorncraft. She met him the day he came over to Jane's place to review the paint color she'd selected for the carriage house. He walked around that day with a clipboard, taking notes. He seemed pleasant enough, but maybe a little rigid. He was pleased with the color Jane selected—historical creds and all that. Cora was not about to rock the historical boat that she and Jane came in on—it worked for them.

So—Sarah Waters was not a little mouse of a librarian. She was possibly involved in drugs, went to bat against the commission several times, and had been quite a collector of some unusual items. Sarah might have been an interesting person to hang out with—sans drugs, of course. What a sorry end for her.

Cora debated what her next step should be. Should she try to talk with Josh again? Possibly Edgar? Or maybe she should contact Cashel and see what he knew about these folks first. That sounded like the most sensible thing to do. Maybe when she told him what she figured out, he'd follow up. Maybe.

He thought it best to leave the investigating to the cops, so he might not want to help.

But the cops' investigation seemed to be focused on Jane, and that was not going to get them anywhere. After all, Jane had an alibi. She was out of town.

But where exactly was she? Where had Jane gone that weekend? Cora didn't even think to ask her at the time where she was going. And it was obvious that Jane had gotten mixed up herself about the times and dates.

Well, it didn't matter where she had been, Cora reminded herself, she knew Jane didn't kill Sarah. And Jane was entitled to some private time.

Cora's eyelids were finally drooping, and she slipped into bed. She was asleep almost before her head hit the pillow.

The next morning, Cora grabbed a cup of coffee, stacked a bunch of muffins into a basket, and high-tailed it to Cashel's office. Her goal was to get out of the house before she was corralled into taking London to school again or into a long social breakfast with her guest teacher and guest. She'd left them both a list of good places to eat in Indigo Gap.

She ran into Cashel on the sidewalk outside of his office, which was across the street from the police station.

"Hey," Cashel said. "Good morning. What are you doing out and about so early?"

"I'm coming to your office. I wanted to talk with

you," Cora replied. Dang, he was looking fine in a dark blue suit and a red tie.

"I'm in court this morning," he said and frowned. He glanced at his watch. "I have about twenty minutes. Let's go to the park."

Sitting on a park bench next to Cashel was not what she planned. Still, there could be worse things. They walked together to the corner, where there was a little park with several benches. He sat down and she followed his lead.

Once again, Cora noted that Cashel's eyes were blue, blue, blue—especially blue outdoors with the sky's reflection and light in them.

Get a grip, Cora. He is Ruby's son.

"What's in the basket?" he said.

"Muffins."

"For me?"

"You may have one, but I'm taking them to the police station."

"I'm sure there's a story?" he asked, reaching for a blueberry muffin and taking a bite. His hair was catching the morning light, giving it a golden sheen. "Okay, spill," he said, with his mouth curling into a kind of lopsided grin, then took a bite. "Mmm, good muffins."

"Thanks," she said and proceeded to fill him in on what happened last night, as well as the graffiti, and the confrontation in the front yard of Sarah Waters' house with her daughter.

"I know you're trying to help Jane," he said when Cora was done. "But it looks like it could get dangerous. I want you to stop."

"I can defend myself," she told him. She didn't feel

obligated to tell him about all the self-defense classes she had been required to take as part of her old job.

"Not much you can do against a gun," he said.

"Nobody had a gun—except your mother," she said, watching him finish his muffin and roll his eyes at the mention of his mom. "All that aside, what do you think?"

"I think you have a unique mind," he said, as a softness came over his face. Cora might have been misreading him—but she thought he genuinely liked her. "I think you care a lot for your friend. But what makes you think the police haven't previously researched this?"

"Because they are investigating Jane. Why would they bother with her if there were other leads?" she responded. A strand of her red hair blew in front of her eye, so she tucked it behind her ear.

"They found a partial print that appears to match hers and they are compelled to look into it. That's pretty serious business," he said after a few moments.

"We both know those aren't her prints. When will the team of experts be here to look at them?"

"They are already here, from my understanding. Look, I need to go," he said and started to rise from the bench.

"One more thing," she said. "Does Indigo Gap have a drug problem?"

"Every place in this country has one—big or small. It's everywhere."

"Thanks for talking with me," Cora said and stood face-to-face with him a moment.

He scratched his chin and eyeballed her, opened his

mouth as if he had something to say, and then looked away as he picked up his briefcase.

"Oh," he said, turning back around. "Giving muffins to the police? Nicely played." He laughed and walked away.

Chapter 21

When Cora still wasn't home after Jane returned from taking London to school, she started to worry. It was ridiculous, Jane knew. If anybody could take care of herself, it was Cora. When most people looked at Cora, they might think she was pretty and sweet and, well, almost pixie-like. But looks deceived. Cora was a warrior.

A creative-warrior vintage-fairy-princess. But still. A warrior.

She noticed a car pulling up to the house and wondered if it was a guest arriving early. When Jane opened the front door, she realized that it was that guy from the historical commission.

"Good morning," she said. "Can I help you?"

"I'm Edgar Thorncraft."

"Yes," she said. "I remember. Is there a problem?"

"I'm checking on the parking situation. I know you're having guests this weekend," he said and used one of his long bony fingers to push his glasses back on his nose.

"There will be cars parked here and in the driveway.

Cora isn't here now, but she informed you about this, right?"

He nodded. "I wanted to make sure the number of guests hadn't grown. We don't want visitors to our quaint historical town to see an eyesore in the form of a big pile of cars in front of one of our most famous houses," he said with a biting tone.

Jane frowned. "As far as I know, our registration has remained the same as when Cora spoke with you. If it's changed, I'll have her call you. Do you have a card?"

"She has my number."

So do I, Jane thought. "Okay," she said. "I'll pass along your concerns." She walked forward out of the house, trying to usher him along. But he stood and observed the house, then turned back to Jane.

"You are Jane Starr, correct?"

She nodded.

"Humph. My sister loves your pottery," he said and then walked away.

"That's so good to hear," she called out after him.

What an odd bird. The words "lacking in social skills" rang in her head. Oh well. She wasn't going to worry about him today. Today was an important day. The retreat guests were arriving, and they were going to have a fabulous reception. Launch day. She could hardly believe it.

If someone had said to her ten years ago that this life was going to be hers, she wouldn't have believed it. Of course, it could all be taken away if by some strange fluke she was found guilty of the murder of Sarah Waters.

As she turned the corner into the backyard and garden that was between the main house and the carriage house, Jane saw some weeds and bent down to pluck them out. When she stood back up, there was Ruby, with her hands on her hips.

"Where were you last night?" Ruby demanded.

"Here. I mean, I was home." Why was Ruby questioning her as if she were guilty of something? She'd noticed Ruby regarding her oddly a few times today. It was unsettling—was Ruby suspicious of her? Or was Jane being paranoid?

"Didn't you hear all the commotion out front?" Ruby persisted.

"No," she said, with her heartbeat escalating. What was going on?

"Well, it turned out to be nothing," Ruby said. "But that Josh Waters was sneaking around the property. Brought over a box of doilies and put it on the front porch."

"What? Why would he do that?"

"Good question. He said that Cora should have them. After all, she paid for them."

"Well," Jane said, making a mental note that a nearby flower bed needed some attention, "I suppose he was trying to be nice."

"At midnight? Nobody is up to any good at that hour of the day." Ruby scowled.

"So what happened?"

"Cora called the cops. They were here. Sirens. Lights, Everything. You didn't hear a thing?"

"No," Jane said. Last night, she must have checked all the doors and windows five times before she went to sleep. She was such a sound sleeper that it had become a joke with her family, how she could sleep through anything. The only time she didn't slept through noise was when London was a baby. "I didn't hear anything, but that's not unusual."

"Where's Cora?" Ruby said.

"I don't know. Maybe she's at the police station because of what happened last night."

"I doubt it. It was resolved pretty quickly. She's not pressing charges. I think she felt sorry for the guy. He is kind of pitiful."

"Is he?" Jane asked, thinking about Cora's suspicion about him killing Sarah.

Ruby nodded. "I've always felt sorry for him. I didn't know him or Sarah well, but he seemed like the clichéd browbeaten husband. Always looked tired, slumped over, followed her around like a puppy dog."

Jane bent down and plucked a few more weeds. "What about their daughter—the one who Cora ran into yesterday?"

"Bad seed," Ruby said. "Very bad seed."

Jane felt a chill travel up her spine and she shivered. Was it a premonition? Or was she just nervous because of the secret she was keeping?

Chapter 22

When Cora walked into the police station, she was pleased to spot Officer Glass from the incident the night before standing behind a desk where the receptionist was seated. He spotted her and smiled. Cora smiled back. The sweetest, most charming smile she could muster.

"Can I help you?" the receptionist said.

"Are you here about last night?" Officer Glass asked. He was familiar with both Cora and Kildare House by now. He'd been to the place twice during the past few days.

"In a way, yes. I would like to talk with you, if that's okay," Cora said.

"I have a few minutes. Come inside," he said and opened the door.

Cora walked down the hallway to a wide office filled with cubicles. Officer Glass led her into his cubicle. Plants and photos of his family donned his L-shaped desk.

"What can I help you with?" he said.

"Well, first I wanted to thank you for coming by the house last night," she said. She handed him the basket of muffins.

"Thank you. I'll share it with the guys. Very kind of you," he said and unfolded the towel on top of the muffins and took a whiff. An expression of pure pleasure came over his face.

"I was wondering if you could recommend an alarm company," Cora said. "I didn't think we'd need it. I researched before we came here and the crime rate is so low. The police here do such a good job. But now I wonder if I might need one. Between the graffiti incident and last night, well, I'm kind of shaken," she said, wondering if he'd believe her. She didn't believe herself, even as she spoke the words.

"Our crime rate is very low," he said. "But I can recommend a few alarm companies." He placed a muffin on a napkin on his desk, reached for a tablet, and started to scratch down a few names.

"I was surprised yesterday when someone mentioned the Waters family had problems with drugs. I mean, here, in Indigo Gap? Drugs?" Cora said.

He set his pencil down and squinted at her.

"I guess drugs are everywhere," she continued. "But it's one of the reasons I left Pittsburgh. I was so tired of the junkies in my neighborhood." Lies, lies, lies. There hadn't been a single junkie in her neighborhood—at least none that she knew of.

Officer Glass merely grunted in agreement.

"Are there any places in town I should stay away from?" Cora asked.

"No," he replied. "It's very safe in town."

"But yesterday I was nearly assaulted at the Waters house," she said.

"Why didn't you call us?"

"I handled it and left quickly."

"What were you doing there?"

"I went for the yard sale—remember, that's why Josh brought me the box of doilies."

"Oh yes, right."

"But I smelled something odd. I thought it was coming from the opium kits and collectibles Sarah had. But now I don't know."

His eyebrows hitched. Cora took that as an invitation to keep talking.

"I'm sure if that family is involved in drugs, you all would know it, and that would be a part of your investigation into Sarah's murder," Cora said.

"I'm not on that case so I couldn't tell you. It's an ongoing investigation so things are pretty hush-hush."

"I wish I knew. It would allow me to sleep better. I mean, I moved here, thinking I'd be safer, and . . ." She allowed her voice to rise a little and batted her eyes. Oh, she was making herself sick! Would he buy into this god-awful acting job of hers?

"I'll tell you what. I'll check into it a little bit and let you know, okay?" Officer Glass said in kind of a condescending voice.

But he meant well. He was trying to help a community member feel safe. She knew that. So she smiled, yet again.

"I'd so appreciate that," she said. Her grandmother's voice rang in her head: *You catch more flies with honey than vinegar.*

"Here's the list of alarm companies we recommend," he said and slid the paper across the desk.

"Thanks so much, Officer Glass," Cora said, extending her hand. "Thank you, I feel so much better knowing you'll help me out a bit."

When he smiled back at her, Cora could've sworn he was checking her out—as in his eyes sparked with a leering quality. No. Could it be? Certainly not. She must be misreading the situation. She tried to shrug it off as she left.

As Cora walked through town back toward her house, she pulled out her phone from her crocheted handbag to check her messages. Dang. Five messages. Three were from the caterer. One was from Jane, and the other was from Ruby.

She listened to Jane's message first. "Where are you? I'm starting to worry about you. It's opening day and where are you?"

Opening day! Yes! Cora knew it was opening day, of course, but had to check a few things off her list before she could get to the rest of the day's activities.

The message from Ruby was typically to the point. "Good morning, sunshine. The caterers are trying to reach you."

Cora's heart began to race. Three messages from the caterer and one from Ruby about them as well. What was going on?

Cora didn't bother listening to the rest of the messages; she just called the caterer directly.

"Hi, Ms. Day, this is Cora Chevalier," she said when Darla picked up the phone. "I didn't listen to your messages, but I saw that you left them. What's going on?"

"We're going to substitute some of the cheese that you selected. I didn't want it to be a surprise. One of our suppliers had some diseased cows or something and has just gotten busted," Darla said.

Busted was an odd word coming out of Darla Day's mouth for some reason.

Is this really why she had left *three* messages and it wasn't even ten AM? *Because of cheese?* Cora thought.

Cora loved her food, but she wondered if Darla was a bit off. Why make such a big deal about cheese?

"Thanks so much," Cora said. "Is there anything else?"

"Would you like to select one of the other local cheeses before tonight?"

"No," Cora said, perhaps a bit too quickly. "I trust you implicitly." *And don't call me back unless there is an emergency,* she wanted to say, but didn't.

"Well," Darla said. "Thank you for that. Very good to know. We'll see you around four?"

"Yes, see you then," Cora said.

Okay, so she wasn't experienced dealing with caterers, but that was making a mountain out of a mole hill. It was one more reason to get the kitchen into good shape so that she could do the cooking and baking herself.

As she rounded the corner to the street where her house sat, Cora observed Jane talking with Edgar Thorncraft in the front yard. She backed up and hid behind a hedge. He was the last person she wanted to see.

Suddenly, she was a bundle of nerves. Tonight was the night—the beginning of their craft-retreat business. And despite her hard work, she sensed her carefully laid plans might unravel.

Chapter 23

Cora, Jane, and Ruby spent the rest of the day checking in their guests and getting them situated. Two women, Martha and Diane, had driven up all the way from Florida. Miranda, with the pretty soft blue eyes, had come from Tennessee. Several of the other women had come from Ohio; they had a crafting group and traveled together to be a part of the retreat.

Cora was basking in the warmth of these women. They were eager to try a new craft or two over the next few days, and so was Cora. She could hardly wait.

She snapped a few photos of some of the preparations— the centerpieces, and baskets, plus the bouquet her uncle had sent. She intended to write up a blog post this afternoon. Keeping up with social media was a never-ending task. But she wanted her blog followers who couldn't make it to the retreat to feel like they were in the loop.

She dashed off to her apartment, and with Luna in her lap, she wrote a post.

Then she lay down on her bed—just a quick wink would help to refresh her for the rest of the afternoon.

She was a firm believer in power naps—necessary to the creative process.

Cora applied pink lipstick and took one last view at herself in the mirror. Not bad. Cora's guests were all now here. The caterers were here. Everything was moving along like clockwork.

She had changed into her beloved 1960s red-and-white minidress and vintage white boots. She slipped the Bakelite earrings on and grinned. "This is it," she told herself, her green eyes blinking back at her.

She glanced over her room and saw Luna curled up in the box of doilies. When she saw Cora giving her a look-see, she mewed. It was her hungry mew.

"Okay, Luna," Cora said. "Follow me into the kitchen."

Kitchen was not quite the right word for it. It was more of a kitchenette, with a fridge and a tiny stove, which she only used to boil water for her daily tea breaks. But it was efficient and Cora liked it—in fact, she liked her whole apartment. Her favorite part of it was the way the ceiling sloped and the interesting nooks and crannies throughout that were turrets and window seats. It was large, the biggest attic apartment Cora had ever seen. But the space was open—the living room, kitchen, and dining room were one huge space sectioned off by nothing more than furniture. Her bedroom and another room were separate rooms. She also had a huge oddly shaped storage room, which made her feel a little bit like Alice in Wonderland.

Luna followed and watched as Cora prepared her food and sat the dish in front of her.

"Your Majesty," Cora said and smiled. Then she gave Luna a scratch on her calico head.

She went back into her bedroom to grab a handmade shawl to wrap around her shoulders. October in North Carolina was not like October in Pennsylvania. Thank goddess for that. But there was still a chill. They had not turned the furnace on yet for the season, but a fire roared in the fireplace downstairs. The old house was drafty.

As she reached for her shawl, she noticed that a few doilies had escaped the box. She picked one up and held it up to the light. It was beautiful, with elegant stitch work. Did Sarah herself make these?

Cora was expected downstairs, of course, but she couldn't help digging around a bit in the box. She marveled at the luscious, lacy doilies with tinges of pinks and purples.

As she reached farther into the box, something solid, cool, and hard touched her fingers.

She flipped the box upside down on her bed.

There, nestled among the delicate doilies, was a small gun.

A gun? What the heck?

It was the smallest and most elegant gun Cora had ever seen. Jewel encrusted. Perhaps a lady's pistol? What did Cora know? She was ignorant about guns, but this one was tiny and pretty. Still, she hated guns. Nothing good ever came of them. She made a mental note to remember to tell Ruby to get rid of her own gun as soon as possible.

But what was a gun doing in this box?

As she mulled it over, she started to wonder if Josh knew the gun was in the box. Or did he, in his haste, drop it in the box so the police didn't see it? Which would mean that he was up to no good, as Ruby suggested. Cora felt a shiver. She pulled the wrap over her shoulders closer.

Just what she needed. A gun in her bedroom at the start of her opening reception. She'd endeavor to sweep it out of her mind and be a good hostess. But later, she'd pay Josh Waters a visit to return the gun. But she promised herself that this time she wouldn't go alone.

She wrapped the gun in one of the doilies and placed it back in the flimsy box. Sarah Waters certainly collected some interesting things—this gun included, if indeed it had been hers.

As Cora descended the stairs, she heard music and laughter from the party already starting on the main floor. She'd hired a local modern bluegrass trio to help celebrate. Strains of the banjo and guitar welcomed her. Her guests gathered in groups across the foyer and into the sitting room. The couch brimmed with women. The chairs were full, and people held plates of food and glasses of wine. Cora gave herself a moment to soak it in.

"You know my date," Ruby said as she came up beside Cora.

"Your date?" Cora turned. It was Cashel, in blue jeans and a gorgeous sweater that Cora was certain someone (probably Ruby) had made for him. It was an unusual shade of green, which brought out the green flecks in his eyes. He looked good. He should wear jeans more often.

"Oh, hi, Cashel," Cora said. "How's it going?"

"I was wondering how your meeting with the police went today. Did you find out anything?" he asked.

"Not yet, but I have feelers out." Cora watched as one of the caterers carried a tray around to her guests. "Good to know you're here, Cashel," she said in a slightly quieter tone. "I have something in my bedroom I need to show you before the night is over."

He nearly choked on his drink as his face reddened.

"Land sakes," Ruby said. "Aren't you brash? And right in front of his mother."

"No, no," Cora said hurriedly, as she realized her poor choice of words. "That's not what I mean. Not at all. I'm sorry." She felt her face heat with a blush.

"Cora." Jane walked over to her. "There's a group of women in the paper-crafting room with questions about tomorrow's schedule. I couldn't answer them."

"Excuse me," Cora said. "We'll talk later, Cashel."

He gave her a crooked, impish grin.

"What did I miss?" Jane said.

"I'll tell you later," Cora said quickly. Leaving the others behind, Cora entered the paper-crafting room, where two women stood admiring the shelves of supplies.

It was the two women from Florida—Martha and Diane.

"Hi there," Cora said.

"I'm a big fan of your blog," Martha said.

"Thanks so much. What can I help you with?"

"Well, we had a question about the schedule," Diane said, pulling it out from her bag. "There seems to be a lot of time between the classes?"

Cora nodded. "I'll be speaking about this in a moment. Won't you join me in the sitting room?"

They followed her in, and Cora clinked a spoon to her glass to get everybody's attention.

"I'd like to thank you all for being here for the first retreat," Cora said, as the crowd hushed and gathered around her. "This place is a dream come true for me. I wanted a place where people could gather and learn new crafts in a supportive, safe, and free environment. With no pressure. As many of you know, when I worked as a counselor at a women's shelter, I realized how healing and how much fun crafting could be. To take classes or hang out working on what you want to do. So, as someone mentioned just now, there's a lot of downtime in the schedule. It is, after all, a retreat. A time you've given yourself to think and reflect while crafting. I'm so happy you're all here."

Cora's eyes met Jane's misty eyes.

"This, ladies and gentlemen, is my best friend, and one of the best potters in the world, Jane Starr."

Jane waved.

"She won't be teaching classes this weekend, as we're not quite ready for it, but if you have any questions about pottery, she's your girl."

A smattering of polite applause erupted from the small crowd.

"And of course, our guest teacher Jude Sawyer will be teaching a broom-making class first thing tomorrow morning."

More applause, a bit louder this time.

Jude lifted his head and gave a little wave. He was flanked by two women, neither of them Ivy, Cora noted. He must have ducked her.

"And where is Ruby?" Cora scanned the gathered crowd to see Ruby, who was raising her hand.

"Our resident herbalist is Ruby O'Malley," Cora said. "She'll be teaching the candle-making and soap-making classes this weekend. But she's always happy to talk about herbs if you have any questions."

"A toast!" Ruby suddenly said. "A toast to Cora." She cast her eyes toward Cashel, and he raised his glass. "Congratulations!"

As all the guests raised their glasses to her, Cora's heart filled with emotion. She blinked away tears and lifted her glass.

It was then that a gunshot rang out.

Everybody stood still—it was like something out of an old movie. All eyes were on Cora, her mouth hanging open.

"That darn neighbor of ours," Ruby said, thinking quick and breaking the stunned silence. "That car of his backfires and it always sounds like a gun. Sorry about that folks—we didn't mean to startle you."

"Yes," Cora said, finally finding her voice. "Please relax and enjoy the food and music."

Her heart pounded. She excused herself as gracefully as she could and headed upstairs to check. Did that shot come from the gun in her bedroom? If so, who shot it?

Cora headed quickly for the stairs, with Cashel and Jane following close behind. Ruby kept the guests busy downstairs, discussing different kinds of wax with a group of crafters, as the three of them made a beeline for the attic apartment.

"What was that, honestly?" Jane whispered.

"I have my suspicions," Cora replied, as they made their way upstairs.

Cora looked at Cashel when they arrived at her door.

"Just before I came down to the party, I rummaged through my box of doilies and inside was a pretty little gun."

"A pretty gun?" Jane said.

"And you think it might have gone off?" Cashel said.

"My cat is inside. I'm hoping she's okay," Cora said as she opened the door.

But the apartment appeared to be empty.

"The gun isn't where I left it," Cora said, shifting through the doilies covering her bedspread. "Luna?" Cora called.

"Luna?" Cora repeated, then searched under her bed to find her terrified cat, who mewed an awful, mournful sob of a mew. Cora pulled her out and brought her to her chest. "There, there, kitty." She stroked and scratched the cat to soothe her.

"But where is the gun?" Cashel asked, looking around.

"There it is," Jane pointed to the gun, which was on the kitchen floor. A bullet hole blackened a nearby cupboard.

"Whoa," Cashel said. "You're lucky you weren't here when it went off."

"But how . . ." Jane said.

"Obviously Luna knocked it off the bed and it fired. It's a good thing she didn't shoot herself," Cora said.

"Why would you leave a loaded gun lying around?" Cashel asked angrily.

"I don't know anything about guns," Cora protested. "I had no idea it was loaded."

Cashel carefully picked the gun up off the floor. He opened the gun and emptied out a few bullets.

"It is pretty," Jane said, admiring the jewel-encrusted weapon.

"We need to return that as soon as possible," Cora said. "Like tonight. I'll never be able to sleep with it in the house, let alone my apartment."

"Okay," Jane said. "I don't think I can go with you because I need to get London to bed and the sitter needs to get home."

"I'll go with you," Cashel said to Cora. "It's no problem."

Jane glowered at Cora. She'd made her feelings about Cora's attraction to him quite clear.

"I think that would be a good idea," Cora said and grinned at Jane, who rolled her eyes and walked off. After all, what could it hurt to bring the handsome Cashel O'Malley with her on this gorgeous October evening? A girl could always use a good friend like him. The fact that he was so scrumptious had nothing to do with it. Nothing at all.

Chapter 24

"I have to go," Jane said, after making her way over to Cora, who was deep in conversation with Jennifer, a woman who owned a yarn shop in Pennsylvania and whose husband had recently passed away after an extended battle with cancer. She really needed this retreat. Her daughters had given it to her as a surprise.

"Babysitter?" Cora said to Jane.

Jane nodded.

"It is getting late, ladies, I'm off to bed," Jennifer said. But several of the other guests sidetracked her with questions about yarn.

Jane left, and Cora began searching for Cashel. She found him and Jude in the kitchen, each with a bottle of beer.

Cashel looked up at her. "Are you ready for me?" He said and winked. Jude laughed.

"As ready as I'll ever be," she said and grabbed his arm, as if to pull him along.

"Do you have the gun?" Cashel asked as they exited the house.

She nodded.

It was only a little after nine PM, but Cora still felt a little odd about visiting this time of night, especially with a gun in her purse. But it was the only place to keep it. Cashel wore a sweater, no jacket, and the gun certainly would not fit in the back pocket of his jeans. They walked off together down the nearly empty streets of Indigo Gap. The historically accurate streetlights helped light the way.

"This gun is surely a collectible," Cora said. "Sarah had so many interesting collections."

"Yes, I read about that in the newspaper. The auction listed everything. I can't believe people collect and pay for brooms," Cashel responded.

"People collect anything you can imagine. But I'm the opposite of a collector."

"Wait a minute," he said and stopped at the corner. The lights fell along the lines of his face in an interesting way. His eyes glowed. "Who had doilies all over her bed today?"

"I can see why you'd think that I collected those," she said and laughed a little. "But what I'm doing is repurposing them. I haven't made up my mind yet what I'll make with them, but that's one of my things. Taking something old and repurposing it."

"Interesting. You're kind of doing that with my mother too."

"What do you mean?"

"Before you bought the place, well, she was a bit of a hermit. You've made her feel like her knowledge is appreciated," he said. "Thanks for that." He sort of leaned in to her, and suddenly she saw Ruby's face in his and backed away from him. Was he going to kiss her?

He raised an eyebrow, but didn't say anything.

Cora decided they should keep moving down the lane and started walking with more purpose toward the Waterses' home. Cashel followed close behind. As the house came into view, she was pleased to find the lights on, which meant that Josh was still awake.

They walked up the sidewalk to the front-door stoop and rang the doorbell. As Cora leaned against the outer edge of the door and waited for Josh to open it, she noticed a crack of light between the door and the frame. The door had not been properly closed. She pushed on it slightly and it opened fully.

"That's odd," Cashel said. "Leaving the door open like that."

"Mr. Waters?" Cora said. "Are you in there?"

"Waters?" Cashel echoed.

The two of them entered the house and both called out for him again.

Items were strewn about haphazardly—pillows, Tupperware, clothing. But as Cora walked over to the tables, where all the garage-sale items had been, she noticed that a good deal of it had apparently been sold.

But something was wrong.

Maybe she should just sit the gun on the table and leave the house. Maybe Josh was in the bathroom. Or taking a shower. She didn't want to disturb him. A sudden overwhelming sense of discomfort came over her. Her skin pricked. She shouldn't be here; she was intruding. Yet, he had left the door open.

She turned and faced Cashel. She reached into her purse to pull out the gun. "I'm just going to leave it here," she said. And then she noticed the tennis shoe.

It was sticking out from under one of the tables— and it was attached to something. Or someone.

"Cashel—" she said and nodded in the direction of the shoe. "Is that—?"

Cashel rushed forward and kneeled down. His hands went to his face as he stood. His normally peachy skin tone was now ghostly pale. He took an audible deep gulp of air.

"Are you okay?" she said, rushing to his side.

Cashel shook his head. "Call 9-1-1."

She reached for her cell phone, and leaned down to get a view of why she was calling the police.

At first she saw something red and lacy, but she blinked her eyes and saw the blood-soaked doilies— lying all around and on top of Josh Waters. A huge blade was lodged in his crumpled and very bloody body.

Cora dropped her phone, her purse, and the little gun. The last thing she remembered was the sound of the items as they crashed to the hardwood floor. Then everything went black.

When she came to, she was on a couch in another room. She woke up confused and bruised. Did she land on her left arm? It hurt like hell. Where was she? What had happened? As her mind caught up to where her body was positioned, a paramedic walked into the room with a glass of water.

"Okay," the paramedic said. "Let's get you sitting up and drinking some water."

"What happened?" Cora managed to say.

"You passed out. Which is a typical reaction to finding a body covered in blood," she said cheerfully. "Perfectly normal response."

"Oh yes. Poor Josh Waters. Oh my God, what happened to him?" Her brain was moving in slow motion. How much time had lapsed?

"I'm okay," Cora said. The room finally stopped spinning. Cashel sat next to her on the couch.

"This is Cashel," Cora told the paramedic, who looked questioningly at her.

"What happened?" asked another paramedic.

"Not much," Cora said. "I passed out because I ran into a dead body surrounded by bloody doilies."

"We shouldn't have come," Cashel said.

"Look, I didn't want that thing in my house. I wanted to return it," Cora said. "I guess it's kind of a good thing that we came. He could have been lying there for days if we hadn't happened on him, poor guy."

"What is your full name, please?" the paramedic whose name tag read "Joy" said.

Cora glanced at Joy, then Cashel.

"I'd rather not give it," Cora said.

"Nothing is worse than Cashel," Cashel said.

"I need your full name, please," the paramedic said.

"Coralie Yves Chevalier," Cora said, begrudgingly.

Cashel's eyes met hers. "That's a lovely name," he said.

"So is Cashel," she said.

"It's the name of my mom's grandmother's home-town in Ireland," he said. "It's where I was conceived."

Was it strange that Cora knew two people who named their children after places they were conceived? Maybe she knew more. There was Brooklyn—yes, that's right. Were there any others?

"The police want to talk with you, of course," the paramedic said, ignoring their conversation. Joy was all business. "Are you up for that?"

"What?" Cora managed to say, as her brain was too busy thinking of names.

"Can you answer some questions for the police?" Joy said.

"Certainly," Cora said.

Joy left the room to fetch the police officers.

"So much for peaceful small-town living, heh?" Cashel said.

"So much for my number one murder suspect. He's now dead," Cora replied.

Chapter 25

Cashel and Joy escorted Cora outside for some fresh air. With all of the frenzied activity in the house, the air inside was stifling. Cora realized that this fresh air was just what she needed. Joy and Cashel stood with their heads together, examining a form. Cora spotted a white card in the grass, just off to the side of the front-door stoop. She bent over to pick it up and read the text, JUDE SAWYER, MASTER BROOM MAKER. Cora stood and felt a little dizzy. As she swayed, she stuck the card in her pocket.

"Whoa!" Cashel said, coming to her rescue.

"There's something I have to show you," Cora whispered.

But just then an officer walked over to them.

"Twice in one day," Office Glass said, spotting Cora. "How are you feeling?"

Cora shrugged.

"Are you up for a few questions?" Officer Glass said, leading them back inside the house.

"Yes, sure," Cora said, but she wasn't certain. Things were still a bit blurry.

"Why did you come here tonight?"

"I came to return a gun that I found in a box of doilies I purchased."

He smirked. "Do you have any idea how ridiculous that sounds?"

"I do," she said. Damn, her head hurt. "Did I hit my head on something?"

"Cashel?" Glass asked.

"Yes, I think she hit her head when she went down," Cashel said.

"Are you okay to answer questions?"

She nodded. "I think so."

"Now, Ms. Chevalier," Officer Glass went on. "How did you come into the house?"

"The door was open."

"I just told you that," Cashel said, with a slight irritation in his voice.

"You know the procedure, Mr. O'Malley," Glass said and then turned back to Cora. "You mean wide open?" he persisted.

"No, I went to knock on it and when I knocked the door opened farther. You know, it wasn't closed completely."

"Why would you walk into someone's house?"

"Well, I had been there yesterday and was aware of the yard sale. I guess I was thinking it was still going on. Look, all I know is I wanted to return the gun. I didn't want it in my house," she said.

He nodded. "Understood." He glanced at Cashel. "We'll be in touch with more questions." He turned to walk out of the room, then turned back. "By the way, the guys at the station loved your muffins," he said.

"Great," Cora said.

"What did your muffin bribery get you?" Cashel asked, after Glass left the room.

"Not much. He's supposed to be checking into a few things for me. Is it okay to leave? I mean, I have a house full of guests. Does this mean Jane's off the hook?" Cora asked.

"What do you mean?"

"I mean, everybody knows where she is," she said stiffly. "Not here. She's at the retreat."

"You're still not thinking clearly. We don't know if both murders were committed by the same person," he said. "But don't worry. It will be okay. She does, at least, have a great alibi for tonight."

Which reminded Cora that she still didn't know where Jane was the night of Sarah Waters' murder. She never told her. Had she told Cashel? How could she ask her without sounding like she suspected her?

"You said you had something to show me," Cashel said.

Cora, still woozy, but gaining her strength, pulled out a card from her pocket. "I found this near the front door. I'm surprised you didn't see it."

"What is it?" Cashel said.

She held it up for him to see. "It's Jude's business card."

They stood in silence.

This meant that Jude must have been in the house sometime before Cora and Cashel. But when? Did he visit Josh to discuss the brooms? The card looked relatively untouched, not worn, as it would if it had been lying around in the elements from whenever he had purchased the broom collection.

"We need to find out what he was doing here," Cashel said.

"You don't think that . . ." Cora said.

"I have no idea what to think," Cashel said. "I think we need to turn this over to the police."

"No!" Cora said. "They will bring him in to question, right? He's supposed to be teaching a class for me tomorrow. And besides, we know he didn't kill Josh. Right?"

"If we keep this to ourselves, we are withholding evidence—evidence that could exonerate Jane."

But it could only exonerate her if Jude was the killer, Cora thought. *And Jude Sawyer was no killer. He was an artist and a craftsman.* "I'm certain he was just here to clear up his purchase of the brooms. One of the sisters wanted them back."

A different officer entered the room. "We're going to ask that when you leave, you go out the back door. Technicians are working on the front door."

"You might want to take a look at this," Cashel said, holding up the card. "Cora found this on her way in."

"Wait a minute," Officer Shimer said. "Where did you find this?"

"Out front, in the grass, near the door," Cora said.

"Okay, thanks," the officer said and nodded. "We'll be in touch."

"What?" Cashel said, noticing Cora's glares. "Look, I'm a lawyer. I'm working to exonerate Jane. I have an obligation—"

"Save it," Cora said. "We'll deal with it. We'll move Ruby up on the schedule tomorrow. Or something."

"They are just going to question him, ask him why he was here. It doesn't mean he won't be able to teach tomorrow," Cashel said. "I know what he told you about his purchase of the brooms, but he could be spinning a tale."

Cora was a bit miffed and feeling a little like a bag in the wind that Cashel was blowing around. Her brain was foggy from everything she'd seen and felt that night. She'd taken quite a knock on the head. As the cold October air hit her skin when she stepped outside, she took a few deep inhalations. It was as if the night air slapped some sense into her. Of course Cashel was right. He absolutely was compelled by his duty to turn that card over to the law. Cora's duty was to warn Jude so that he could take matters into his own hands.

Chapter 26

When Cora returned to the house, a few of the retreaters, including Ivy, were gathered in the sitting room near the fire, chatting and knitting. Knitters were always up late at every retreat Cora had ever attended. What was it about knitting?

"Hello," Cora said in possibly a too-friendly voice for such a late hour.

Members of the group glanced at her and some nodded. They appeared to be deep in conversation or a meditative state. The fire. The needles. The yarn. It was mesmerizing them.

"Well, I think that's it for me. I'm going to bed," said Jennifer.

"Good night," Cora said.

Cora sat down in her preferred overstuffed chair. Next to it she kept her basket of whatever project she was working on. These days it was an embroidery piece. She planned to make a fabric book of samples. She picked up the thread and needle and found her rhythm. The retreaters were all quietly working.

The moment was a much-needed pause in her day,

sitting there with other crafters, just enjoying their own craft and one another's company. About thirty minutes later, Jane walked in the room with a bowl of popcorn and set it down on the table.

"I see you've gotten my message. Is Ruby with London?" Cora asked Jane, who nodded. She placed her project back in the basket and sat it next to the chair.

"Has anybody seen Jude?" Cora asked, as she rose from the comfy chair.

"I think he went to bed," one woman offered.

Cora approached the steps, with Jane following.

"Which room is his?" Jane said, then in a lower voice. "What's this about?"

"I'll show you. Remember, the teachers get the bigger rooms," Cora said as they walked up the stairs. "We'll talk later." When they reached his room, she knocked on the door. "Jude?"

There was no answer.

Cora knocked again. "Jude? Are you in there?"

Still no answer.

"Where can he be at eleven-thirty at night?" Jane said.

"Maybe he's just a sound sleeper. Or maybe he went for a walk?"

"Right. There's nothing open this time of night, is there? Oh wait, the bar down the street—what's the name of the place?"

"Ludwig's," Cora said. "Is he a drinker?"

"How would I know?"

Cora shrugged. "You know, last night I thought I saw him coming out of Ivy's room."

"You *thought* you saw him?"

"Well, I was pretty certain. But, of course, it's none of my business," Cora said, twisting a piece of hair.

"Ivy is in the living room with the knitters."

"Yes, so he's not with her, in any case," Cora replied.

"Well," Jane said, with her hands on her hips. "We might have to wait until morning to speak with him. I need to go home."

"I'll keep an eye out for him," Cora said. "But I also need to get to bed. Big day tomorrow."

As they left Jude's door and the hallway and walked down the stairs, Jane gave Cora the once-over. "Girl, you look horrible."

"Pardon me if I look a mess. I just happened on a murder scene."

"Are you okay? Come to my place and let's finish that bottle of wine. You need to wind down before you can sleep, don't you?"

Unwinding with Jane was tempting. But it was so late. She knew she'd regret any late nights.

Who was she kidding? Cora was not going to sleep anytime soon.

"Okay," she said. "I'll come with you. One glass of wine might do me right."

The two of them made their way to the carriage house, and Cora filled Jane in on what happened. Ruby sat reading an herbal magazine in the main room of Jane's place.

"What happened? You look like hell," she said to Cora.

Jane explained what happened as Cora took up residence on the couch, tucking her feet up beneath her.

"I'll be back with the wine," Jane said as she headed to the kitchen.

"How horrible for you," Ruby said to Cora. "I'm so sorry you saw that. But I'm glad Cashel was with you."

Cora couldn't help but roll her eyes. *Cashel*. She'd think about him tomorrow.

Jane walked in with three glasses and a bottle of wine. "She asked that Cashel not give Jude's card to the cops, but don't you know that's exactly what he did."

"What card?" Ruby asked.

"Oh, sorry. I thought Cora told you," Jane said. "She found Jude's business card on the doorstep of the Waterses' place."

"And you told Cashel," Ruby said. "And he gave it to the cops?"

"Well, he had to, of course," Cora said.

"Of course," Ruby said, and then after a moment she added, "I don't know where I went wrong with him. He's as straight as an arrow." She drank from her wine glass.

Cora couldn't help but laugh.

"He's a good guy," Cora said, her eyes meeting Jane's.

"So now you're searching for Jude so that he can go to the cops, head them off at the pass, sort of," Ruby said.

Cora nodded. "That's about the size of it. But we're not sure if he's in his room or not."

"Well, we know where he was earlier—at Sarah Waters' house," Ruby said, and poured herself another glass of wine. "How do we know that Jude didn't kill Josh Waters?" Ruby asked.

That question made Cora's head spin. It had been there beneath the surface of her thoughts from the moment she found the card. The cops had been there to visit him the day he arrived, for mysterious reasons.

And Becca had wanted Sarah's broom collection back, though Jude had paid for it fair and square. So he said.

Was a broom collection worth killing for? Was anything worth that?

"What's going on in that pretty little head of yours?" Ruby said.

"Trust me," Cora said. "You don't want to know."

Jane knew. It was as if she could read her mind. "Take another drink of wine, Cora. It's going to be okay. I promise. Tomorrow, Jude will teach his class. Nobody needs to know anything. At some point, one of us will take him aside and warn him, before the cops get here. It will be fine."

Cora sank back into the couch cushion and drank deeply from her wineglass.

"Yes," she said. "All of that will happen. But none of that may matter if a killer is in our midst."

Chapter 27

After drinking a few glasses of wine, Cora left Jane's place feeling a little more relaxed. The clouds concealed the moon and stars, and it was dark along the garden path to the main house, which still twinkled with a few lights, enough for Cora make her way along the path.

As she approached the house, she glimpsed movement out of the corner of her eye. Something dark. Something—or someone—on the bench near the house. She blinked. A pale face came into view as it lifted. It was Jennifer.

"Oh, hello," Cora said. "I thought you went to bed."

"I couldn't sleep," she replied. She sat wrapped up in a dark coat and several scarves, making her normally round person look even more round.

"You should try that claw-foot bathtub, take a nice bubble bath. It might help to relax you," she said. The room was the best in the house, Cora mused. Jennifer's daughters wanted the best for their mom.

"Maybe," she said, looking up at the sky. She crossed

her arms for warmth in this brisk night air. Her cheeks were red.

"Such a cloudy night," Cora said. "It's so dark."

"It suits me. Suits my mood, I suppose," she replied.

"Jennifer—"

"Oh, I'm sorry," she said, waving her hand. "I'm feeling a little lost these days without my husband. We were married forty years."

What could Cora say? That was a long time to be married—long time to be with one person, every day, every night. That loss must be devastating.

"Would you like to sit down?" Jennifer said and placed her hand on the bench.

Truthfully, Cora was a little too relaxed from the wine, and wanted to slip under her quilts and drift off, but this woman needed a friend, even a not-quite-sober one. She sat down—and was only too happy to do so.

"It must be strange to be without him," Cora found herself saying.

Jennifer nodded. "Oh, I know, he's gone and doubtless in a better place and all that. But I still feel cheated. He took care of himself. He didn't smoke. He ate good food. We wanted to grow old together. It feels like a big 'screw you' from the universe. Cancer sucks."

Cora nodded. "It's just going to take you some time to get your bearings. Don't push yourself. Take care of yourself."

"I have no great cause for self-pity. I've got wonderful daughters, grandchildren." She took in some air. "Plenty to live for. I know that, intellectually, you know? But grief is a cold hard rock I can't seem to get over."

Cora thought about her own losses. Her parents and

grandparents. The dark cesspool of grief. "You never get over it, Jennifer."

She raised her chin and leaned back and regarded Cora, as if it were the first time she saw her.

"You just find a way to live with it. The rock? It becomes a stone, but it's always there," she said. "I lost my parents when I was quite young. My grandparents pretty much brought me up. Then, I lost them, too."

"I had no idea," Jennifer said in a hushed voice.

"We all suffer loss," Cora said. Just now her thoughts slipped from her parents and grandparents and moved on to Josh Waters and his family. Had they been informed yet of his murder?

"Yes, but you are so young," she said. "How did you manage?"

Cora had thought about this for a long time. She supposed her grandparents helped her to get over her parents' accident. After they died, dear Uncle Jon tried to step-up but he lived in France until recently. She'd found that by helping others through their difficult time, and not dwelling on her own pain, it soothed her grief. And so that's what she told Jennifer, who sat and listened to her story.

"It sounds kind of like a platitude or cliché or something," Cora said and smiled. "But it's what worked for me."

"You are wise beyond your years, my dear," Jennifer said, after a few moments of quiet consideration.

A smile spread across Cora's cold face. She was certain her face was red and splotchy from the fall night air.

"Is it okay if I go into the paper-crafting room tonight? I mean, are there allotted hours?"

"You can craft any time of the day or night," Cora said. "C'mon, I'll walk in with you."

"I'm going to make my daughters some very special thank-you cards," Jennifer said.

"That sounds awesome," Cora said as she led Jennifer back into the house through the screened porch.

They walked into the house and headed for the paper-crafting room, where another crafter was situated and working. Miranda, with the pretty blue eyes, looked up from her scrapbook.

"Well, it looks like I won't be alone," Jennifer said.

"I've got a lot more to do," Miranda said. "I'm on a roll."

"So am I," Jennifer said, after a few minutes.

When Cora went to bed that night, she lay and thought about the two paper crafters she left in the room, surrounded by pretty paper, embellishments, and all the tools they needed. They both seemed intent on finishing their projects tonight. She wondered if she'd see them in the morning. If not, it would be fine, of course. In fact, it would be better than fine—bonding over crafts, even late into the night, was exactly what she wanted to happen.

Chapter 28

Cora rose early the next morning. She wanted to clean up the kitchen before the caterers came. Plus, she had a blog post to write and wanted to make certain the supplies were in order for Jude's class. She crept into the craft room early in the morning, just as the sun was coming up, filling the room with glowing pink hues. She checked the supply baskets and, once she was satisfied, headed back to her room for a shower.

By the time Cora made it to Jude's class, it was already in full swing. Nobody saw her enter the classroom—not even Jane, who appeared to be as enraptured by Jude as everybody else.

He held up a small hearth broom, which was beautifully plaited at the top. The broom straw was made up of vibrant shades of purple and red, with actual blooms woven into it. "Brooms are not only beautiful, but they are useful. This is one of the reasons I love the craft. I come from a long line of broom makers. I've always known the beauty and utility one broom can offer."

Cora caught Jane's eye and nodded at her. Jane

started to make her way to the back of the room toward her as Jude continued.

"But for generations, brooms stood for many other things besides beauty and utility. A woman's broom said a lot about her. In the days of practicing wise women, brooms became a symbol of power and, yes, flight, but not the way we imagine it," he said.

Nervous laughter rippled in the room.

"Magically speaking, depending on where you lived in the world, and what witchcraft tradition you ascribed to, brooms were used to sweep good luck into the home and to sweep unpleasant energies out. If you were going to curse someone, you'd take your broom and sweep the unpleasant thoughts and energies into another person's doorway. No need for fighting or guns, then, if you had a good broom."

Much laughter ensued, as Ruby entered the room with two steaming cups of coffee and handed Cora one.

"Thought you might need this," she whispered.

"Thank you," Cora said, thinking that yes, this was exactly what she needed. The warmth of the coffee cup seeped into her hands and traveled up her arms.

She continued to watch Jude. Could he be a killer? Why hadn't the police been to see him yet?

"For centuries," Jude said, "brooms have also been symbolic of passage between the worlds or movement from one phase into another. And so it's now time for me to demonstrate the broom we'll be making this weekend."

Damn, he was good, Cora thought. He captivated the women who were in the room. She thought about him coming out of Ivy's room. That was entirely his business, but it was something she was keeping in mind, as it surely said something about the man. Something she felt she needed to be watchful about. After all, he was working for her.

"I talked with him earlier," Jane whispered to Cora as Jude led his demonstration.

"Oh?" Cora said.

The room was shuffling around a bit as the crafters were gathering their supplies, getting ready to follow along with Jude as he taught.

"He said he dropped by to see Josh and talk with him about the broom collection," Jane said.

"And?"

"Well, he said no one answered the door, so he left his card. Simple as that," Jane said.

Cora drank from her coffee cup.

"But when Cashel and I arrived, the door was cracked open slightly. Didn't he see that?" Cora asked.

Jane shrugged. "I don't know. I didn't ask. But what he said makes sense, right?"

"I don't know. Maybe too much sense," Cora said.

"Why are you so suspicious?" Jane asked.

"I don't know," Cora said, after a moment. "Could be I'm a little on edge, after last night."

"Do you really think he could kill someone?" Jane said.

It was a terrible thought. Cora didn't take the idea of accusing someone of taking another person's life lightly. But someone had done it. Just last night. Just down the street. Cora couldn't get the bloodstained doilies out of her mind—nor the blade handle sticking up from Josh's chest. As she studied Jude, she tried to vanquish the suspicions from her mind. Of course, Jane was right. They had no real reason to accuse him of such a heinous act. And with each sip of coffee, Cora brightened.

Ruby tapped Cora on the shoulder. "Darla needs to see you in the kitchen."

The three of them exited the craft wing and headed for the kitchen, where Darla Day and her crew were already gathering for the brunch buffet.

The kitchen was full of staff chopping, prepping, and plating. It smelled like cinnamon, apples, and melting butter.

"We could use some help," Darla said. "Mostly carrying food out to the table."

A wave of hunger overcame Cora as the food smells filled her nose. She reached for a miniquiche and popped one into her mouth. It was cheesy and spicy. She needed another one.

"You said you'd help," Darla reprimanded her. "Not eat all the food."

Ruby and Jane dug into the pimento cheese and were spreading it onto crackers.

"Lawd, that is the best pimento cheese I've ever had," Ruby said.

Ruby appeared lively today, and her excitement about the cheese made her gray eyes sparkle. She was dressed in a peasant denim skirt and purple blouse with a crochet-fringed vest.

"Thanks," Darla said. "That's Steve's granny's recipe."

She pointed to Steve, who was chopping fresh peppers for the vegetable tray. He smiled, shyly, at Ruth.

"Where's your granny from?" Ruby asked.

"Low country, ma'am," he said.

"Makes sense. Great spice in that cheese. Nobody does spice like the women from the low country," Ruby said.

"Take this tray, please," Darla handed a tray of the miniquiche to Cora. "And can you take the biscuits and jellies?" she directed Jane.

Darla herself lifted a sliver tray of apple hand pies and led them into the room where the decorated tables sat.

The sunlight streamed into the room through the lace curtains and shone on the centerpiece of fall wild-flowers, flanked by large candles situated in wide jars. The candles were much smaller than the jars but were seated in a bed of acorns. The effect was stunning.

"Needs no glitter," Ruby said.

Cora swatted at her, teasingly.

"I forgot the napkins," Darla said to Jane. "Do you mind?"

"Sure," Jane said and left the room.

"I'm surprised she's here today," Darla muttered, as she fussed over the trays.

"Why?" Cora said.

"Well, I wouldn't want her working for me if I were a start-up—with her being suspected of murder," Darla said.

"Darla Day, I never pegged you for a stupid woman," Ruby said.

"Well, I never!" Darla said.

"Yes, you have and we all know it," Ruby said.

Darla's face turned red, and she left the room in a tizzy.

Cora's mind swirled in anger and embarrassment.

"Sorry," Ruby said to Cora, who was standing there with her mouth open.

"Sorry for what?" Jane said, walking into the room with an armload of napkins. "Where did Darla go? What am I supposed to do with these?"

Chapter 29

During the brunch, Jane pulled Cora aside. "What is going on? Why is Darla being so nasty to me?"

Cora didn't want to lie. But she wasn't sure she could tell her the truth. So, instead she just took a bite of her miniquiche.

"She read the paper, of course," Jane said. "She thinks I'm a killer. Did you tell her I'm innocent?"

Cora took another bite of her quiche before answering.

"Of course I did, or maybe it was Ruby. In any case, we defended you. She's a good caterer, but I'll find someone else for the next retreat. What an ass."

Jane exhaled. Her body seemed to relax.

They observed the retreaters; some were gathered around the table, stocking their plates, while others were scattered about, sitting and eating. Ivy walked across the room and handed Jude a plate. He looked up at her and thanked her. But it was a clear indication to the other women that something may have been going on between them. Cora noted that knowing glances were exchanged.

Her initial feeling about a man teaching at a retreat full of women was that it would not be a good thing. She was right. The energy was different when a man was around. She wanted her retreaters to be able to relax— not twitter around, serving the teacher. Or sleeping with him. She nearly blushed at the thought. Some people had no scruples.

Ruby came up to the two women. "I saw them early this morning in the garden," she said, indicating Jude and Ivy.

"Isn't she married?" Jane asked in a hushed tone.

"That she is," Cora said. "Or at least that's how she registered."

"Oh well," Ruby said. "To each his or her own. We've no idea what her life is like."

"True enough, Ruby, but let's hope she's not making whatever her situation is worse."

She and Jane exchanged knowing glimpses. They had seen so many cheating wives and husbands, and as a result they were both a bit jaded.

"Well, we better mingle, ladies," Jane said.

They split up and walked through the crowd. Ruby was pulled aside to answer some questions about different kinds of wax.

Another group was gathered on the couch, inspecting an almost-finished minibroom.

"Can I see that?" Cora said. "It's lovely."

"Thank you," said Linda, a soft-spoken woman from South Carolina. "It's one of mine."

The woven handle fit nicely in Cora's hand. The weaving was sturdy, and as the handle reached the top, it formed a crescent, with the broomcorn splaying out from it, in plumes of golden yellow and deep crimson.

"It needs a knot here," Linda said, pointing to the joint. "I think I might make another one of these. I seem to have a knack for it."

"I sure don't," the woman next to her said. "I'm getting there, but not as quickly as Linda."

"Keep plugging away. You'll get there," Linda said to her. "I can't knit worth a damn and you zoom through it."

"You know, that's the way it is. It's part of the beauty of crafting. You don't know what you'll be good at. How fast it will take you to learn it. But it's all fun," Cora said.

"And these brooms are so useful," Linda said. "So it's not one of those things that you make and sit it in a corner or stack in a dresser somewhere."

"Why did you choose the small hearth broom, rather than the full size?" Cora said.

"It seemed more manageable," Linda replied. "Though I may give the full-size brooms a go. I do love the sticks you chose. Very gnarly and beautiful."

Jude came up to the group and took the broom from Cora. "Look at the gorgeous weaving of the handle. So nice and tight."

Linda blushed. "Thanks, Jude."

Jane came up beside Jude.

"Excuse me, Jude and Cora, I need to see you for a moment in the paper-crafting room," she said.

Cora took one look at Jane and knew something was wrong.

"Excuse us," Cora said. The three of them walked together to the room, where two uniformed police officers sat, along with Cashel and one other man.

Cashel introduced the man as Detective Thomas Brodsky. "He has a few questions," he said.

"Ms. Chevalier, I've checked the report from last night and I'd like to ask you about the door," Detective Brodsky said. "How open was it?"

"About this much," she said, holding up her hand, and with her thumb and her index finger indicated about an inch.

"The door was open," the detective said. "And you went in. Why would you do that?"

"Well," Cora said. "I thought the yard sale was going on still. Besides that, I only had one thing on my mind, Detective. And that was to return the gun that I found in the box of doilies Josh Waters had left here."

Detective Brodsky appeared as if he were trying not to smile. "Do you have any idea how ridiculous that sounds?" he said.

Did all police and detectives feel like they had to point that out?

"Ridiculous or not, that's the truth. I was there," Cashel said.

"Okay, so, the door was open by the time you'd gotten there. Which was what time?" Detective Brodsky said.

"About eight-thirty," Cora replied.

"What time were you there?" The detective eyed Jude.

"It was right before the reception. I suppose it was around five. I looked at the clock because I knew I had to be back to mingle and to eat."

"What happened when you arrived?"

"I walked up to the door and I knocked," Jude said. "Nobody answered so I left my card. It's that simple."

"Did anybody else see you there?"

"I don't think so."

"Were you alone?"

Jude looked down at his hands, then back up at the detective.

"Were you alone?" Det. Brodsky asked again, this time with an edge to his voice.

"Ivy was with me. Well, she waited for me at the sidewalk. She didn't walk to the door with me," he spit out, with some effort.

Jane and Cora exchanged looks.

"Who is Ivy?"

"Ivy Renquist," Jude replied. "One of the guests here."

"What were you doing at the Waters'?"

"As some of your officers know, one of Sarah's daughters wanted Sarah's broom collection back. I had paid for it, fair and square, but it started to bother me and I wanted to talk with Josh, without police or lawyers, and see if we could come to some arrangement," he said. He was calm and cool, as if he were questioned by the police all the time. It wasn't making him nervous at all. Cora, on the other hand, had to focus on breathing.

"I see," said the detective, after moment, nodding his head and narrowing his eyes as if he saw something nobody else did.

"The door was closed when I knocked, I assure you. I am certain I would've noticed if the door was open. I slid my card right in the door jamb."

The more Cora listened, the more it made sense. Why had Cora ever suspected him?

"Who found the card?" the detective asked Cora and Jane.

"I did," Cora said. "It was in the yard, sort of right near the door."

"Sounds to me like someone—your killer—entered

the house between the time Jude was there and the time we got there," Cashel said.

"Yes, thanks for that," the detective said a bit sarcastically.

"Do you think this murder has to do with Sarah's murder?" Cora asked.

"That would seem to be the million-dollar question," the detective said.

Chapter 30

After the police and detective left, the doorbell rang. It was Edgar Thorncraft.

Cora opened the door and took him in: bow tie, cardigan, tiny mustache. She doubted he was trying to make a fashion statement. Or was he?

"Can I help you, Edgar?" she said.

"I wanted to thank you for keeping your word on the parking situation," he said. "The town is full of tourists this weekend."

That was the most pleasant thing Edgar Thorncraft, chair of the historical commission, had ever said to her.

She beamed. "Why don't you come in and help yourself to some brunch?"

"Well . . ." he began, but as Darla walked into the room, his eyes widened. "She's the caterer?" he said in a low voice.

"Yes," Cora, said lowering her voice to match his. "And I'm afraid it's just not working out."

"She looks familiar," he said. Darla clearly agitated him. *Odd*.

He turned to leave.

"Mr. Thorncraft," Cora called after him. "Please stop by Sunday night for our chocolate reception. I'd love for you to meet my great-uncle and his wife, who are coming in from Virginia."

"Thank you," he said. "I might just do that."

And with that, he was gone.

Cora found Jane talking about pottery glaze with a small group of crafters, who dispersed soon after Cora's arrival. She then told Jane about Edgar.

"He really doesn't like Darla," Cora said.

"I'm not sure he likes anybody," Jane said. "Or if anybody likes him. He's keeping a close eye on us. That irritates me."

"He takes his job very seriously," Cora said.

Cashel walked up beside them with a plate of food. "Mom said I should help myself," he said. "Nice spread."

"Darla Day is our caterer. Do you know her?" Cora said.

Cashel shrugged. "Not at all." He scooted his fork around on the plate and brought up a bit of cheesy hash browns.

"Edgar Thorncraft certainly doesn't seem to care for her," Cora said.

"He doesn't care for most of us," Cashel said, brushing it off.

"He seems to like us," Jane said, grinning.

"Now, that's more interesting than him disliking someone, I'm afraid. But what's not to like—two attractive, intelligent, talented women in a gorgeous house, who are on their way to great things."

Jane crossed her arms. "You are such a smooth talker."

"That's why he's a lawyer," Cora quipped.

Cashel's mouth curled into a grin and a laugh escaped. "What? It's true."

"How goes the case?" Cora asked.

"I checked out your alibi, or should I say, alibis," he said to Jane.

"Alibi*s*?" Cora said.

"Yes, both men checked out," he said, and popped a minibiscuit in his mouth.

Cora glared at Jane. "Both men? What is he talking about?"

"Excuse me," Jane said. "Ivy looks like she's upset." She took off quickly, leaving Cora alone with Cashel. Cora started to follow. "I'll take care of it," Jane said, with a tone signaling Cora to leave her alone.

"What was that all about?" Cashel said.

"Jane hasn't told me what her apparent alibis are."

"But you're her best friend."

"Trust is an issue for her. But then again, I'm not one to talk."

"You trust me, don't you?" Cashel said, bumping his shoulder into her. It was a little flirtatious, but she didn't have time for it.

"Who were the men Jane was with?" she said.

"Huh?"

"Who were the men who are her alibis?"

"I can't tell you that," he said with an impish grin.

"Do you want me to trust you?"

"I'm sorry. I'm her attorney. She can tell you. Ask her."

"Evidently she doesn't want me to know." *But why?* Cora could only think of one reason: Neil. Jane wouldn't have been off with Neil that weekend—would she?

She saw Jane wrapping her arm around Ivy, who

seemed distressed, and walking her out onto the front porch. What was going on there?

Darla walked by with a tray and stopped to also watch Jane comfort Ivy.

"You'd never know that she was a violent woman, would you?" Darla said.

"Darla," Cora said. "As I am paying you handsomely for this weekend, I'd thank you to keep your opinions to yourself. Also, there's something you should know about Jane. She's one of the gentlest souls I've ever known. She didn't kill anybody. I don't care if they find her fingerprints all over the house, the body, or wherever, Jane would not harm a soul." *Unless someone was attacking her with a blade, that is.*

Darla drew back, lowered her head, and muttered an apology as she left the room.

"Was that wise?" Cashel said, after laughing.

"What do you mean?"

"I've always heard it's not a good idea to piss off your caterer."

Chapter 31

"Ivy, are you okay?" Jane asked as she led Ivy to the front porch. "Perhaps we should go for a walk?"

Ivy gaped at her. "Walk? Why? What's that going to do for me? Bring him back to me?—Men!—I'm tired of them ruling my life. You know?"

Jane didn't answer immediately. "I know exactly what you mean," she finally said. But the woman had hopped into bed with Jude the first day she met him. She was married. It was hard to feel sorry for her.

"I mean, I'm no fool," Ivy continued. "I thought Jude and I could have a fling and then he'd go back to his life and I'd go back to mine. I know it must sound horrible. I know I must sound like . . . a slut . . . or something. But I just wanted a little something just for myself. For once."

Ivy studied Jane, as if she were expecting answers. Jane thought she might have some, but she was certain Ivy wouldn't like those answers. So instead, she said nothing and handed her a tissue from her pocket.

* * *

Jane had lost track of Cora. And she hoped that Cora had lost track of her.

After her encounter with Ivy on the porch, Jane was heading back to her place for a break. Sometimes she just had to get away from the crowd. Tonight, London was staying with a friend—so, at this point, a moment of solitude beckoned. The crafters had settled in and were working on their brooms—except a small group that were knitting. The knitters were hard-core. The phrase "hard-core knitters" rolled around in her brain and made her grin.

She pulled the collar of her sweater tighter around her neck. The sun was still in the sky, and it was warm out, but the wind had a chill to it. As she shuffled along the garden path, soaking in the fall flowers they had planted along the red brick path to her house, she thought she heard someone behind her. She moved faster. She didn't want to be bothered with niceties and pleasantries. She had had enough socializing for one day—though she knew she'd have to do more later. She craved a bit of replenishment.

The next thing she knew, a figure stepped in front of her and blocked her path.

"What are you doing?" Cora said.

"I wanted a bit of a break," Jane replied. "Everything seems to be rolling right along. Why? Do you need me?"

"I don't care if you're taking a break," Cora said, with an edge to her voice. "I want to know—were you with Neil the night of Sarah's murder?"

There it was. It was hard for Cora to even utter his name. Jane knew that. How was she going to explain this to her? Her mind raced.

"Should we go into my place and drink some wine?" she said, after a moment.

"No, I don't think so. Not until you tell me what's going on." That was unlike Cora, to pass up a glass of wine. *She must be very upset,* thought Jane.

"I'll tell you what happened, but you have to make me two promises," Jane said. *Could she really do this?*

"Okay," Cora said. "What are they?"

"First, you have to let me finish before you jump down my throat."

"Well, that tells me everything I need to know."

"You promise or I won't go on."

Cora crossed her arms and pursed her lips.

"The second part of the promise is . . . well . . . try not to blow what I'm going to tell you out of proportion like you always do."

"What? I do not."

"Do you want to hear my answers, or not?"

Cora nodded. "Okay, I promise."

"Neil called me." Jane watched, as Cora bit into her lip. Literally. Her face reddened and twisted.

"He wanted to talk," Jane said. "It was a moment of weakness, I suppose. I thought I'd meet him somewhere neutral—not close to home. He still doesn't know where we live. But he is London's father. And he said he was clean and wanted to talk. I thought I should see for myself. I know what you would've said. And you would've been right. He is my weakness. And he lost the right to be in my life and certainly in London's life."

Cora was now rocking on her feet. She gently kicked at some marigolds that had grown over onto the path.

"But the closer I drove to our meeting place, the more I realized it was a mistake, so I pulled over in the next town," Jane said. "I rented a hotel room and lay in bed and sobbed myself to sleep. Please believe me. It wasn't pretty.

"When I woke up, I was starving," she said. "So I went to into the hotel restaurant and ate, then went to the bar and had a drink," she said, then gulped. "And I met a man."

Cora gasped. Then went back to biting her lip. Her face was turning every shade of pink.

Jane's heart quickened. Cora was her closest friend. But she was a private person and some things you didn't share until the right time, or if at all. And, she was kind of embarrassed.

"Well, one thing led to another and we spent the night together in the hotel," Jane said.

"Get out!" Cora said and shoved her a bit. "What? That's not like you!"

"You promised!" Jane reminded her.

"Your story's finished, right? I don't get to talk about this ever?" Cora said with a wide grin.

"You promised to not blow this out of proportion, right? You know what I think about men coming into my life. I have London. She is my priority. I need to make certain any man who comes into my life is good enough for her," she said.

"And?"

"It's too early to tell," she said. "We spent that weekend together and we've kept in touch. The attention has been nice. But that's as far as it's gotten. He lives in Hendersonville."

Just then, they heard people coming up the path. As they drew closer, Jane saw that it was Linda, the woman who made the wonderful broom, followed by Jude. They stopped, and Jude cleared his throat. Linda reddened when she saw Jane and Cora. Jane had just comforted Ivy, who had, in essence, been dumped by Jude. Was Linda the reason why? What kind of a cad was Jude?

"Hey," he said. His voice was ragged. "We're taking a bit of a stroll. I wanted to check out Ruby's candle-making class. Is that her cottage?" He pointed to the carriage house.

"No, that's my place," said Jane. "The cottage is a little farther down the path. You'll see it if you keep going."

People were often surprised by how much property was behind Kildare House, as most of its depth was hidden by trees, fences, and gates.

"Thanks," Jude said, and he and Linda kept walking. He turned and peeked back over his shoulder and gave the women a hangdog grin.

Was he really going to Ruby's place? Or was he planning to ravage poor Linda somewhere in the garden? wondered Cora.

She looked at Jane, who rolled her eyes.

"What's with him?" Jane asked.

"Remind me to not hire another male teacher," Cora said. "This is part of what I meant when I said they change the energy in the room."

Jane laughed. "Point taken."

Cora laughed as well.

"Are we good?" Jane said. "I really was going to tell you all about this at the right time. So are we good?"

"Of course we are," Cora said. "Now about that wine . . ."

Chapter 32

Ruby's garden cottage sat on the very back edge of the property in a glade of what at first appeared to be shrubs or weeds with specks of color, which upon closer view were revealed as dying flowers. It was the fall, after all. During the spring and summer, it was another matter; Ruby loved to educate guests about the herbs that surrounded her stone cottage. The rock pathway to the front door was lined in marigolds—a bit of order in a chaotic, but still somehow charming, garden.

The "simple" candle-making class was in full swing when Cora and Jane slipped in the door to watch Ruby in action. They were both a little more lighthearted after having a glass of wine together.

"This is fun and easy," Ruby said. "For those of you who don't want to make candles from scratch. We'll be making candles from scratch tomorrow afternoon." She held up a sheet of cream-colored beeswax. "But for tonight, you are going to roll this around a candle wick, basically. We've added a little creative element in that you have some herbs to sprinkle on your sheet. So when the candle burns, you'll smell the herbs. Some of them are quite potent—so a little dab will do.

"A few blow-dryers are scattered around the room. Take turns if you must. Just heat up the wax enough to make it pliable.

"Right side down, sprinkle the herbs all over the inside of the sheet," she said. "Now it's important to know what the qualities of each herb are that you choose. You know some say herbs offer magical qualities."

Cora's and Jane's eyes met. Ruby was skating a fine line here. They had warned her to go light on the witchy–new age woo-woo stuff because they didn't want to offend anybody.

"You can get into the magic of candle making by getting detailed with the meaning of colors and so on. But since we're focusing on the herbs, I'll tell you a few of the beliefs about some of the herbs here. For creativity, we have lavender," Ruby said. "For psychic power we have honeysuckle, yarrow, mugwort, and thyme. For protection, rosemary, fennel, and sage. For love, rose, lavender, gardenia. And for money, cinnamon, chamomile, and basil."

"Pass me the money herbs, please!" Miranda said and laughed.

"I want the love and money herbs," Diane said.

"Don't we all," Ruby said, and then fired up her blow-dryer, as the group laughed.

Cora and Jane walked around Ruby's living room, which had become a makeshift classroom. The idea for the small group to meet here was Ruby's. She felt welcoming guests into her home was more intimate. Plus the other retreaters were busy with broom making, knitting, and whatever else they decided to do with their crafty weekend. Cora hoped they were allowing themselves plenty of space and time for reflection and renewal.

The scent of honeysuckle pricked at Cora's nose.

"So, after you've warmed up your sheet, decide if you want to make smaller candles by cutting the sheet, or if you want to keep them long. Then sprinkle your herbs on it. Cut your wick to be slightly longer than the length of your candle and wrap your wax around it.

"If you want, cut a diagonal from the top left-hand corner of the sheet to about halfway down the center of the right-hand side and tightly roll up the beeswax, so the candle becomes tiered as it takes shape. Experiment with different angles of the diagonal, cut to create a variety of tiered beeswax candles.

"Gently press the end of the sheet into the candle to seal it. The idea is to give it as seamless an effect as possible."

"She's fabulous," Jane said to Cora.

She nodded in agreement. Ruby was proving to be a wonderful teacher.

Her phone buzzed, and she stepped out of the cottage to answer it.

"Hello," she said.

"Cora Chevalier?"

"Yes, speaking."

"This is Officer Ted Glass. Remember how I told you I'd look into things for you?"

"Yes," she said, her heart nearly leaping out of her chest.

"I think you better come down to the station so we can talk."

Cora looked over at the main house and then at her watch. Did she have time to run down to the station?

"When would be a good time?"

"I'm about ready to go on break in, say, ten minutes. We could grab a cup of coffee and I can tell you what I found out. How does that sound?"

Cora hesitated. She hated to leave the retreat and besides that—coffee with a cop? Why did this not feel right? But, at the same time, she did wonder what he might have found out. They needed to clear Jane of this murder suspicion, and that's all there was to it.

"I'll be right there," she said. She dashed back inside Ruby's cottage and yanked on Jane's arm.

"What?" Jane said as she followed Cora outside.

"I want you to come with me to the police station," Cora said.

"What? Why? I'd rather not."

Cora told her what Officer Glass had said.

"Interesting," Jane said. "Did I mention to you what Ruby said yesterday? She told me the Waterses' daughter had a horrible drug problem."

Cora nodded. "That's the same track Officer Glass is on. So are you up for it?"

"I don't know. Is this a good idea? I mean, I am a suspect."

"Not quite a suspect. A person of interest." Cora corrected. "Come with me. We'll call Cashel on the way and see what he says. If he says no, you can just wait outside for me."

"Why would I want to do that?"

"I have a weird feeling about this meeting. It's probably nothing. But I'd feel better if you were around."

"You and your weird feelings," Jane said and sighed.

"You know they are always right."

"Unfortunately, I do," Jane said.

Chapter 33

Cora and Jane walked together to the police station. Even though there was a bit of a chill in the air and the sun was beginning to lower in the sky, it was a pleasant evening for a walk.

Jane's cell phone buzzed. "Yes," she said as they kept walking down the red brick sidewalk.

Cora noticed that people were getting their homes ready for Halloween. The folks in the pink Victorian displayed three jack-o'-lanterns on a bale of hay. The next house over was more witchy. Sitting on their porch was a cauldron with a cardboard witch hunched over, peering into it. The next neighbor offered a yard full of inflatables—ghosts, Frankenstein, and Dracula. Cora wondered how they had gotten away with that, given the strict code. Maybe it was set aside for Halloween. She had so much to learn about her new hometown.

"Yes, baby, I miss you, too," Jane said into her phone. "But are you having fun?"

Cora loved the fall harvest decorations at the next house. Brightly colored fall produce—pumpkins, squash, black-eyed Susans—added a splash of color to the front of the gray house.

"Okay, London, I love you, too," Jane said and then put the phone back in her bag. "That was my baby. She's staying at Zelda's house tonight. I like her mom and dad. They don't seem to be bothered by everything that's going on."

"No person with a brain in their head would be," Cora said. "It's all going to be straightened out. And these people who are so rude will be eating crow."

Jane looked out over the town. "I hope you're right."

"Is there something you're not telling me?" Cora said. "I mean, other than the fact that you have a hot guy stashed away somewhere."

Jane laughed and shook her head. "The rest of my life is an open book. The guy remains my secret until I see where it's going. Is that okay with you?"

"No," Cora replied. "I want details!"

Jane just laughed and kept walking.

Awnings were being drawn, lights shut off, and doors locked as the shops were closed for the evening. A group of retreaters were heading into the local diner and waved to Cora and Jane.

"It's a great group of women," Cora said. "They seem to be relaxing and fitting right in."

"It's great that they're going out and supporting the other local businesses. That does my heart good," Jane said. "Maybe that will save our failing reputation. Craft retreat houses a potter-killer."

"Let's hope it doesn't get that bad."

"I should be afraid to enter the police station, given my record here," Jane said as they neared their destination. "But it's just so welcoming."

"I agree," Cora said. "Let's hope that Officer Glass has something interesting to say."

When they entered the station, the woman behind the reception desk smiled up at them. "May I help you?"

"Hi," Cora said. "I'm here to see Officer Glass."

"Are you Cora Chevalier? He's been expecting you. He'll be out in a moment," she said and picked up the phone. "Please have a seat."

"It's odd, isn't it?" Cora said. "I've been in a lot of police stations. They are usually austere and unfriendly. Usually, kind of dumpy. But not this one."

"Well, this is Indigo Gap," Jane said.

When Officer Glass entered the room, he smiled at Cora, then frowned when he saw that Jane was with her. Cashel never returned her call, so she assumed it was okay tag along.

"This is Jane," Cora said. "I asked her to come along. She obviously has a vested interest in the case."

"I know who she is," Glass said, quickly recovering from his initial disappointment. "I, uh, thought we'd go and have some coffee right around the corner. That okay? The only thing better than having coffee with one beautiful woman is having coffee with two."

"Aren't you a charmer?" Jane said.

Cora was glad she'd brought her along. Her vibes were never wrong. She had an inkling this married man was feeling out her situation. Wanting to know if she'd be game for an affair—and she was not. With him. Or anybody else. She hoped that by bringing Jane along, she had sent him a clear enough signal.

"Here's the thing, ladies," Officer Glass said, after they were situated at a table at the nearby Blue Dawg

Coffee Shop. "This is not my case, so some things are not open to me. I'm sorry about that."

"Is that what you called me here to tell me?" Cora said, after taking a drink of her coffee.

"No," he said and lowered his voice. "I wanted to say that I don't think drugs are the issue in this case."

"What makes you say that? I thought Josh Waters was stoned when I saw him and I'm certain I smelled something odd," Cora said.

"He probably was high," he said. "We found out that he was diagnosed with an untreatable cancer. He had a prescription from Pennsylvania for medical marijuana."

"Wow," Cora said. "I didn't see that coming." She was certain it wasn't pot that she had smelled. But perhaps it was pot and some other substance mixed together. A wave of sadness rolled through her. "That's so awful."

"But what about Becca?" Jane said. "She has a history of drug abuse."

"She does. But she's clean. Because of her record, we check her periodically. She has to take regular drug tests."

"But she seemed very disturbed," Jane said after a minute.

Ted Glass sat back in his booth and took a drink of his coffee. "She is fragile," he said. "The loss of her mother . . . she is so torn apart by the way her mom died. And now her dad is gone, too. She must be devastated."

"What about her sister?" Cora said. "Where is she?"

"That's a good question," he replied.

"So," Cora said. "The two main causes of a murder,

statistically speaking, are drugs and domestic violence and it seems like they've been eliminated in these cases."

Jane sighed. Deep and long. "That's not exactly what I wanted to hear."

Chapter 34

Officer Glass was called back to the office just as they were finishing their coffee. They said their good-byes and went their separate ways.

"What are you going to do?" Jane asked, as Cora stopped while they were walking back to the house.

"I just remembered that I wanted to research the Waterses' divorce records," she said and continued to walk. "But it's too late to go to the courthouse."

"Why would you do that now? Both of them are dead. What does it matter?" Jane said.

Cora didn't have an answer. But she did know that sometimes things were written about a divorce that might leave clues to other parts of the lives of those involved. Hobbies. Children. Money situations. Money was always a hot-button issue and a good enough reason for many murders.

"I want to see for myself," she said. "I'm not sure I trust Officer Glass's impressions."

"He was up to no good. I saw the way he leered at you," Jane said. "Aren't North Carolina records online?

Let's go back to the house and check. That way we can check in on the retreaters."

"That's right. We can do it online," Cora said. "I always have to remind myself that almost everything is online now."

"So funny, being the big craft blogger that you are."

"I know, right?" Cora snickered.

The two of them walked back to the house, with the sun setting behind them. It was one of those autumn sunsets that blazed across the sky with bright oranges and fuchsia streams.

They said hello to the group of crafters huddled around the fireplace in the living room. *The group from Florida must be cold,* thought Cora.

"Everything okay?" Cora said.

"Yes, the fire is great," Martha muttered.

"Do you have dinner plans?"

"None for me, thanks. I had enough with the brunch and there's still leftovers in the kitchen," Diane said.

Jane and Cora sat down with the crafters as they worked. The fire crackled. Cora reached for her basket and worked on her embroidery project. Jane placed more wood into the fireplace.

Working with her hands often became like a meditation for Cora. Between the rhythmic motions and the fire, she felt grounded and centered. The chatter between the crafters was pleasant, but once again her mind turned to Josh Waters and the bloody doilies. She and Jane stayed with the other crafters for about an hour, then excused themselves.

"If you need anything, holler," Cora said, placing her embroidery back in the basket and setting it aside. "I'm

planning to come down later and take some photos of
what you're doing for the blog."

"Cool," Diane said. "As long as the pictures are of the
crafts, not me!"

The group laughed and agreed as Jane and Cora left
the room. As they climbed the stairs, Cora smelled
pizza.

"Someone must be eating in their room," Cora said.

Then they heard talking and laughter through the
door of one of the rooms. A woman's and a man's voice.

Jane's eyes widened. "Do you think—"

"Shhh!" Cora said and then pressed her ear up
closer to the door.

A bed was creaking. There were definite moans and
sighs. Cora felt her face heat.

"You have got to be kidding," Jane said.

Cora motioned for Jane to follow her up the stairs
to her apartment. When they both were inside, they
exploded in a fit of giggles.

After they calmed down, Cora felt anger take the
place of amusement. "I mean, it's none of my business
who he sleeps with, but geez, how unprofessional can
he be?"

"Wait a minute. It *is* your business," Jane said, picking
up a slip of paper from the floor. It was a note that had
been slipped under the door. "It's from Ivy, explaining
that she had to go because of the situation with Jude.
She's embarrassed and begs our forgiveness. She felt
she couldn't stay, now that he's taken up with Linda."

Cora almost cried as dread came over her. She had
wanted to create a safe space for women to explore and
relax. This was not good.

"I'm going to have to talk to Jude," she said, and a slight wave of nausea started in her stomach.

"I'd wait a few minutes, if I were you."

"Oh, I'll wait until tomorrow. That will give me a chance to calm down," Cora said. "What an ass. To come here to teach and then be sleeping with my re-treaters. Not just one, but two. No more men after this!"

She sat down at her desk, and Luna popped into her lap. She ran her fingers over the cat's back.

"I suggest we contact Ivy and offer her the next retreat for free. What do you think?" Jane said.

"I don't know. I feel sorry for her, but she chose to hop into bed with him. Plus she's married. I'm not sure we need this kind of drama—from anybody," Cora replied as she clicked on her computer. "Let me think about it."

Luna curled up on Cora's lap, and Jane leaned over to see the screen. Within moments, Cora had pulled up courthouse records.

"Wait, those aren't divorce records," Jane said. "What's that?"

"Reported robberies. I clicked the wrong tab," Cora said.

"But there's Sarah Waters," Jane pointed to the screen.

"Hmm. Looks like there was a robbery at the Waterses' house about a month before she was killed. A couple of opium kits were stolen. And they were insured for three-point-two million dollars?" Cora said.

"What? That can't be right. Three-point-two million?" Jane exclaimed.

"I agree. It's excessive, but the broom collection that Jude bought from them was pricey as well. This kit had jewels of some kind on it. I'll never understand the collector mind-set," Cora said.

"Or their wallets. Who is willing to spend that kind of money on a broom, or an opium kit, just to sit and look at?"

"I wonder if Sarah ever received that insurance money. Sarah was still working at the school when she was killed. It doesn't seem likely that she had millions socked away," Cora said.

"Who would she have left her money to? Her daughters? Her ex-husband? I mean, she hadn't remarried. She was divorced for years, way before the robbery."

"Well, let's start with the divorce settlement and work our way to finding a will or probate records," Cora said. "Divorce records can tell us a good bit, even if the divorce was years ago."

The two of them read over the divorce records that Cora quickly found. Josh had apparently requested the divorce on the grounds of marital infidelity on Sarah's part. He took almost everything in the proceedings, except the house.

"There's no mention of millions, then," Jane said.

"But they didn't have millions then," Cora pointed out.

There was a list of ordinary things—cars, the house, jewelry—plus Sarah's own collections, which she kept along with the house. They had a grand total of $300,000 in assets. Even though Sarah had owned the highly-valued collectibles, no mention was made of the value or of an insurance policy. Maybe the policy came later.

Then Cora and Jane moved on to her estate and will, which once again listed all of her assets, but sans millions she would have made if she'd filed that insurance claim.

"We know her items were insured, now. At least that's what the newspapers say. I wonder what happened with the insurance claim after she was robbed," Jane said, tilting her head.

"It's possible she never contacted them," Cora offered. "There's no mention of a huge amount of money in any of the probate records. Of course, I think some of this is pending. It's happened so recently."

After a few minutes more of reading, Jane asked, "Could she have been awarded money and then just never listed it in her assets?"

"That would be fraud and maybe tax evasion. I think," Cora responded. Spirals of curiosity zoomed through her. What was going on here?

"Well, they have both been murdered. It seems the killer must be after something," Jane said grimly.

Chapter 35

Cora knew about marriage disputes, but she didn't know anything about insurance fraud. As she lay in bed that night with Luna curled up next to her and the moon shining through her lace curtains, she mulled over what she knew about the murders. In a way, it comforted her to know that it was likely not a drug situation that led to the Waterses being killed. She turned over on her side, trying not to disturb Luna. Her thoughts drifted to Jude. How was she going to approach a grown man about the fact that he was sleeping with her guests? She felt like a chaperone at a craft camp for teenagers, and she resented him for making her so uncomfortable. Poor Ivy. It once had been hard for her to believe that women cheated on their husbands—but at this point, at the ripe old age of thirty-two, Cora had seen everything. Well, almost. She had never seen a broom worth thousands—or an opium kit worth millions.

The next morning was gray and cloudy. The weatherman had said it was going to rain, and it looked like an accurate prediction. As Cora descended the stairs, she saw a group of early risers like herself, already drinking coffee and chatting.

"Good morning," she said. "How is everybody this morning?"

They all said good morning in turn, and then Cora went into the kitchen for coffee. She came back into the living room with her coffee and sat in an overstuffed chair next to the fireplace, which was still giving off a bit of heat from last night's fire.

"Are you having a good time, Martha?" she asked the guest sitting next to her.

"Oh yes, I love it here," she said. "I've made a broom and a couple of candles already and we still have two days left. It's been productive."

Diane tittered on the other side of her. "I've told her she needs to relax a bit while she's here and not worry about what she can accomplish."

"Keeping busy helps me to relax," Martha said. "It sounds crazy, I know."

"As Cora says on her blog, there is something to that," one of the other crafters piped up. It was Miranda, the woman from Tennessee with pretty blue eyes and dimples to match. She was a knitter, and if she wasn't drinking coffee and eating a croissant, she'd be knitting right now. "I know knitting helps me to think."

"I hear you," a guest named Piper said. Piper was a long lean woman with fingers to match. Cora observed her yesterday manipulating the broom straw easily with those fingers. Her nails were painted bright purple.

"I was just reading an article about the health benefits of crafting," Jennifer chimed in.

Jude came into the room. Had he just awakened?

No, Cora realized, he must have been out and was just now getting in.

"Well, where have you been this early?" Miranda asked.

"Out for a run," he said. "How's everything, ladies?" Cora watched him turn on his trademark charm.

The assembled women seemed to respond, as they sat up a bit straighter, smiled, and murmured niceties back to him.

"I need to get in the shower," Jude said. "I'll see you all in a bit." And then he was gone.

"He's absolutely beautiful," Diane said, in a wistful voice.

"He's all right," Martha replied.

"He needs to learn to keep it in his pants," Miranda said, and reached for her knitting needles.

Cora's face heated. "What?"

"He was sleeping with Ivy. Now he's sleeping with Linda," Miranda said. "We've been watching the shenanigans. It's been quite entertaining."

"I'm so sorry about all this," Cora said. "This is not at all what I had in mind for the retreat."

"No worries," Diane spoke up. "As Miranda said, it's been quite entertaining."

"Does everybody know about this?" Cora managed to say, her face so hot now that she felt it might ignite.

"Well, we all do," Martha said. "We're not sure about the others. They've kind of kept to themselves."

Cora frowned. She'd have to talk with Jude as soon as she could. He was distracting her crafters. They were here to craft and reflect—not gossip about who was bedding whom. Still, she mused, they didn't seem to mind all that much.

She drank more of her coffee and felt herself perk up a bit more.

"I love the way you dress," Diane said to Cora.

Today, she wore another seventies vintage dress. It was a red minidress, with a Peter Pan collar and white polka dots. She wore it with modern leggings, which helped update it a bit.

"Thanks," Cora said. "You know, it's part of my mission to wear as many vintage clothes as possible. I found this in a shop in New York City. I thought it was in great shape. It looked as if it had only been worn once or twice. So wasteful."

"We don't have many vintage stores where we live," Diane said. "But I've found some great things at the Goodwill. It takes so much time to dig through everything."

"Yes, it does, but it's so worth it," Cora said, nodding in agreement.

The group quieted for a few moments before Martha said, "How about that murder? Do you know anything about it?"

Cora almost choked on her coffee. "Excuse me?"

"I read about this man who was murdered night before last," Martha explained.

"Yes . . . a tragedy," Cora hedged.

"Did you know him?" Martha persisted.

"Not really," Cora said, trying to downplay her involvement. Had her voice just gone up a octave? She squirmed a bit in the soft chair.

Luckily, Jane walked into the room with a couple of

boxes from Mac's Doughnuts, a local family-owned doughnut shop. "Hey, everybody, look what I brought. Doughnuts, anyone? Consider it your reward for getting up early."

Thank God for Jane—and her doughnuts.

Chapter 36

Cora allowed Jude a few minutes for coffee and a croissant, and then she pulled him into the paper-crafting room, shutting the door behind her.

"What's going on?" Jude said, sitting down at one of the crafting tables.

Cora handed him the note that Ivy left. He read it over and placed the note on the table, then made eye contact with Cora. "I'm sorry," he said. "It should never have happened. I don't know what I was thinking."

"So this is all true?" Cora said, sitting down across the table from him. She had expected a denial. At least he was being honest.

"Yes," he said. "I'm afraid so."

"Look, it's not my business who you sleep with . . ."

"Yeah, yeah," he said, shifting around in his seat. "I know. But you hired me and I'm working for you?"

His face paled and jaws tensed; one of his cheeks twitched. Humiliated, he couldn't even look at Cora. A ball of nerves and tension formed in the pit of Cora's stomach. Oh, how she hated confrontation. Why was she so embarrassed, when his behavior was the problem? She was certain his philandering would stop, now.

"If you want to have a relationship with Linda or Ivy, you can contact them after the retreat, okay?" she said.

"Relationship? Hell no," he said, lurching back a bit and causing his chair to squeak. "Look, Ivy kind of flung herself at me. She's a lot older than me, but I figured we could have a good time and then move on. But she started to get a bit clingy. She also had this wild temper."

"This all happened in one day," Cora said, more to herself than him. They met, slept together, and things went wacky—all in one day. And Jane wondered why Cora didn't get involved with men?

"Yeah, I know. It was like, bam, she was in love. I was upfront with her from the get-go. Then Linda came along and we hit it off and one thing led to another, as they say," he said matter-of-factly. The humiliation appeared to be gone. "I'm sorry Ivy felt like she had to leave," he said.

Cora's hands formed into fists. Suddenly all she wanted to do was to ask him to leave. Her mind was racing. She knew her retreaters wanted to take his next class. But who did he think he was?

"Really?" she piped up. "You can't understand why a woman who you had just slept with didn't want to see you with another woman? You can't be that clueless."

He lurched back in his chair again, looking as if he had been slapped.

"You are thirty-five years old. It's not like you are an eighteen-year-old boy," she added, concentrating on keeping her voice even and not shrill. "I know you're Mister Popular in craft circles. But, you're no rock star.

In fact, the more I get to know you, the sorrier I feel for you."

"Feel sorry for me? Why?" his mouth curled into a grin. "Okay, so I have a weakness when it comes to women."

Cora saw this conversation was going nowhere. She stood up. "Break it off with Linda—gently. Blame it on me. And keep it in your pants or you will be asked to leave and never come back." She surprised herself by the forcefulness in her own voice.

But it shut him up. *All about "weakness" and grins, is he?*

With her knees shaking slightly, her pulse racing, Cora left the room and headed upstairs to her apartment. She didn't even peep at the crafters who were gathered in the living room. She needed a few moments to herself.

She walked into her apartment and plopped down on her fluffy, inviting papasan chair and took some deep, cleansing breaths.

Men! Jude was too old to be acting as if he just discovered sex. She'd seen this extreme version of the Peter Pan syndrome before, but it was almost as if he had feigned his initial embarrassed reaction. The rest of the time, he had been cool and calm about bedding two of her guests. That was not the kind of retreat she was running. It wasn't supposed to be like this at all.

Supposed to be, she reminded herself. Those words were often triggers for depression and disappointment. *Okay, this isn't what I planned, but I need to focus on the positive things going on this weekend, all the friendships developing, the great crafting, and move forward. Lesson learned.*

She glanced at her box of doilies. How could she

ever consider them now without remembering poor Josh Waters?

Her class started in ten minutes—a thirty-minute class on making pumpkins out of old burlap sacks. She had had a hard time making up her mind which craft to do, until she found those sacks in the basement. These miniclasses were offered as little creative breaks through the day. She sighed.

Jude would be teaching this afternoon, and tomorrow was Ruby's class on soap and candle making. Then, the final party. If she made it through this weekend, it would be nothing short of a miracle.

Her head still ached. Images of bloody doilies kept popping into her brain. And the image of poor Josh Waters, lying there with a blade sticking out of him, surrounded by doilies, poked at her.

She needed time to process this—but time was the one thing she didn't have. A room full of retreaters was waiting for her class to begin, her best friend was still being accused of murder, and her guest teacher was sleeping around. What else could go wrong?

Chapter 37

"Look at how wonderful those pumpkins are. I mean, who would've thought?" Martha said, admiring the pumpkins Cora had fashioned out of burlap sacks.

"The stuffing is old plastic grocery bags," Cora said.

"How many of us have plastic grocery bags full of other plastic grocery bags?" Linda asked and laughed. They all raised their hands.

"Thanks for helping me make my point, Linda," Cora said and grinned. "To make the pumpkins, you stuff bags into one another and tie them with some jute." She demonstrated as she held up the thick fiber, and all the crafters followed. "Now look at your sack. You can cut it into a square. Or an oblong shape. Or leave it as it is. It's totally up to you."

The room filled with the sounds of the shuffling around of bags and scissors, accompanied by chatter.

"Then gather the corners of the burlap at the top of your plastic bag," Cora said, demonstrating once again.

"In order to get the pumpkin shape, wrap the burlap with jute as if you were wrapping a present. Be sure to pull tightly on the jute to create grooves in the burlap.

As you get closer to the end, bend the burlap to create a bent stem. Then wrap the pumpkin stem with jute."

"I like mine, but it's way different than Linda's," Diane said, holding up a short plump pumpkin and an oblong one with a much curlier stem.

"That's part of the beauty of this," Cora said. "Every pumpkin is unique. Just like real pumpkins."

"I have boxes of old burlap bags I could be using for something like this," Diane said.

"Everybody has boxes of things they could reuse," said Cora. "The whole point to upcycling is repurposing the things around us. We remake them into something useful and beautiful instead of being packed away in boxes."

"I love your cup and saucer bird feeders in the garden," Diane said. "I'm not sure which I like better. The hanging feeders or the ones on the poles. Very clever. You made those, right?"

Cora nodded. Making bird feeders out of old cups and saucers was one of her favorite upcycling crafts. It was a craft with seemingly endless variations. It could be as simple as gluing the cup and saucer on a stick and placing it in the yard, or as fancy as hanging crystals off it. She'd even used melted forks and spoons as part of the design.

"Yes, and the directions are on her Web site," one of the other crafters said. "I made them, too. Your directions are always so easy to follow."

"I tore up one of my aunt's old quilts and made different things with it for people in our family. A table runner. A wall hanging. Place mats. And a vest. And I'll tell you something . . . it was strange. But it was a cathartic experience for me. My aunt died a painful death and she loved to quilt. But there was only this one quilt of hers left. So I split it up. It was like, I don't know . . . I think it was the best way to remember her," Diane said.

Cora suddenly knew she had to do something with those doilies in a box in her apartment. And why hadn't she seen that it would help her properly deal with all these recent events? She needed to replace the bad memories with good ones. Now, what could she make . . .

As the class exited the room, Cora smelled cinnamon and nutmeg and knew the caterers were setting things up in the dining room. She went to check on the preparations.

Darla mumbled a greeting to her. What was wrong with her? What had happened to the cool, crisp woman that she hired to cater this first retreat? It was as if she was almost a different person. She was barely put together, on the verge of frumpy, with her apron askew and her hair unbrushed.

"Are you okay?" Cora asked.

"Yes, sure," Darla replied, grabbing a tray off the kitchen counter. "Just working."

"You look kind of . . . tired," Cora said.

Darla left the room with the tray of food, ignoring Cora's comment. Cora caught the eye of one of Darla's helpers. He frowned and then went back to work.

What was going on?

Cora heard Jude's voice in the hallway before she saw him. "Darla, please," he said as he followed her back into the kitchen. "Don't be like that."

Cora stood rooted to her spot, dumbfounded. She

hadn't been aware that the two of them even knew one another. Was she yet another of Jude's conquests?

Darla shot Jude a pointed glare, cluing him in to Cora's presence.

"What is she being like?" Cora said.

Jude turned, flummoxed, and managed a smile. "Cora—I didn't see you there."

"Obviously," Cora said. "What's going on here?" Bad vibes were zinging through her. Was she being paranoid?

Jude Sawyer, brilliant broom maker, lover of women, was not quick on his feet. His mouth hung open and his hands fluttered at his sides. "You know what? I don't know what's going on and that's the truth," he said and then stomped out of the room.

"Well then, perhaps you can fill me in," Cora leveled her gaze at Darla.

"It's a personal matter," Darla said. In other words, she wasn't going to tell her anything.

Cora started to steam beneath her vintage clothes. "Please deal with your personal situations on your own time," she said.

Darla looked at her for a moment before her face crumpled and she turned away.

Oh God, was she crying?

"Darla—"

"Just go away and leave her alone," one of her helpers said. "She's had a bit of a rough morning. We'll get it together and make sure your guests are taken care of."

"I didn't mean to . . ." Cora said.

The man threw her an icy glare, and Cora had nothing left to do but leave her own kitchen.

Chapter 38

After cleaning up the craft room, Cora and Jane strolled through the other rooms to see how everything was going. The crafters were gathered in small groups, eating and chatting. Some were in the dining room, others were in the living room, and a few stood in the foyer.

"The food is so good," Jennifer said to her as she walked by.

"So glad you like it," Cora said, thinking no matter what evil thing she could say about Darla, she could not say her food was bad. No, indeed.

The brunch was coming off without a hitch. Darla and her crew worked like a fine-tuned symphony. Jude was in the craft hall preparing for his next class, where they would be focusing on options for the knurl—the part of the broom that fastens to the stick. He was famous for making colorful weavings that held the broom together at its knurl, or joint.

Cora and Jane pulled Ruby aside.

"What do you know about Darla?" Cora said.

"Not much," Ruby said. "What do you mean? What's going on?"

"She's been accusing Jane of the murders and now she's disheveled and we had words in the kitchen. She cried," Cora said. "I felt horrible. But at the same time, I'm paying her good money."

"What were your words with her about?" Ruby asked.

"Jude," she replied.

"He's turned out to be more trouble than he's worth," Jane muttered.

"Wait—you mean . . ." Ruby said.

"I don't know what's going on between them," Cora said. "He followed her into the kitchen. And he didn't answer me when I asked him about it."

"Did you do a background check on either of these people?" Ruby said.

"Jude Sawyer? The internationally famous broom maker? No," Cora said. "With Darla, I got several references and tried her food. What kind of a background check do you mean?"

"I mean the police kind. You know, to see if they've been convicted of any crimes," Ruby said. "Even if they don't have a criminal record, those checks can tell you a lot. Previous addresses, names, divorces, and so on. I'll call Cashel to see if he can run a check on both Jude and Darla."

"Wait," Jane said, her eyebrows knitted together and voice raised a bit. "Just because they were having a fight doesn't mean we should go snooping around in their backgrounds. I mean, what's the point?"

The three of them regarded one another. Cora was trying to put into words the sensation she had in the kitchen when Jude and Darla had been arguing, but she couldn't. Maybe she was being unusually paranoid, what with a killer on the loose.

"I should've done those checks beforehand," Cora said, with firmness in her voice. "I think it would be fine to run them now to see what it brings up. But I'm most suspicious of Darla. How does she even know Jude enough to argue with him?"

"Well, this is a small town," Ruby said. "And even though Jude is not from here, they might have met up at some other event."

"I agree that her behavior has not been professional. But does it warrant a background check?" Jane said. "We just won't hire her again. I think this is invading her privacy. Don't we need to get their permission?"

"Not if we're not using it for employment purposes. It's not going to hurt to do the check," Ruby said. "Cashel can do it. No problem." Ruby said it with a note of finality.

"If someone did a check on me, they wouldn't like what they saw," Jane said in a hushed voice. "You can't judge people on their pasts."

Cora's heart sank.

"It's a good place to start," Ruby said. "Sorry to say it, but it's true. I backed Cora into a corner the other day after hearing nasty gossip about you, Jane. I know your secret. Just know that if I read your report and saw that you almost killed your first husband in self-defense that tells me about your character. It tells me you are a strong woman, darling. What you did was not a bad thing. You were defending yourself and your baby. Now let's find out what's going on with those two."

Jane's mouth dropped opened. She eyed Cora for an explanation.

"Sorry," Cora said. "I meant to tell you."

As she thought about Ruby and Cashel, and so on, it occurred to Cora that Cashel might be able to help her figure out the insurance claim business with the Waters family. "Can you tell Cashel to call me?" Cora said. "I want to ask him a question." If he could run background checks, surely he had access to other kinds of information. Why hadn't she thought of that before?

When Cora turned around, she was greeted with the sadly familiar sight of two uniformed police officers entering her front door, along with the detective she had met earlier. One of the officers was Ted Glass. *Again.* The group of women in the living room looked up from their knitting and eating, startled.

"Coralie Chevalier?" asked Officer Glass.

"Yes, you know that," Cora said.

"Jane Starr?"

Jane nodded.

"Is there someplace we can talk?" Detective Brodsky said.

"We can go in here," Cora said and opened the door to the paper-crafting room. Two women were inside at the table, scrapbooking. They looked up and smiled.

"Should we leave?" one of the crafters said.

"No, no," Cora said. "We'll go in another room."

Cora led the police to another room.

The fiber-arts room was not quite ready for guests, but it did contain chairs and tables, surrounded by colorful yarn and fabric, yet to be entirely organized. The scent of wool and felt greeted them as they entered the room, which was on the other side of the foyer from the paper-crafting room.

"What's going on?" Cora said after they were all seated.

"Should we call Mr. O'Malley?" Jane said.

"You can, if you wish," the detective said.

"I'll call him," Cora said. She noted the time on her cell phone. Jude should be getting started on his class now. Cora hoped the retreaters were happily busy and none too concerned with the sudden police presence.

"My mother just called," Cashel said after Cora dialed him and said hello. "I'm running your reports now. What is it?"

"The cops are here," Cora said.

"Where is here?"

"At my place."

"What do they want?"

"They have more questions."

He sighed. "I'll be right there. Don't say a word until I get there."

"Okay," she said. Then she turned back to the police. "Can I get you some coffee? We might have some muffins left. Please help yourself while we are waiting on Mr. O'Malley."

Jane resembled a deflated inflatable. Her shoulders hunched as she sank into herself, staring at the felted wool. Her hands were in her lap, her knuckles white.

"Can I get you something?" Cora whispered to her.

Jane shook her head. Her eyes held a fear that Cora wished she had never seen. It sent shivers through her as it took her to the night that Jane had been brought to jail for the attempted murder of Neil Jones.

Jane had been a husk of herself and moved like a

zombie through the police procedures. Her hands were stained in blood and her skirt was covered in it.

She had shot the man she loved. Then she tried to save him by bandaging his wound. Thankfully, London had been sleeping over at a friend's house.

Yes, she had shot the man she loved. The dream of a British man that she met while studying art in London. They had a few wonderfully happy years, before moving to New York, then the pressure of his theater career had gotten to him—and the drug use and violence started. The night Jane shot him was the night he came at her with a blade. It was him or her. And Jane was a survivor—a mother who ached to be there for her daughter. She wasn't going down without a fight.

Cora knew this place of strength and steel in her friend was still there. As she sat surrounded by the police, Cora struggled to see some shred of evidence that the survivor in Jane still thrived.

Chapter 39

"I thought you had new questions," Cora said. After Cashel had arrived, the questioning had begun, first with Jane and now with her, and Cashel overseeing things. She answered the detective's questions—the same questions they'd answered before.

"Standard procedure," Brodsky said. "We wanted to be certain we've gotten everything correct."

"Have you found out who vandalized Jane's place?" Cora asked them, just as it was appearing they were getting ready to leave. "What did your paint analysis reveal? Anything?"

"Unfortunately not," Officer Glass said. "It was standard stuff found in any store that carries paint. Not helpful at all."

"Have the fingerprints experts found anything?" Cora asked.

"They're still working on it," Brodsky said. "It takes time. This isn't like on a TV show, you know."

"I know that," Cora said. "But how long does it take to examine something and see if it matches?"

"Remember that we only have half of a print," Brodsky

said. "This just means they have to go through several variations of possibilities with that print," he said. "Believe me, if you want your friend to not be charged, you want the team to be as thorough as possible."

That was a good way to look at it. Cora's stomach settled a bit. She wanted to press the detective more—but he seemed to be in a hurry. And she had a craft retreat to run.

"I'd like to talk with you more," Cora said to him. The uniformed officers were almost out the door. Brodsky turned and handed Cora a card. "Call me."

"I will. I've something I'd like to run by you," she said.

He stopped. "Pertaining to this case?"

She nodded. "Yes, I've been doing some research."

"Cora," Cashel interrupted, his hand on her shoulder. "This isn't the time."

"Research?" The detective ignored Cashel. "Look, I'll swing back around later today. If you don't see me by, say, three, give me a call to remind me." He turned around and started walking down the sidewalk. "This ought to be good," he said to one of the officers, who laughed.

Cora's face reddened. "Was he making fun of me?" she said to Cashel.

"I told you the cops don't want you poking around in their business," Cashel said.

"But this *is* my business. Jane is my friend and my business partner. She's been unjustly accused of murder. They keep coming to my house, keep asking me the same questions. They seemed to be spending a lot of time on Jane and me, when the real killer is out there somewhere. It's troubling," she said. "And as her lawyer, I'd think you'd be more troubled than what you appear."

"I am," Cashel responded. "But we need to do things by the book. Everybody has a role to play. The cops are doing their job. I'm doing mine." He pulled her arm until she was closer to him and looked directly in her face. "You've got to trust me, Cora."

As she stood there and saw the passion in his eyes, the way his jaw set firmly, something was exchanged. A heat? A longing? Or was she mistaken? He was asking her to trust him about this case—but was he asking more? Asking her to trust him, as a person? As a friend? More than a friend?

"What's going on here?" Jane said as she approached them. "Are you two going to kiss? Fight? What?" She laughed nervously.

Cora stepped back from Cashel as he let go of her. "Um," she said. "Ah, we were discussing the case."

"Yes, the case," Cashel said, weakly.

"He's trying to tell me to back off from investigating, to leave the cops to it," Cora said, regaining her composure.

"That's a good idea," Jane said. "I told you we shouldn't be poking around."

"Poking around?" Cashel said. "What have you two been up to?"

Cora thought a moment before answering truthfully. "Honestly? Not much. The retreat is getting in the way. But I did research the divorce and estate records and stumbled on news of a robbery at the Waters place a month before Sarah was killed."

"What?" Cashel said. "How . . . ?"

"I used to work with battered women. I know all

about husbands and wives and how bad it can get. So I thought I'd start there," Cora said.

"We need to talk about this," he said, watchful. "Can we go up to your apartment?"

"Why, Mr. O'Malley, I thought you'd never ask," Cora couldn't help but say and laughed.

"I'm going with you," Jane interjected. And she wasn't laughing.

Chapter 40

"Jude is clean, by the way," Cashel said as they entered Cora's attic apartment. The small sitting room was a bit of a mess. Her new doilies were still spread over the couch, as she was still waiting for inspiration.

Cora scooted around the room, picking up the colorful doilies.

Cashel dropped a pile of paper, presumably Jude's background check, onto Cora's coffee table. "Take a gander."

"I trust you," Cora said, placing the doilies in a pile on an end table.

"You trust me and yet you're conducting your own investigation?" he said.

"He's got you there," Jane said, plopping down onto the papasan chair. She always sat in the same place when she visited.

"You can't go poking into police affairs when you're not a cop," he said.

"Wait a minute. I've done nothing illegal. What's wrong with my poking around a bit in the hope that I can help clear my best friend?" Cora said, sitting down on the sofa. "Please sit down."

"I don't want to," Cashel said. "Tell me what you've found out."

"It's not a big deal, really," Jane said. "We read the divorce and probate records. Anybody can do that. You know that."

"Yes, of course," he said.

"We learned Sarah was having an affair. That's why they divorced. And the only thing she wanted was the house. That tells us something about her character, doesn't it?" Cora said. "We also know that someone was involved in drugs or alcohol at one point because I ran across an interview with Josh Waters talking about drug addiction."

"That would be his daughter," Jane said. "Ruby told us, remember?"

"But we also found out that Sarah was robbed a month before her death," Cora said.

"I remember that now," Cashel said. "Several jeweled opium kits were taken, or something like that. Worth an outrageous amount of money."

Cora nodded. "I wondered about the insurance claim on it. When I scanned the list of items in Sarah's estate, I saw no mention of millions. What happened? Did she make a claim? If so, where is the money? How do we find out?"

"They always say to follow the money trail in murder investigations," Jane said. "Is anybody doing that?" Jane leveled her gaze at Cashel.

He sighed. "I'm your attorney, not a PI. My focus is on those fingerprints. It's very simple. If you didn't kill Sarah and Josh, then you will be cleared when the experts are done examining the prints."

"In the meantime, we are losing customers and our current customers are asking questions about Josh's murder," Cora said. "We have a vested, as well as a personal, interest in this case. The faster it's solved, the better it is for Jane and for the business."

Finally, Cashel sat down next to Cora. They all sat in silence for a few moments before Jane spoke up.

"You said that Jude was clean. What about Darla?"

"Darla?" Cashel replied. "I couldn't get a thing on her."

"What do you mean?" Cora said, sitting up.

"Her records are sealed," Cashel said. "At least at the level of security that I'm cleared on."

"You mean you can't access her records? Isn't that odd?" Jane said.

"Why would the records be sealed?" Cora asked.

"The only time I've seen this has been in cases of either stolen identity or witness protection," Cashel explained.

"Witness protection?" Cora said.

"I don't think it could be either of those things, really," he said. "I know I've seen her around town for a year or so. It's not like she just showed up, which is what you'd expect for witness protection."

"Unless it happened when she was very young," Jane pointed out.

"But what about stolen identity? Do you mean she stole someone's identity—or that someone is stealing hers?" Cora asked.

"Either one, I suppose," he said. "You can take legal

steps to seal your records and you might want to do that if your identity has been stolen."

"Well, she's the least of our worries. As soon as this first retreat is over, I'll never hire her again," Cora said.

"What exactly has she done?" Cashel asked.

"She's mentioned Jane's trouble several times to me, and been rude about it, plus I walked in on a strange exchange between her and Jude," Cora said. "She's extremely unprofessional. Your mom thought it best to run a background check on her."

"My mom, huh?" he said and grinned. "You know, she has great instincts."

"What about this insurance business?" Jane said. "How do we find out if a claim was made and, if it was, what happened to the money?"

"First, we'd need to find out who Sarah's insurance agent is or was—maybe via her attorney. I can make some inquiries, ladies, if you insist on pursuing this," Cashel said. "Probably by the time I find out, Jane will already be off the hook and it won't matter."

"Let's hope so. Let's hope this all ends as quickly and as you suggest," Cora said. "Though I have to say, that never seems to be the case with us. We are full of complications," she joked, trying to lighten the mood.

"In the meantime, our caterer could be someone other than she claims to be," Jane said. "I don't like that. I have a child to protect."

"So far, she doesn't seem to be dangerous, perhaps just a bit overwrought," Cora said reassuringly. "But believe me, I have my eye on her. Perhaps it's best that you keep London at her friend's house another night."

"Already on it," Jane replied, getting up from the papasan. "Well, let's go. We have a plan."

"We do?" Cora said.

"Yes—Cashel is going to find out about the insurance policy, you and I are going to keep an eye on Darla and Jude, and run this retreat, as if nothing else is going on," she said. "And we are all leaving this apartment right now, together."

Cashel looked at Cora to see if she agreed with the proposed plan.

Cora merely shrugged in response.

"Okay. Let's go."

Chapter 41

"So we've already made a traditional broom," Jude said. "Although some of us are still working on it." He looked over at a group of women, who giggled in response. Cora, Ruby, and Jane had all joined Jude's latest class and were seated with their guests.

"But I wanted to give you a smaller, simpler version of a broom that you might be able to make in less than a day," he continued. "This is commonly known as a cobweb broom. This should be simple, after having done the larger brooms. I do things a bit backward—I started with the harder project." He smiled.

"Thanks for that, Jude," Diane said, flatly. She was not impressed with the man. She had his number. In fact, Jane was certain most of them did by this point.

"We've gone ahead and soaked, drained, and prepared your broomcorn," he said. "Now, as with your other brooms, where the knurl—remember that word? Knurl is where the brush meets the stalk, right? Okay, where the knurl is, after you've secured it, you can get more creative. The twine we've selected for yours is orange, green, or black. Colors of the season."

The crafters started working on their brooms. Ruby was moving right along with hers rather quickly.

"I'd like to add that after you're finished, you can decorate these brooms with dried herbs or flowers," Ruby said. "You can hang them up. They make lovely wall or door hangings."

"Yes," Jude said. "My mother has a broom that she decorates for each season with fresh flowers, greenery, or herbs."

"What a great idea," Linda chimed in.

Jane scrutinized Linda and wondered why Jude was attracted to her. She was plain. Not unattractive, but just plain. What would someone like Jude see in her? It didn't make any sense. Ivy was cute and perky; Linda was neither of those things. Even when animated or excited, loving what she was doing—as she clearly was now, making a broom—she was simply plain. Jane hated herself for thinking like this, but nonetheless, it didn't make sense. Jane supposed Linda could have done a little something more with her appearance, if she tried.

She was one to talk. She knew she could try harder, as well. But she was not interested. She supposed that Linda wasn't either.

Jane's only interest, other than her daughter, was her art, which she had not gotten to since the retreat plans took over her life. As soon as it was over, she'd be back at her wheel, with her hands on the clay.

David understood. He was a potter, as well. For them to meet like they had was kismet, plain and simple.

"Hey," Cora said, sidling up next to her. "What do you think of my broom?"

Jane inspected it. "It needs work," she said and laughed.

"I think I need to trim it here and that will offset the crooked part over here," Cora said. "What do you think?"

"You may be right," Jane said. "I like the black twine."

Darla poked her head in the door and interrupted their conversation. "Can I see you, please?" she said to Cora.

Cora set her broom down and turned to face Jane, nodding for her to follow. Cora was tired and worried—Jane saw the circles beneath her eyes, the tiny lines of worry at the corners. She knew that Cora was tough, but stumbling upon a dead body was not something many people could handle. She was holding up well—especially after conking her head.

Jane followed Cora and Darla as they walked into the kitchen. Smoke was billowing out from the oven.

"What the—" Cora said.

"It's under control, but we burned the pies," Darla said quickly. "We'll get it cleaned up and make new ones. But this means that we will be here longer than I expected and I'll have to pay my crew overtime. I'm so sorry." She looked pale and tense.

But not as tense as Cora.

"Take a deep breath," Jane said quietly to her friend.

"I apologize," Darla said. "This weekend has gone nothing like I had planned. Several team members are down with the flu. My kitchen's oven has broken down, so I'm having to use yours. We're working with a skeleton crew. I'm a bit frazzled."

"We can help," Jane said. "Just put us to work."

Cora still hadn't uttered a word. She inhaled deep, audible breaths.

"Okay, well, we need to remake the pies. I've got dough chilling now, but how about making the filling?" Darla said.

"I can do that," Jane said. "What about Cora?"

"Can we get Cora to whip up some brownies? Double chocolate, for the chocolate reception tomorrow," Darla replied.

"Cora?" Jane said, bumping her with her elbow. Her little fairy-warrior friend was fading fast. "Hey!"

"Uh, yeah," Cora finally said. "I can make the brownies."

Jane realized that Cora would feel better if she were working and busy. But she also figured that Cora was wondering what else could go wrong this weekend. Jane wondered the same thing.

"Things could be worse," Jane muttered to Cora.

"Really? How?" Cora said. "No. Don't answer. I don't want to know."

Chapter 42

After matters were back under control in the kitchen, and Cora had calmed herself down, she wandered through the house to touch base with the guests—none of whom had anything bad to say about the food or the service. No matter how much Cora didn't like Darla, it seemed she kept her shenanigans away from the guests.

Cora walked out onto the front porch. One of the many things she loved about this big old house was its wraparound porch. The sky was now bright blue with swaths of white cottony clouds. In the distance the mountains were covered with colorful trees in shades of crimson, orange, and gold, getting ready to shed their leaves.

"It certainly is a beautiful day," a voice rang out. Edgar Thorncraft was walking down the sidewalk and heading for her front gate. It squeaked loud and ferociously when he swung it open. Cora really needed to get that fixed.

"Hello, Edgar," she said. "How are you doing today?"

He walked up the sidewalk and approached the porch steps. "I'm doing well, yourself?"

"I've been better," she said and sat down on one of the wicker chairs.

"Not going so well, then?" He asked with an air of concern.

"It's going okay," she said. "The guests are none the wiser, at least. How can I help you?"

"Right now, I'm just enjoying this view," he said. "You know my grandmother and I used to walk up here when I was a boy."

The Kildares had been situated like a royal family surveying their subjects.

"I admit I didn't think the old place was going to sell. The historical society wanted it, but it didn't work out," Edgar said. He stood with his hands folded in front of him.

"Please sit down. I didn't know the historical society was interested in Kildare House," Cora said. "I fell quite in love with it." And she had. Even with all its problems, she still loved it. She loved the window seats, the nooks and crannies, and her attic apartment spanning the length of the house. She loved the creak of the third step up from the landing, where the stained-glass window stood. She loved the sighs and moans of the old pipes and always settling floor and ceilings. Kildare House was a grand old lady with a ton of character and great bones.

"Oh yes," he said, taking a seat in a wicker chair next to hers. "There were several serious buyers interested in this place. One of them was Sarah Waters."

A weird pulse jabbed through Cora. "Where would the school librarian get the money for a place like this?"

He shrugged. "I have no idea. Maybe she sold something—you know, one of her collectibles."

"Quite a collector, that one."

"Aren't we all?" he said, with a smirk.

"What do you collect, Edgar?" she said, but he never had the chance to answer. Just then one of the retreaters came outside and joined them on the porch.

It was Diane, one of the women from Florida. "It's so beautiful here it hurts my eyes," she said. She had her craft basket with her and started working on her cobweb broom. "I had to get out of the house and get some fresh air."

"I hear you," Cora said. "I feel the same way."

The three of them sat in silence for a few moments. Cora viewed the town of Indigo Gap, so lovely with its artisan shops, quaint little restaurants, pretty churches, and old cemeteries. Her mind led her straight to death. First Sarah and then Josh. Both were gone—but why?

Sarah had wanted Kildare House. And yet, her own house was the only object she kept from her divorce. Cora had thought that meant she was attached to the place. Maybe not. But it certainly wasn't the only item that was worth money. Sarah owned many collectibles— especially the rare jeweled opium cases, which had been stolen.

Cora hoped Cashel would turn up something in his research about Sarah's insurance. That might lead them directly to the murderer. *Follow the money,* she reminded herself.

It occurred to her that Edgar might know something

about the robbery. But she wasn't certain she should bring it up with a guest within earshot.

"What do you know about opium cases?" Cora asked him, settling in her mind to keep the conversation general and light, while still trying to ferret out some information.

"Not much," he said. "It's not my cup of tea. But they are lovely. Sarah's collection was beautiful. Especially the ones that were stolen. They were worth a lot of money, but of course only to the right people. I wouldn't have paid a dime for them. That's the funny thing about collecting."

"I found it shocking how beautiful drug paraphernalia could be," Cora said.

"I know, but they still contained drugs. Not something I'd personally go for. But Sarah was an odd bird, to say the least." He clicked his tongue on the roof of his mouth and shook his head.

Cora was a little uncomfortable with him mentioning Sarah's name with Diane sitting so close by. But Diane seemed occupied and not too concerned with their conversation. In fact, she looked downright meditative as her fingers worked over the weave of her cobweb broom.

"What do you mean by 'odd bird'?" Cora said. Edgar flinched. How odd. She noted how birdlike he himself was—he resembled an ostrich. Long and skinny, with a large nose and beady eyes.

"She collected odd things. She loved history, yet she was always wanting to make changes to her house, one of the most historic in the village," he said.

That's right! Cora had forgotten that Sarah and Edgar had gone head-to-head on a number of issues. She had been so distracted by the theft and possible insurance money aspect of the case that she had forgotten about Edgar's history with Sarah.

"It's so annoying," he said. "If you buy a historical house in a historical town, knowing full well what those implications are, why fight the rules? Why not embrace the way things are? It's good for the whole town."

Something about the way he said those words made Cora think they were really meant for her.

"Given her attitude," he said, "you can imagine my surprise at her donation."

"Donation?" Cora said.

"She left the historical society quite a large sum of money."

"But, how? Josh said she left everything to him," Cora said.

"Yes, the house and her belongings, but evidently she had some money tucked away and she endowed much of it to us About three weeks before she died." When the man smiled, his demeanor seemed fake and almost sinister. He should be happy—but for some reason, this bit of news did not make him happy.

"Could it have been her insurance money from the theft?" Cora said. This would make sense as to the reason it wasn't mentioned as part of her estate.

"I have no clue," he replied. "I know nothing about that woman's finances. In fact, it turns out I knew nothing about her at all." A sorrowful expression came over his face. Cora knew that Sarah's marriage to Josh had ended due to infidelity. Had Sarah and Edgar been having an affair?

Chapter 43

After Edgar said good-bye and went on his way, Cora walked back inside and into the kitchen to find a well-ordered mess. Darla and her small group of helpers were finishing up, but they were moving at a pace that could only be described as lacking. Cora didn't fancy them hanging out in the kitchen any longer than necessary. She wanted her guests to feel free to wander in and out of the kitchen anytime at will. Sure, they could continue to do so with the caterer there—but it wasn't quite the same thing.

Darla still wasn't herself. The woman who had been so cool, calm, and collected was a mess as she moved through the kitchen packing up a few boxes, preparing for tomorrow's chocolate reception, and chastising her help—one of whom stood at the sink, finishing washing pans, the other sliding something inside the fridge.

Darla attempted to lift a box full of napkins and plates, and Cora stopped her. "Let me help you," she said, taking one edge of the box. The two of them walked carefully out the back door to the van, which was already open. Cora and Darla managed to cram the box inside.

"Thank you," Darla said, shutting the door.

DAY CATERING was written on the side of the van in bright red letters, prompting Cora to remember the police said that a catering van had been spotted in the neighborhood the morning Jane's door was vandalized.

"You're welcome, Darla," Cora said, noting to herself that she needed to check her calendar to see if Darla and her crew were around that day.

"Are you okay?" Darla asked. "You seem out of sorts."

I could say the about you, thought Cora. But instead she said, "I'm a bit stressed and tired. It's nothing." She didn't want to alarm Darla, but Cora's guts were warning her. This woman was up to no good.

They wandered back to the kitchen, where the crew appeared ready to go.

"We'll see you tomorrow afternoon," Darla said, gathering up her purse and a few other items.

"See you then," Cora said and watched them walk off. One more day, she told herself, and then this first retreat would be over. Then they could take steps to make certain these little blips wouldn't occur again. Step number one: no men allowed on the next retreat. Step number two: background checks on all incoming parties. Number three (most important): no more murders.

This weekend had not gone as Cora had planned, but some good things were happening, too. She walked out into the living room, where a group of knitters were sitting and chatting. Jennifer and Miranda were off in a corner, laughing and knitting—maybe this was the start of a lifelong friendship. Another group were finishing up their brooms and talking about dinner plans.

Cora liked to hear that. The more her crafters went out and about in the town, the better for her and for local businesses. The locals would eventually come to appreciate her sending customers to them. She was hoping to forge alliances with several of the restaurants in town so she could offer retreaters discounts on meals and so on.

Seeing that everything was under control, Cora thought it safe to sneak back to her apartment and check some e-mails. She liked to respond to questions that came in about projects on her blog fairly quickly. As she walked up the steps, the sun was coming through the stained-glass window. Their patron goddess of the arts gazed over them all.

When Cora opened the door to her place, Luna began circling her legs.

"Did you miss me, Luna?" Cora picked her up with one hand and headed for her computer. The cat took her customary position on her lap. Cora logged in to her e-mail account. She had several new e-mails about her acorn project. But there was one from Cashel. She opened that one first:

Hey,

Found out that Sarah's insurance agent, Peter True, is here in town. I've got an appointment with him later today—about the same time Detective Brodsky will be paying you a visit.

Will touch base later.

Fondly,
Cashel

Fondly? What did that mean? Her head swam with possibilities that she didn't have the time to think about now.

She had forgotten about Detective Brodsky's return visit. She checked the time. He would be arriving soon.

She clicked on an e-mail from something called Big Island Craft Retreat:

Dear Ms. Chevalier,

We would like to invite you to be a special guest at our beach craft retreat. We would like you to teach a class on blogging for crafters. We would like to also extend this invitation to your other teachers. Details to follow, but do let us know if this is something you'd be interested in.

Yours,
Mathilda Mayhue

Interested? Oh yes, how lovely this would be! What perfect timing! By the time she, Jane, and Ruby came back from the beach retreat, this nonsense with Jane and the murder would have completely blown over with the locals.

But in the meantime, plans for the next Kildare House retreat were coming together. Cora hoped that any negative publicity wouldn't reach the women who were already registered. She and Jane had always wanted to do a "wildcrafting" retreat, where the crafts came from nature. Things were falling into place—they'd heard back from a local Cherokee basket maker, and were waiting on special permission from the park system to allow them to pick flowers, grasses, and so on, from state lands. Cora and Jane were so excited about the possibilities.

The learning curve for this retreat was going to make the next one go much more smoothly. But then again, how could they have ever planned for murder?

Chapter 44

"Hi, Detective Brodsky," Cora said. "Please come in and have a seat. Can I get you anything?"

"Thanks, but no," he said and promptly sat down on her couch. They were in Cora's apartment—she had left word for Ruby to send him upstairs when he arrived. "Nice place you have here."

"Thank you," she said. "Now what can I do for you?"

The detective scooted around on the couch for a minute, trying to get comfortable on the small couch. He was middle-aged, frumpy, and balding. Where were those hot young TV detectives when you needed them?

"You said you wanted to talk with me," he said. "You wanted to run something by me." He used air quotes around "run something by me."

"You know my friend Jane Starr is currently a person of interest in the Sarah Waters murder case," Cora said.

He nodded, with an air of impatience.

"So I've been trying to poke around a bit on my own. I appreciate how busy you guys are," she said. One of his eyebrows lifted. Just one. *Oh dear.* "Are you sure I can't get you some iced tea or water?"

"No, thanks," he said. "I'd like to hear what you've been up to."

"The only thing I've gotten a chance to do is check out the Waterses' divorce records. You see, I used to work in a women's shelter and I understand how to access these things. They are public, of course."

He nodded. "Go on."

"I'm aware that in most cases a murder victim knows their killer. I also know that husbands are the first one the police investigate and there's a variety of good reasons for that."

"Yes, but her husband was her ex-husband," he said. "They've been divorced amicably for years."

"True, but exes still kill and they must've still been quite close since she left the house and all of her belongings to him," she said. The detective didn't react. "I didn't find anything unusual with their divorce settlement and so on—except that she didn't want anything but the house. She clearly wanted out of the marriage. I'm guessing she had moved on with another man."

The detective nodded. "Yes, but this was, like, six years ago," he said. "It has little bearing on this case. I assure you. You seem to be wasting your time. You have a business or something to run, don't you?"

She ignored his veiled insult and kept going.

"I mistakenly clicked on some other records. Turns out Sarah Waters was robbed a month before her murder."

The detective crossed his arms.

"Pricey items were stolen," she said.

"That's all true, yes. But what does that have to do with anything?"

"I figured since it's obvious that Josh Waters didn't

kill his ex-wife, the next best thing is to try to follow the money trail on this."

He laughed and shook his head.

"What's so funny?"

"You are so delightful," he said. "You're trying to help your friend. I get that. But if she is innocent, it will all work out. I promise you."

Cora was nonplussed. "Did you know about the robbery?"

"Of course I did," he said. "We never found the thief. Contrary to popular belief, we don't have a magic wand and always get nice little happy endings to all of our cases. God knows I wish we did."

"I know that. I've worked with the police for years. But I also appreciate how overworked you all are. And I also know what you're up against, in terms of time and budget constraints. So sometimes it's hard to follow up on every lead. I thought I could help."

"You know what?" he said. His face softened. "I think I will take that iced tea. Is it sweet?"

"Yes," she said, rising from her chair and heading toward the kitchen area of the open floor plan apartment.

As she poured the iced tea, the detective's cell phone rang. After answering and muttering a few words, he hung up and slipped it back in his pocket. She handed him a glass of sweet tea. He took a long drink of it and sat it down on a coaster on her table.

"Thank you," he said. "That is the best sweet tea I've ever had," he exclaimed.

Cora beamed. "I've been practicing. They say good sweet tea in the South is the key to a good social life."

Cora sat back down. "So you think the murder had nothing to do with the theft?"

"I didn't say that. We're investigating a number of leads," he said. "Rest assured, we are being as thorough as possible."

Cora felt foolish. Of course they were doing the best they could do and she should back off. She could hear her therapist clicking her tongue in disapproval. She had done it again—starting to behave as if she could fix everything. Although she had wanted to help, and it had all come from good intentions, it was that same impulse that had gotten her into such trouble countless times.

The detective eyed the apartment. "That is pretty cool," he said, pointing to the chandelier that she had fashioned out of old silverware.

"Thanks," she said. "It's one of my upcycling projects. I take old stuff and make new things with them."

"I like it," he said. "So you used to be a social worker?"

"I was a counselor in a women's shelter in Pittsburgh," she said.

"What brought you here?" he said a little too nonchalantly. He was profiling her. She might as well give him a full picture.

"I developed an anxiety issue and needed to retire. I started writing this craft blog, which took off and now have decided to try out craft retreats.

"I noticed how much crafting helped some of the women at the shelter. Keeping our hands busy, making something useful, beautiful, it's meditative. So," she said. "Here we are."

He took another drink of iced tea and sat it back

down on the coaster. "What about these? Did you make these?"

She nodded. "Yes."

"Clever," he said, and then something else caught his eye. "What's this?" he said, noticing the stack of papers Cashel had left earlier.

"Oh," she said, waving her hand dismissively. "Something I should have done before I hired them. Background checks. We had Cashel run them for us."

"Do you mind if I look them over?" He picked the report up and starting reading it.

"Not at all. You can get those reports yourself, right?"

He nodded. "But what's interesting to me is that this is obviously faked," he said.

"What?"

"Jude Sawyer has a record a mile long and none of it is on here."

"What?" Her heart lurched.

"I've never heard of this firm that this record came from. Did you say O'Malley ran this?"

She nodded.

"Odd. He should know better," he said.

"Wait, wait," Cora said. "Did you say Jude has a record? What kind of record? I mean, are my guests in danger?"

"He's on probation for involuntary manslaughter."

She didn't hear him right, did she? "Come again?"

"Involuntary manslaughter," he repeated.

Cora's stomach churned. Was she trembling? Where was her medicine? If this didn't bring on a panic attack, she didn't know what would. She stood quickly and knocked over a stack of craft magazines sitting on the table.

"Are you okay?" Brodsky said.

"I need to get something. I'll be right back," she said and went to the bathroom. Just as she was popping one of the pills into her mouth, the detective came up behind her.

"Can I see those pills?" he asked.

She reluctantly handed him the bottle.

"That's what I suspected," he said, wryly. "I take the same ones."

Chapter 45

"I adore salt glazes," Jane said. "But you must be careful with them. You must dedicate one kiln to them because the salt ruins the kiln for any other type of glaze."

"I didn't know that," Miranda said. "I've been reluctant to try, but I admire the look of the glazes."

Jane's phone beeped, alerting her to a text message.

I'm okay, but had to take a pill. Please come to my place. Brodsky is here.

"Excuse me," Jane said and left the small group of women she was chatting with.

By the time Jane entered the apartment, Cora was on the couch, drinking a glass of water, and Detective Brodsky was sitting next to her, with his arm wrapped around her. He pulled away when he saw Jane.

He nodded by way of greeting. "Ms. Starr."

"Detective," she said. "How are you, Cora?"

Cora wasn't supposed to be having panic attacks anymore. This new way of life was supposed to be helping her.

"I'm fine," Cora said. "Really. I took a pill and I'll be fine in a minute."

Jane sat next to her on the other side of the sofa. "What's going on? Why are you upset?" She glared at the detective. "What did you do?"

"Me?" he said. "Nothing. I told her the truth."

"What are you talking about?" Jane said.

"Jane," Cora said. "The background check on Jude that Cashel ran for us is a fake."

"What?" How could that be? What was going on?

Cora nodded. "Turns out Detective Brodsky here knows that Jude is on probation for manslaughter."

"Involuntary," Brodsky pointed out.

"Oh my God. What happened?" Jane said, barely getting the words out of her mouth.

"Calm down," Cora said. But it was easy for her—she had just taken a happy pill. Jane had just walked into the situation.

"Evidently, it's the best kept secret in the crafting community," Cora said. "We should have thoroughly checked him out before hiring him. This is my fault."

Jane remembered Jude going into the paper-crafting room with the two cops—but what did he say they had been talking about in there? Her mind sorted through the memories of that day. "He said he had purchased Sarah's broom collection and one of her daughters wanted it back. Was that a lie?"

"That's a good question. I've got no answers for you," the detective said. "This is the first I've heard of it. But I wouldn't have necessarily been kept informed about it. It's not my case."

It then hit Jane with a hard cold thud. "You know, if

he's lying about one thing, he could be lying about everything."

"Where are you going with this?" Cora said.

"I'm wondering about Josh Waters' murder. He said he never went in, that he knocked on the door and left his card. Now I wonder," Jane said. Her brain was on fire—a million possibilities were sparking.

"Hold on," Detective Brodsky said and reached for his phone. "Ivy Renquist corroborated his alibi. She was with him."

"Ivy wouldn't lie to the police, would she?" Cora said.

"It's certainly been done before," Brodsky said wryly.

"As far as I'm concerned, Ivy is capable of anything," Jane said. "Plus, she's a married woman who hopped into bed with a man she barely knew at a craft retreat, for God's sake. She must be troubled."

"What?" Brodsky said. "You didn't tell me about this, Cora."

"Yeah," Cora said. "Jude slept with Ivy and then became enamored with another one of our guests, Linda. Ivy left because she was so embarrassed."

"I'd like to know more about this manslaughter case, involuntary or not. I have a daughter to protect," Jane said.

"I don't know the details," Brodsky said. "Not my case. But involuntary manslaughter indicates an unintentional killing."

"An unintentional killing for which he's still on probation?" Cora asked.

Brodsky nodded. "He'll likely be on probation a good long while. Anything he does is up for intense scrutiny by the police. That's just the way it is," he said.

"So, how are you feeling now?" He handed her the glass of water. "You need to keep drinking this."

The tough detective turned gentle before Jane's eyes, leading her to surmise that he was a kind man. She drew in air.

"What's wrong?" Cora said.

"I'm glad I sent London off for the weekend," she told her.

"Me, too," Cora said.

The detective's cell phone went off, and he stood to answer it. He walked toward the kitchenette and spoke in a low tone.

"He's a good guy," Cora said.

"I can see that," Jane responded.

"Gives me hope," Cora said. "This weekend has been a mess, hasn't it?"

Detective Brodsky walked back over to the couch, his phone call ended.

"Sorry, ladies, that was my wife," he said. "I need to get going. Saturday dinner. I promised." He grinned sheepishly. "You know, she was sorry to cancel this weekend."

"You mean she was one of the ones who canceled?" Cora said.

"I asked her not to come because of the case. I thought it wouldn't be appropriate since I'm working it," he said.

So that's what happened, Jane thought, and wondered if not all of the locals had canceled because they believed she was a killer. Something in her stomach settled. Something she didn't realize had been unsettled. Like a breath you were holding in and didn't realize until you let it out.

"Oh," Cora said, glancing at Jane, then back to Brodsky. "I hope she will come to the next one."

He nodded. He handed Cora and Jane each a card. "This has my number on it. Use it if you need to."

With that, he turned and left the apartment, leaving Jane and Cora to sort through this new information.

"Nothing has really changed, right?" Cora said. "I mean, we just need to get on with it. Tomorrow, he's out of here. We never will have him back."

"Plenty has changed," Jane pointed out. "If Ivy was lying about Jude, he may have been the person who killed Josh Waters. In which case, we have a killer teacher on our hands."

Chapter 46

The whole situation left Cora's head spinning. But mostly it was Jude. Jude was on probation for a serious crime. How could that have slipped by her?

"You're thinking about Jude, aren't you?" Jane said.

She nodded. Jane knew her too well. "I didn't think to run that check."

"Next time, we will," Jane said. "Live and learn. How are you?"

Cora sat up straighter. "I'm fine. It was just a shock and I started to—"

"Let's not give it any energy. I know what happened. It's okay, sweetie. It was bound to happen. You handled it—that's what matters."

Cora exhaled. She was right.

"So, this doesn't leave us much in the way of our murder investigation," Jane said. "We've been sidetracked."

Cora drank deeply from her glass of water before setting it back down. "We still don't know much, do we? We do know that Jude was attempting to visit Josh Waters that night and we know that Ivy was with him."

"But Jude wasn't here when Sarah was killed. He lives in Tennessee," Jane said.

"That doesn't mean he wasn't here," Cora pointed out. "He'd obviously been here before."

"We could ask him when the last time was."

"We could. We will. But now, I . . ."

"He makes you nervous, now?"

"Of course," Cora said. "I mean, he's killed someone. And now we're thinking again that he may have killed Josh. He's sleeping under my roof."

"I can't help but think . . . I don't know. He seems so normal," Jane said.

Cora stood and walked to her kitchen to place the glass in the sink. "Sometimes you just can't tell. I know we always joke about our intuition, which is usually right. But sometimes it's more difficult." She placed the glass in the sink with a thud. "Not that I've known any murderers—that I know of."

"The detective did say involuntary. Let's keep that in mind," Jane said, standing up, and the box of doilies, which had been sitting on the arm of the couch, fell over. She bent down to pick up some of the scattered doilies. "These are gorgeous. I'm not a big doilies person. As in, I'd never have one in my house." She grinned. "It reminds me of little old ladies. I can't help it."

"I think I can make something out of them. I just haven't decided what," Cora said.

"I have an idea. Why don't you bring the box downstairs and work on it in the sitting room, where the retreaters are. They might have some good ideas. It will get your mind off everything."

"That's exactly what I need. Dr. Jo always said that the best thing for a panic attack was to get my mind on something else. I'll focus on this for a couple of hours, then it's back to the murder investigation."

Jane rolled her eyes. "Maybe we should let it rest. Let Cashel deal with it."

"Speaking of Cashel . . ."

"Yeah, we need to tell him about those reports. Let me handle it," Jane said. "I need to return his call from earlier anyway. I also need to check in with London," she said. "I miss her."

Cora took the box of doilies from Jane. "I miss her, too."

When the two of them entered the living room, they were surprised to see almost all of the crafters there—some working on brooms and some knitting. Others were eating and chatting. It was a lovely room to walk into; a warm energy filled the place. Cora sat on the floor next to the fireplace and spread out the doilies.

"Oh!" came a squeal of delight from Diane. "What do you have there?"

"I bought these doilies at a yard sale and am trying to figure out what do with them."

"You could frame them. Check this out," she scooped one up in her hand and held it up. "It resembles a spider-web. Look how intricate it is. This would be gorgeous framed."

"They would be pretty framed," Linda chimed in.

"I agree," said Cora. "But I'm not much of a framer. I'd like to make these useful. Find some sort of function for them other than just looking pretty."

"I've seen them made into table runners," Linda said, sitting down on the floor next to Cora. She helped

Cora spread them out. "You've certainly got a treasure here," she said. "They look like they're all handmade."

"I think they are," Cora said. "You never know what you can find at a yard sale," she said, trying to sound cheery, but images of Josh Waters played in her mind. Poor Josh. Poor Sarah. What was the world coming to?

She placed one doily next to the other and saw they could fit together nicely. Perhaps a table runner was not a bad idea.

"You, know, I've seen doilies made into curtains," Diane said. "It's a bit froufrou for me, but it's clever."

"I could see curtains or table runners," Cora said, fitting together the doilies on the floor like pieces of a puzzle. Linda placed a pink one next to a white one edged in purple. Cora realized that it was going to be a challenge not only to piece and fit them just right but also to make certain the colors touching one another were complementary. She stood and placed the whitest of the doilies against her red skirt, just to see the effect.

"A skirt!" Martha said from across the room. "You could make a skirt."

"What? Really?" Cora said. *A doily skirt? It could be very tacky,* she thought.

"If it was done well, it could be gorgeous," Linda said, as if reading Cora's mind.

"And it would be fantastic on you. You're thin enough to carry it off," Martha said.

"I'm not much of a seamstress," Cora said, more to herself than the crafters.

"I am," said Linda. "But I think you need someone who can crochet and sew."

"Exactly," Diane said. "You don't want people to see

how it's put together. You need someone who can do both. I think I can do it."

"Or I can do it," Martha said.

Cora grinned. "Why don't you both do it? Work on it together?"

It was perfect. Two of her guests working together on an impromptu project. She loved the idea of the women working together to create an upcycled skirt. Visions of old-fashioned quilting bees danced in her head. She was curious as to what they'd come up with— it could be the tackiest skirt ever. But it could also be gorgeous. She was willing to give it a go.

As Cora placed one doily after the other, changing them around, making sure the colors and patterns looked good together where each doily touched, she couldn't help but mull over what she knew about Jude. Could he have killed Josh Waters? How about his wife? What motive would he have? Did the broom collection have anything to do with it? Or had he been lying about everything?

He had been to Indigo Gap before. He seemed comfortable in the town and went on and on about how he had always thought Indigo Gap was one of the prettiest towns he'd ever visited. Other than mentioning that he worked at the mill, which was miles outside of town, when was he last in town? And where was he now, anyway?

She placed the purple-fringed lace next to the yellow fringed.

"That looks good," Linda said.

"I like it, too," Martha said, coming up behind them. She was eating leftover pimento cheese spread on slices of rye bread.

Cora contemplated her guests. The knitters were still knitting in the corner. Some were eating, others were drinking. Someone laughed. This is exactly what Cora had imagined when she had wanted to start a craft retreat. And an unexpected group project added to her satisfaction.

Other than the oversexed broom maker on probation for manslaughter, the nasty caterer, and that fact that her best friend and partner was still under suspicion for murder, of course.

Chapter 47

Several hours later, the crafters' collective quiet was interrupted by Ruby entering the room and asking if anybody wanted to go to dinner with her. Several of the women in the room said yes.

"Cashel wants you to call him," Ruby said to Cora.

Cora sighed and set aside the skirt. "I'll be right back," she said to Linda and Diane.

Ruby followed her into the kitchen. "Have you seen him?"

"Who?" Cora said.

"Jude," Ruby replied.

"Not recently. I have no idea where he is. He's most likely out for dinner. Who could blame him for wanting some downtime to himself?" Cora said. "He's been 'on' with these women since he's gotten here."

"In more than one way," Ruby said, eyebrows twitching.

"Unfortunately, yes," Cora said. "What does Cashel want?"

Ruby shrugged. "He didn't say. I'm just his mother, the woman who bore and birthed him. He doesn't tell me anything."

Cora rolled her eyes. "That's a little dramatic."

"You think?" Ruby said and grinned. "Well, listen, I'll let you get to it. I'm hungry." With that, Ruby took her leave.

Cora dialed Cashel on her cell phone, and he answered on the first ring.

"Cashel O'Malley." He sounded very official.

"It's me, Cora," she said. "Ruby said that you wanted me to call."

"Yeah," he said. "How's it going?"

"Okay," she said.

"First of all, I'm sorry about those fake reports. I had no idea. My office assistant only just started dealing with that company. They were cheap, but I suppose there's a reason for it."

"I'll say," she said.

"It happens," he said, with a note of defensiveness in his voice. "The other thing I wanted to ask you is about this Ivy Renquist."

"What do you want to know?"

"I wanted to give her a call and ask her about that night . . . the night that we found Josh. But I can't seem to get any answer. Not even a machine. I thought that was curious. So I'm calling to check with you to see if I have the right number."

"Okay, what do you have?"

He read the number to her, and she jotted it down. "Hold on," she said. She grabbed the folder near the phone that held the registration forms the guests had filled out and flipped through them. After a minute, she got back on the phone.

"Cashel," she said, "Where did you get that number?"

"The police report," he said. "Why?"

"It's wrong. This is Ivy's number." Cora read off the number.

"So she gave the cops a fake number."

"Maybe she was distraught," Cora said. "The two numbers are similar. Maybe the cop just wrote it down wrong."

"I'm not certain either one of those possibilities is something I believe," Cashel said.

"What do you think?"

"Sounds like Ivy Renquist is hiding something."

"Well, she did cheat on her husband. That's something she'd want to hide for sure."

"Have you seen Jane?" Cashel asked.

"Not recently. She had some phone calls to make," Cora said.

"You may want to check in on her," he said with a stiffness in his voice. "The fingerprint experts want to see her first thing Monday morning. It doesn't look good."

"What?" Cora's heart raced.

"Calm down," he said. "I may be entirely misreading this. But they do want to see us. So the results must be ready."

"Do they expect us to wait until Monday morning?" Cora said, trying not to panic.

"Well, the court isn't open on Sunday," he said.

"What will happen if they think her prints match?" Cora said.

"They will need to prove she killed Sarah," he said. "And if Jane wasn't there at the murder site, they won't be able to do that. I'll call in a few of my own experts. Try not to worry too much, okay?"

After they finished their conversation and hung up,

Cora sat at the kitchen table with a pen and paper. She always kept a pen and paper handy. Doodling was a great way to think.

She found herself writing names, instead of doodling—Jude and Ivy. She picked up her cell and dialed Ivy's number. A machine answered.

"Ivy? This is Cora Chevalier calling to see that everything is okay with you and you made it home all right. Give me a call back when you can."

Did Ivy intentionally give the police the wrong number? Cora wondered. If so, did she really think she could get away with something like that? She'd known a lot of women who cheated on their husbands. People tended to think it was only men who were unfaithful, but that wasn't the case. Cheaters of either gender were either wholly egotistical and thought they'd never get caught—or they were desperately unhappy and felt like they had no other choice. Which one was Ivy? She didn't appear to be egotistical. In fact, she had been quite embarrassed by her own behavior, hadn't she? So she was desperate and unhappy, then. Which didn't make Cora feel any better at all.

Chapter 48

When Jane opened the door to her carriage house, Cora eyeballed her. She was pale and too light on her feet. Dark circles edged her eyes.

"Are you okay?" Cora said.

"You know they called me in for Monday, right?" Jane said. "I'm a bit of a nervous wreck about it. Cashel said it didn't look good. I've no idea what that means."

"I don't get it, either," Cora said, following Jane into the house. There was an open bottle of wine on the coffee table, and Jane went to fetch a second glass. "You have alibis."

"Yes, I do," Jane said as she filled Cora's glass. "But Cashel said they are weak alibis. Neil is . . . well, you know. Let's just say he doesn't have the best character. And for some reason Cashel's not impressed with David either."

"David? Is that his name?" Cora had imagined another name. A sexy name. A name suitable for a one-night stand. Armando. Erik. Rhett. Not David. Geez, how disappointing!

"They'll use his statement, but evidently, he must

have a record, or something, which is troubling for a whole bunch of reasons," Jane said. "But typical for me. Next time I spend the weekend with a sexy stranger, I'll be sure to ask about his record."

"That will be a real mood killer," Cora said and sipped her wine. It was moscato; sweet and light. It tickled her tongue.

Jane couldn't help but laugh at Cora's comment.

"I love it when you laugh," Cora said. Jane didn't laugh a lot—she didn't smile a lot, either.

"I know I'm innocent," Jane said. Her smile vanished as quickly as it had appeared. "Yet, sometimes I feel like I'm guilty."

"Let's figure this out. I need something to write with."

"What are we figuring out?" Jane said.

"Who killed the Waterses, of course," Cora said, after Jane handed her the tablet.

Jane wrote down the name of everybody in the family, again.

Daughter: Dee Waters
Daughter: Rebecca Saunders
Sarah's Boyfriend?
Josh's Second Wife

"Do we know their names?" Jane said, pointing to the last two people on Cora's list.

"No," Cora said. "But I wondered if Josh's wife's name would be in his obituary."

Jane was already searching on her phone. "Here it is. Charlotte. Charlotte Bow Waters and their two children, Andrew and Christy."

"That's right, he had kids with the new wife," Cora said. How sad that those kids would grow up without their dad.

"The funeral will be in Pennsylvania," Jane read aloud. "But what about the daughters?"

"Which daughters?"

"Sarah and Josh's daughters."

"Oh right. Well, one of them, Rebecca, assaulted me in their front yard. She's kind of scary. The other one was or is in England, the last anyone knew, but nobody seems sure."

"Could Rebecca have killed both of her parents?" Jane said. "Is it possible?"

Cora mulled that over. It had occurred to her once before. But someone had said she was grief stricken over her parents' deaths. Was it Cashel?

"I suppose it's possible," Cora said. "Though I hate to even think about that. It seems too much to ponder, a daughter killing both parents."

"I'm certain it happens," Jane said. "Families . . ."

"Yeah," Cora agreed. She sat her wineglass down. Her mind sorted through the other possibilities. "What about Sarah's boyfriend?"

"Any idea who that was?" Jane said.

"I have an idea," Cora said. "But how would we find out for sure? I mean, it's not something that would be in the obituary."

"No, but it is something that would be on the grapevine, if you know what I mean," Jane said with a grin.

"Let me call Ruby," Cora said.

"Good idea."

"Everything okay?" Ruby asked after answering.

"Fine for now," Cora said.

"Did you ever get a hold of Ivy?" Ruby asked

"Not yet," Cora replied. "But listen. Do you know who Sarah Waters was dating before she was killed?"

"Yes, I do," Ruby said. "Why?"

"We're making a list of other possible suspects in her murder."

"Why would you be doing that?" Ruby said. "I'm sure Cashel has everything under control."

"I'm sure he does," Cora said. She didn't mean to suggest otherwise and was sorry that Ruby thought she had. "Just humor me."

"She was dating Edgar," Ruby said. "If you think he'd kill anything, you've got another thought coming to you. The man is a priss. I never knew what she saw in him. But he's the one that broke up their marriage. It went on for years. I don't know why they never married," Ruby said.

"Interesting," Cora said. "Thanks so much, Ruby."

"No trouble at all," she said and clicked off the phone.

"Edgar Thorncraft? Really?" marveled Jane, who'd been listening in to Cora's conversation with Ruby.

"We never knew Sarah," Cora responded. "I knew her in passing. You knew her—barely—from the school. So, it's hard to imagine her with Edgar."

"Yet, she left everything to her first husband," Jane said. "Something odd is going on there."

"But Edgar? He's . . ."

"He's a cold person," Jane said.

"True. But a killer?"

"Knowing what we do about families and romances, it appears as if Edgar and the Waterses' daughters should be at the top of the suspect list," Jane said. "Trouble is, it's almost Saturday evening. And it's not like we can go visiting. And even if we could, what would we say? Did you kill your girlfriend, Edgar?"

"We'll be seeing Edgar tomorrow," Cora reminded her friend. "He's coming to the reception. I don't know how I'll manage it, but I'll question him."

"What about Rebecca?"

Cora thought a moment. "Well, do we have any muffins left?"

"We might."

"Let's take a basket of them to her."

"What? When?"

"Let's get it together and do it now."

"Isn't it a bit too late?" Jane asked.

"We can go over and check it out. If it looks like she's settled in for the night, we'll let it wait until tomorrow. What do you say?"

Jane shrugged. "No time like the present. But what will we say to her?"

"Just leave that to me," Cora said. "I imagine that whether she killed her parents or not, she's grieving. I can handle Rebecca Saunders."

Chapter 49

"Maybe she's not staying here," Jane said, after they had knocked on the door and had rung the doorbell of Sarah Waters' former home several times.

"She's not," said a voice from behind them. Jane and Cora turned to see a man, probably in his seventies. Neither of them had ever seen him before.

"We brought her muffins," Cora said. "Do you know where she is?"

He nodded. "I'm Harv Masters. I live next door. She's quite depressed. I'm not sure she could take a visit from anybody right now."

"Is she staying with you?" Jane asked. "I'm Jane, by the way. This is Cora. We've moved into the Kildare House."

"I know who you are," he said, shaking their hands. "And yes, Becca is staying with us. We're doing the best we can for her." He looked at Cora. "You the woman with the doilies?"

"The doilies from the yard sale? Yes."

"Perhaps she would like to see you after all," he said.

"Follow me. By the way, this place is a crime scene, again. Nobody is supposed to be here. I've been keeping an eye out." He pointed to the yellow crime-scene tape on the door, which Cora and Jane had ignored.

Harv led them to his backyard. A woman was sitting on a back porch, finishing what looked like a slice of apple pie. But Cora didn't want to ogle the pie.

"You were right," said the woman. "There was some-one over there." She stood as they approached.

Cora introduced herself and Jane. "We were looking for Rebecca. We're delivering his basket of muffins from Kildare House."

"How kind of you," the woman said. Cora took a closer view. Was this Rebecca? Was this the same woman who had attacked Cora a few days ago? That rage-filled woman was not this placid person now standing in front of them, was she? Cora was shocked by the change.

"Becca?" Harv said. It was her!

Becca took the basket from Cora. "Thanks so much. Do I know you?"

"We met briefly in the front yard of your mother's house," Cora explained. "You were quite distraught."

"Oh," she said. Her faced reddened. "I do apologize. It was such a shock—the whole thing, my mom's death, her things being sold . . . I just . . ." She shrugged. "I am not handling it well. I'm so glad Harv found you. I wanted to apologize to you."

"Please have a seat," Harv said, as he brought over two more lawn chairs that had been stacked against the outside wall. It seemed rude not to sit, though Cora and Jane had not planned to be gone from the retreat for long.

"Becca, how are you doing now, if you don't mind my asking?" Cora said after they all sat down.

Becca was checking out the muffins. She took one, then handed the basket to Harv, who grinned.

Becca didn't smile. But her bearing was much better than the last time Cora had seen her. "It's a bit much to take actually. Both of my parents are dead. I feel very alone. Even though I'm not. I have a husband, friends, and so on. But I still feel so alone."

Cora wondered about the whereabouts of her husband.

"I think it's going to take a lot of time and patience with yourself," Cora said. "Grief is a tough one. When we are dealing with the loss of parents, it's rough. And with one gone it's hard enough. And then it's of course all compounded by the tragic nature of their deaths. Please give yourself some time." *It was almost as if she were talking to herself. Both of Cora's own parents had died after a horrible accident. Here one day, gone the next.*

"Cora used to be a counselor," Jane explained.

"She also knows some pretty fancy self-defense moves," Becca said.

"Ah, yes," Cora said. "A requirement of my old job. I worked at a women's shelter in a tough neighborhood in Pittsburgh."

"What are you doing here?" Harv asked.

Cora sighed and told them her story. How did it end up that she was talking more about herself than finding out more about Becca Saunders?

"Can I get you something to drink? Where are my manners?" Harv said.

"No, thanks. We really can't stay. We have a house

full of guests. But we did want to deliver the muffins and offer you our sympathy," Cora said.

Becca scrutinized her fingers. Her hands were crossed on her lap. Her fingers twitched every now and then.

"You know, I wish I had gotten to know your mother," Cora said. "She had the most interesting collections."

Becca brightened a bit. "She did. In fact, she could be a bit of a hoarder. She'd get obsessed about something. It could be an item mentioned in a book or an article and she would go crazy, buying everything she could. She needed to possess it," Becca said.

"They never did find out who stole the million-dollar opium kit," Harv said.

"Those opium kits are gorgeous. I never knew," Cora said.

"Who would have? But there are drug paraphernalia societies and collector's groups and so on. She was involved in some of them. But she stopped collecting them after my sister's overdose," Becca said.

"Oh?" Cora prodded.

"My mother associated her collection with what happened to my sister," Becca said. "It was horrible, what my sister went through and what she put the rest of us through."

"Where is your sister now?" Jane said.

"I wish I knew. The last account we had was that she was somewhere in England. We've hired a private detective to try to find her. She stands to inherit some money," Becca said.

"Money? Edgar Thorncraft mentioned to me that

Sarah left her money to the historical society," Cora said.

"She did," Harv said. "But this is big money. Her insurance policy payout is supposed to be split between Becca and her sister. The opium kit that was stolen was insured for over a million dollars."

Cora watched Becca's reaction. She seemed resolute. Would she have killed her mother for the money? It seemed absurd. She'd get the money eventually, anyway. Why kill her mother to rush the thing, unless she were desperate for money? Unless she hated her mother? But that didn't seem to be the case.

"Where do you live, Becca?" Cora said.

"I live in Asheville. My husband is a surgeon there. He's trying to clear his schedule. He should be here tomorrow."

Cora doubted money was an issue for Becca and her husband.

"We heard that your mom was seeing Edgar?" Jane asked gently.

"They were two peas in a pod," Becca replied.

"But they fought like cats and dogs, sometimes," Harv said and laughed, as if he were remembering a private joke.

Becca seemed to be cheered a bit by their visit. Cora knew that it often helped the grieving to talk about their loved ones. But she also knew it could be rough for them, too, if they weren't ready. After making a bit of small talk, Becca returned to the subject of her parents' murders.

"I just don't understand why anybody would want to kill either one of them," she said.

"We've discussed this, and we know you'd have no reason," Harv said to Jane.

"Thank you," Jane said quietly.

"None of it makes any sense," Harv said.

Becca guffawed. "Does murder ever make sense?"

"Unfortunately, sometimes it does," Harv replied.

Chapter 50

"So much for that," Jane said as she and Cora walked along the streets of Indigo Gap back to the house.

"Do you think we can cross her off our list?" Cora asked.

"It would be a shock to find out that she killed anybody, but I always say never say never," Jane responded.

"Remember Jill?"

Jane nodded. Jill was a girl that grew up in their old neighborhood. She was always sweet. She went to college, became a nurse, married a dentist, had kids, and one day killed them all—her husband, her kids, and herself. She had a complete psychotic break. It happened. People sometimes just broke.

"I don't think Becca is like Jill," Jane said, after a moment.

"Probably not, even though she is fragile," Cora agreed. "Dang, it's getting cold." She wrapped her sweater in tighter around her.

"It is October," Jane said.

The two of them walked down the cobblestone street. The sun was starting to set, and the mountains took on their blue haze, tinged with deep purple. Streetlights were beginning to glow.

A few people were on the sidewalks. A woman dressed all in pink walked by them and nodded. A group of retreaters rapped on the window of the diner when Cora and Jane walked by. They smiled and waved back. They turned the corner and were almost at the florist shop. Cora had wanted to order some flowers for her Uncle Jon and Beatrice, but it seemed as if the shop were already closed, as the curtains were drawn. A man walked toward them down the sidewalk. It was Edgar.

"Hello, Edgar," Cora said with as bright a note in her voice as she could muster. Weariness washed over her. What an exhausting day. Jude. The detective. Visiting with Becca. Now Edgar.

"Good evening, ladies," he said and smiled. "Where are you off to this evening?"

"Just getting some fresh air," Jane said.

"It is a pretty evening, isn't it?" he said. "I would've thought you'd be too busy entertaining to enjoy it."

"We're heading back now," Cora said. Why did she feel guilty about this? Her business was none of his concern. Besides, the crafters didn't need her there all day and all night. In fact, most of them had their own plans for this evening.

"What are you up to?" Jane asked.

"I am heading over to the diner," Edgar replied. "I take my Saturday night dinner there now. I used to—oh, never mind," he said, a hollow expression coming over his face. "Saturdays used to be different. That's all."

"You miss her," Cora blurted out.

His eyes locked with hers.

"Yes, of course, I do," he said. "She was my life."

He glanced away from them, embarrassed. There was more to Edgar Thorncraft than met the eye. More than bow-ties and ever-wagging fingers.

"I'm sorry," Cora said and touched his shoulder briefly. "Do you want to talk about it?" As she turned to face him, she glimpsed movement in the florist shop. A curtain moved. Or was that just the streetlight reflecting?

"Not really," he said. "Talking doesn't change anything."

Cora's heart sank. Poor guy. He was an uptight, reserved man. Not the kind of guy she usually hit it off with. But he was okay. And he was no killer. She felt it then and there in her bones. "She was my life," he had said. Cora believed him.

"You will come to the reception tomorrow night?" Jane said. It broke the uncomfortable air that seemed to settle over the three of them. Jane grinned. "You know, it might be my last night of freedom."

"Don't say that," Edgar said. "I surely hope you are wrong."

Cora's cell phone blared.

"Cora Chevalier," she said after she accepted the call, moving down the sidewalk a bit. She hated taking calls during a conversation.

"Cora?" a voice said on the other end of the phone.

"Yes?"

"This is Ivy Renquist. I'm returning your very confusing phone call."

Confusing? What had she said in her message that was confusing?

"I'm sorry about that," Cora said. "I was just checking to make sure you made it home okay. We were a bit concerned about you."

"Home from where?"

"From the retreat. You left early and not under good circumstances. I'm so sorry about that."

"I'm sorry, Cora, but I think there's been a misunderstanding. You called me to cancel days ago. You said there was a mistake and the retreat was full. I never came."

"But there was an Ivy Renquist here," Cora said, her voice tripping around herself as she tried to figure out this new development.

"Well, it wasn't me. Could there be another Ivy?"

"Anything is possible," Cora said as she tried to gather her wits. "There must be some awful mistake."

"I bet it's a computer glitch," Ivy said. "Damned things."

"When I figure out what happened, I'll let you know," Cora said.

"Was my credit card charged?" the real Ivy said.

"I assume it was," Cora said, sensing her face heat. "I'm so sorry. I will take care of this immediately."

"Thanks so much. Please let me know," Ivy said and then hung up.

Cora stood there on the sidewalk, deep in thought. What had gone on at the retreat this weekend? How could a woman take on another woman's identity and nobody catch it?

"Cora?" Edgar said. She hadn't noticed the way Jane and Edgar had moved in closer to her. "Is everything okay?"

"The reason we can't get a hold of Ivy Renquist," Cora said to Jane, "is that she never showed up."

"What? You're not making any sense."

"The woman who was here was not Ivy."

"Well, who was she?"

"I think we better find that out. Immediately," Cora said. "Sorry, Edgar, but we need to get back to the house."

"Yes, yes, well, I'm off to dinner. Good luck," he said.

Cora and Jane practically ran all the way back to Kildare House.

Chapter 51

Once they arrived back at Kildare House, Jane found Jude, who had been out for a run. She also stumbled across Ruby and thought it best for her join them in Cora's apartment, as well. Most of the crafters were gathered in the sitting room and a few were still out on the town. Cora longed to sit in her chair and work on her embroidery, basking in the fellowship of the other crafters, but this was an emergency that could not wait. Someone had breached security and maybe ripped off the real Ivy Renquist. Cora was furious.

"We found out that Ivy is not who she said she was," Cora said bluntly once the four of them gathered in her apartment.

"What do you mean?" Ruby asked.

Cora recounted her earlier conversation with the real Ivy.

"I checked already and our intruder, whoever she was, paid for the retreat in full in cash. So she was not after Ivy's credit card," Cora said.

"So what was she after?" Ruby asked.

"Maybe she was after Jude?" Cora said. All eyes turned to him.

"Well, she did get me, if that was the case," he said. "Quite a few times, actually." He grinned.

Ruby smacked him in the stomach. "Really, Jude. What would your daddy say about you and your hopping from bed to bed? Your mama and daddy raised you right. I know they did."

His face reddened. "Sorry, Ruby," he muttered.

"In any case, besides all that, I wondered, Jude, if she might have mentioned anything about where she lives or whatever. We need you to think. This is a serious crime," Cora said.

"It's also a serious security breach," Jane pointed out. "She somehow got our list of attendees, called one of them, and told them we were sold out and she shouldn't bother attending."

"People can figure anything out these days with the computer and Facebook and all that," Ruby said. "That's one reason I don't mess with all that. "

"So Jude, did she say anything about a place? Another city? Town?" Cora persisted.

"We didn't talk much," he said sheepishly. "But she did mention the coast a few times."

"Which coast?"

"Somewhere near Charleston," he replied. "Some island . . . Edisto?"

"Edisto is a small island off the South Carolina coast," Ruby said. "Have you contacted Cashel about any of this?" she asked Cora.

"I called Detective Brodsky and Cashel already. They are coming over in the morning," Cora said.

"This could be a wild-goose chase," Jane said. "I'm frankly not sure I believe anything you say," she leveled at Jude.

"I've never lied about anything!" he protested.

"We know about your record," Jane said.

"Whoa!" he said. "Sometimes the record is not quite accurate. That's all I'm saying. I served my time. Six months in jail. It's over. Behind me. I'd like to keep it that way. I don't go around broadcasting it, but I can't hide it even if I wanted to."

"Jude," Cora said. "You're not on trial here. But you understand our concern."

"Yeah," he said, looking on the floor, then back to Cora. "I'd like a chance to explain myself," he said. "I've just made a few very bad decisions."

"That's what they all say," Jane said.

His mouth twisted into a frown. "I purchased some broomcorn from another country. It was laced with arsenic. I wasn't aware, of course. One of the people at my workshops, well, she cut herself and somehow the arsenic got into her bloodstream. I had no idea, believe me. All I knew was it was cheap. I'd never want to hurt anybody, let alone kill them. But she died and I was responsible. It was a freaky thing that happened and I feel terrible. I was negligent, but I meant no harm."

A silence permeated the room while they all took in this confession.

"All right, Jude," Cora said, feeling a bit guilty for making a snap judgment. But then again, he was so careless that someone died from his mistake. Even if it was an accident—and she was certain it was—he was guilty. But she could not get sidetracked and needed to stay present, in this moment. "Let's come back to here and now and Ivy. Is there anything else you can remember?"

He shook his head. "She talked about the island, her house there, and her collections."

Cora's heart fell to her feet, and she felt the air escape her lungs. "Collections?" She managed to say.

"Could that be a coincidence?" Jane asked, voice raised.

"What do you mean? What kind of coincidence? A lot of people collect things. Brooms. Doilies. Whatever," Ruby said. "It's no big deal."

"But Sarah Waters' priceless opium kit collection was stolen," Jane said.

"And then she was killed," Jude said.

"Wait a minute. Let's not get carried away here," Ruby said. "You're making many connections that probably don't exist. It doesn't do anybody good to jump to conclusions."

"You sound like Cashel," Jane said.

"I do? I do! Damn," Ruby said and grinned. "I guess he's rubbing off on me. But the point is this woman was probably after Jude. She got him. He lost interest and she left. End of story."

"An illegal, creepy story," Cora said. "Assuming someone else's identity? Seducing a man you barely know at a craft retreat?"

Sometimes Cora thought she had become jaded doing the work she did in Pittsburgh. Sometimes she thought she had seen everything. But clearly she hadn't.

"Yes, but none of that points to her stealing a jeweled opium kit," Ruby said.

Jude had been sitting on the edge of the sofa, taking

everything in. "But there is something else," he said. There was weight to his words, as if he had something important to say. All three women leaned in closer toward him.

"One of the things the fake Ivy collects is opium kits."

Chapter 52

"I hate to admit it," Detective Brodsky said in a tired voice. "But this is clever detective work on your part."

Cashel nodded in agreement.

"I've got an APB out on this woman," Brodsky said. "You've given me a detailed description of her and with the small population of Edisto—if that is where she lives—we should be able to nab her."

"I assume that not many residents are collectors of opium kits," Cashel said dryly.

"We'd need to search her place and confiscate her kits to see if they match what was stolen, but I'm betting they do," Brodsky said.

They were all gathered in Cora's apartment, as she didn't want to alert any of the crafters having coffee downstairs. They were on their own for breakfast this morning, as the only food served would be at the party later that night.

"Thank you," Cora said. "But I was trying to find the Waterses' killer, not the thief of their opium kits."

"Well, justice will be served in the burglary, in any case," Cashel said.

"Let's hope that Monday morning it will be served, as well," Jane said quietly.

"Actually, I may have good news on the graffiti front," the detective said. "I stopped by the office earlier today. The police followed through with questioning the service folks in the area. There was a florist van." He pulled out a small notebook from his jacket. "Let's see . . . yes. A florist. He checked out, he was delivering flowers to one of your neighbors. The UPS van checked out, too. Those guys are fully tracked at all times. But there's news on the catering van. It said 'Day' on the van."

"Oh, that's our caterer," Cora replied. "Of course she was here. I had a hunch about this!"

"Around what time was she here?" Detective Brodsky asked.

"Let me check," Cora said. "That was the day before the retreat actually started." She clicked on a file on her computer. "Hmm. It doesn't look like she was actually here until the next day."

"Perhaps she was here for another job in the area?" Cashel chimed in.

"Could be. We'll check it out." Brodsky slid his notebook back in his pocket.

"Speaking of Darla Day," Cashel said. "Her background check came back utterly blank. I know the first one we ran was false. But I ran another one and there's still absolutely nothing on her. "

"I find that hard to believe," Brodsky said. "I'll check that out myself. At the least she has to have bank records. A business license and so on. Right?"

"One would think," Cashel said.

"I've got to go," the detective told them. "I'll be back

in touch. I'm not sure how quickly I can move on any of this. But the APB is out."

Cora walked him to her apartment door. "Thanks for everything," she said.

"How are you doing?" he asked.

"I'm much better, thank you," Cora said.

"I'm off, too," Ruby said. "I'll walk down with you. I'm teaching a soap- and candle-making class this morning. I better get ready."

They all said good-bye to Brodsky and Ruby as they headed off, which left Cashel, Jude, Jane, and Cora.

Cora sat down next to Cashel. Jane was watching her every move.

"So we may have solved at least one crime," Cora said.

"Two crimes, actually. Identity theft and possibly the case of the missing opium kit," Cashel said. "Perhaps we should celebrate."

"No, thanks," Jude said. "I've also got a class to teach. I'm such an idiot. I should have followed Ivy that night."

"What night?" Cashel asked, as he got up to leave. It was clear there would be no celebration after all.

"The night of Josh's murder."

"Wait. She was with you, right?" Cashel said. "I mean, that's what you both said."

"Yeah, she was," Jude said. "And like I told the cops, she was there when I knocked at the door."

"But?" Jane said impatiently.

"But we went our separate ways after that. We walked over to the main street and she said she had some shopping to do and would catch up with me later," Jude said.

"Did you tell the police that?" Cashel asked.

"I don't remember. Probably. I don't know. I can't remember if they asked about the rest of the night, or just when we were at the Waterses' place. If they had asked, I certainly would have told them exactly what I told you."

"Can you stay until Monday morning?" Cashel asked, glancing at Jude.

"For what?"

"We might need a statement from you on Jane's behalf."

Jude looked at Jane. "I'll do anything to help," he said, and then the two men left the apartment.

"Jane?" Cora said when they were gone.

"Hmm?"

"Do you think that Ivy or whoever she was could've killed . . ."

"I think we are skimming the surface of the woman who pretended to be Ivy Renquist. Anything is possible."

Exhausted, but wired from the countless possibilities, Cora sighed a deep sigh. "I can't think straight," she said. Jude killed a person by negligence. An intruder was in Kildare House for two days. That same intruder might be guilty of the theft of priceless opium kits. Lessons learned the hard way—she would need to put more security measures in place. Stolen identities were not a part of her business plan.

Chapter 53

Later that morning Cora walked into the craft wing and was greeted with a myriad of scents—lavender, rose, cinnamon, vanilla. Some of the crafters were making soap, some candles, and Ruby was in her glory, fussing over the herbs.

They had poured the soap and candles into the molds and were preparing for a break. But first, they each selected herbs to sprinkle into the cooling soap. Cora snapped some photos. Natural light filled the room this morning. The variety of colors and textures, along with the herbs and molds, played well on her camera's lens—bits of lavender in the cream-colored soap. The green spiky rosemary leaves mixed with calendula flower and chamomile. The swirled cinnamon. Plus the crafters were all dressed in earthy colors. Cora imagined a lively photo essay. She'd publish it on the blog, along with Ruby's soap recipe and instructions.

She hadn't heard from Cashel or from Brodsky yet, and she considered that a good sign. And she didn't see Jude hanging around. Had he gone out for another run? The man did enjoy his runs, she mused. Maybe that's why he was in such good shape.

A stab of guilt zipped through her when she considered she leapt to the wrong conclusions about him. He simply had no judgment when it came to women. Most young men did not. He was thirty-five years old, and her grand-père always said not to bother with a man until he was past thirty. Their judgment was clouded by hormones. Jude's "development" seemed to be behind the curve. Or, perhaps he would always be stuck in that Peter Pan syndrome.

Ruby walked up to her.

"It smells great in here," Cora said.

Ruby nodded. "I love making soap. It's so satisfying."

"I need your recipe and directions. I'll feature it on the blog. And I'll mention that your soap is for sale and link it to your Web site."

"That sounds good," Ruby said. "I had a full class this morning. Even the knitters came. Any word?"

Cora shook her head and took a drink of her coffee. She'd had two cups, but the caffeine hadn't kicked in yet. She was weary and anticipating the end of this weekend. Except that then it would be Monday, which was the day Jane had to report to the court. But Jude would be there, wouldn't he? He would help deflect suspicions from Jane to the Ivy impersonator.

Cora sighed.

"I know," Ruby said, wrapping her arm around her. "It's going to be okay."

"Lawd, it smells like a cheap perfume factory in here," a woman's voice said. Cora turned around to find an older redhead, with strands of gray through her hair.

She wore glasses, but her blue eyes were bright and lively. She sneezed and then said, "Excuse me."

"Bless you," Cora said.

"Thank you," the woman said with a soft, lilting Virginia accent.

"Can I help you?" Cora said.

"I'm looking for Coralie," the woman said.

"Coralie?" Ruby said, bewildered.

"That's me," Cora said. "I'm Coralie Chevalier."

The woman's face lit up.

"Well, my word, look at you! Jon didn't say how gorgeous you are!"

"What?" Cora said.

"Of course not, we are a humble people." Cora's Uncle Jon walked into the room.

"Uncle Jon!" Cora fell into his arms and nearly came undone. "You made it! And this must be Beatrice. *Aunt* Beatrice." Cora hugged her new aunt.

They say you can tell a lot by the way people hug. If that was the case, Beatrice was open, warm, strong, and healthy. It was hard to believe she was in her eighties.

"This place is gorgeous!" Beatrice said. She sneezed again. "But I'm sorry. I can't stay in this room right now," she said. "My nose is a bit sensitive."

Ruby crossed her arms defensively.

"That's fine, let me show you around," Cora said before Ruby could say anything. "But first let me introduce you to Ruby, our herbalist."

Beatrice held out her hand. "Herbalist, heh?" She gave her an appraising look.

"That's right," Ruby said, stiff-lipped. "Pleased to meet you."

"I have a cousin who's an herbalist. Lives up in the mountains of Virginia. Her name's Rose Hill."

"*The* Rose Hill?"

"I suppose so," Beatrice said, shrugging.

"I've taken a few classes with her," Ruby said, brightening somewhat toward Beatrice.

"It's a small world, isn't it?" Beatrice said.

Cora's phone buzzed. She looked at the screen and saw that it was Detective Brodsky.

"I'm so sorry. I have to take this," she said and moved to another part of the room.

"How are you?" Brodsky said when she picked up.

"Good. Do you have any news for me?"

"Yes, but not the news you were expecting, probably. We discovered who the graffiti artist was. The person who spray-painted 'killer' across Jane's door."

"Who? Do I know him?" This was good news.

"It was your caterer, Darla Day. We found the paint in her van. "

"What? Why would she do such a thing?" Cora felt her chest tighten.

"I don't know. She's in holding and she's not talking. We picked her up not long after I left your place. She was headed over to your house to set up for the party tonight. I have no idea why she did it," he said. "When I find out, I'll let you know. In the meantime, your caterer is indisposed."

"I see," Cora said. What was she going to do about the chocolate reception? They were expecting a full house. This was going to be a disaster.

"Thanks for filling me in," she said and hung up. When she turned around, she saw her Uncle Jon looking at her.

"What's wrong?" he said. Beatrice was by his side.

"The caterer for tonight's event can't make it," Cora said.

"What? Why?" Jon said.

"I'll explain it to you later," she said. "In the meantime, I need to figure out what I'm going to serve. It's supposed to be a chocolate reception. Everything in chocolate. Pies, cake, bread . . ."

Jon grinned and grabbed Beatrice's hand. "I think we've got you covered. Beatrice is quite the baker."

"Let's take a look-see at your kitchen, shall we?" Beatrice said.

"Wait—you are my guests. I can't put you to work," Cora said, embarrassed.

"We are family. Of course you can put us to work," Beatrice said in a tone that allowed no argument.

Chapter 54

"What's going on?" Jane asked as she entered the kitchen, where Beatrice and Jon were happily making chocolate pie filling.

Cora introduced Jane to Bea and Jon, who apologized for not shaking her hand since he was up to his elbows in pie filling.

"We need to get these pies done and chilling before the reception," Beatrice said.

"But where is Darla?" Jane asked.

"She's being detained by the police," Cora responded. "It turns out that she was your vandal."

"What?" Jane's voice rose a decibel or two.

"Calm down," Cora said. "She's been caught."

"But why would she do that?" Jane said. "Unless she wanted people to think I killed Sarah."

"Killed who?" Beatrice asked as she stirred a huge bowl full of dark, creamy fluff.

"We've had a couple of murders in town," Cora said weakly.

"Murders?" Jon said with his voice raised. "I thought you said this was a safe place."

"It is," Cora said. "Or at least I thought it was."

"I don't know if I like the sound of this," Jon said. "Your grand-père would not want you in such a situation."

"It's okay," Cora said, trying to reassure Jon. "There hasn't been a murder here in, like, twenty years. And these two murders are aberrations."

"I've heard that before and it never turns out to be the case," Beatrice said, opening the fridge. "Thank goodness they left you dough for the crust," she muttered. "It's good and chilled."

Cora dug around in her cupboard and found two pie plates. Two. "Do you have any pie plates?" she asked Jane.

"No," Jane said. "But I bet Ruby does. I'll go ask."

"Well?" Beatrice said. "What is going on with the murders?" She rolled out the pie crust and Cora marveled at her expert handling of the crust. Before she knew it, two pie crusts were in the plates, edges crimped, and filling poured in—and all the while Cora was explaining what was going on with the murder cases.

Jon stood at the sink, washing out one of the mixing bowls. He wanted to get started on his "famous" chocolate bread. "So, you say they found Jane's prints at the scene of the first murder?"

Cora nodded. "They are only half prints and Jane's prints are so smooth that it's hard for them to match them exactly. But they are similar enough for them to have questioned her several times about it."

"Well, we know that she had nothing to do with it and I'm sure it will work out," Jon said.

Jane entered through the back door of the house with four more pie plates.

"Perfect!" Jon exclaimed.

She set the plates on the counter with a clank, and Beatrice went to work.

"I've been thinking," Jane said to Cora. "There's only one reason Darla would paint 'killer' on my door."

"She wanted people to think you did it," Cora said.

"But why?" Jane said.

"Because she must be the real killer," Beatrice said.

"Exactly!" Jane said.

"Now," Jon said, wiping his hands on a dish towel. "Hold on. You shouldn't accuse someone of murder without real proof. That's what's been done to Jane, after all."

"Why else would Darla have done it, Jon?" Beatrice asked.

He shrugged. "Maybe she was covering up for someone else?"

The air in the kitchen was getting warm since the oven and stove were both lit and several people were crowded into the small room. But a chill swept over Cora. Either Darla had killed Sarah and Josh Waters, or she knew who did.

Which made sense as Cora thought back about Darla's hostile attitude toward Jane. It wasn't that she didn't like Jane, or that she had been listening to rumors; she was probably seizing on an opportunity to distract the locals from the trail of the real killer. Clever. Or, it would have been clever had she not gotten caught.

"I keep thinking about that blank background check," Jane said.

The scent of the chocolate pies baking in the oven started to fill the room, and Cora's stomach growled. She hadn't gotten a chance to eat breakfast yet. She reached for a banana.

"She could just be a bad seed," Bea said. "Someone who likes to stir things up. She may know nothing at all."

"True," Jon said.

"We've had our fair share of murder in Cumberland Creek, our little town," Beatrice said. "I've followed the investigations pretty closely."

Cora peeled the banana and listened intently. Beatrice certainly didn't seem like she was eighty-five years old. She moved around the kitchen like a much younger woman. Plus, her mind was sharp as a tack—and then some.

"The last murder in our town had to do with money. It was a lot of money. But it seems if you follow the money trail, often that leads you to the murderer," Beatrice said. "How is the police investigation going?"

"I think Detective Brodsky is doing a good job," Cora said. "Murder investigations take time. Josh was killed only a few days ago."

"Take my advice," Beatrice said. "Don't rely on the cops to get your friend off the hook."

Ruby heard that as she walked into the room.

"I think we are going to be good friends," she said to Beatrice.

Beatrice looked up from pouring filling into a pie crust. "Then don't just stand there. Get busy. We have a reception to pull together."

Chapter 55

With the pies filled, baked, and chilling, and chocolate bread in the oven, Beatrice and Jon were now discussing what kind of cake and cupcakes to make. Cora suggested pumpkin faces or some other fall or Halloween decoration for embellishment.

"That sounds a bit cutesy to me and you want this to be elegant, right?" Beatrice said. "Maybe we should just color the icing fall colors."

"I have an idea. You all make the cupcakes and I'll decorate them. One of my readers sent me a photo of some cupcakes that exude elegance, but are actually simple," Cora said. "It involves making a few flowers and embossing the top of the cupcakes with gold-dusted sugar. I'll use some of my templates that I've used for paper crafting."

"What will you emboss it with?" Jon said, confused.

"Gold-dusted sugar. I have some gold chocolate around here that would be perfect," Cora said, wiping her hands on her apron and then slipping it off. "I need to go and mingle a bit with the guests. I'll be back shortly." She said. "Thank you again, Uncle Jon and Aunt Beatrice. I'm not sure what we would've done without you."

Now, if she could slip out of the house without anybody noticing, she could head to the police station. Would they allow her to speak with Darla? She felt a pang of guilt as she waved to the group of crafters who were gathered in the living room. She would make this as quick as possible—she wanted to get back to her crafters.

"How is everything?" she called out.

They all nodded, smiled, and murmured pleasantries. They were having a positive experience—which was good. It was a good thing someone was. Cora's aunt and uncle were working in the kitchen. It was humiliating! They were guests!

But Jon was also an investor in the business, she reminded herself. He was eager to see the place succeed.

She thought about taking her car, but she knew everybody would hear her pull out of the driveway so she hoofed it down to the police station instead. It would take a little longer, but she was a woman with a mission. And the mission was to find out exactly what was going on with Darla. Why did she paint "killer" on Jane's door? Was Jane correct in thinking that it was because she knew who the killer was and wanted to help cover up? Or was she the killer herself?

It was all hard to imagine. But then again, so much of what had happened recently was hard to imagine.

As she entered the police station, it seemed empty and quieter than usual, probably because it was a Sunday.

This might work to her advantage.

"I'd like to see Darla Day," she said to the woman behind the counter.

"I'm sorry," the woman said. "Who?"

"Darla Day," Cora repeated.

"There is nobody here by that name," the woman told her. "Are you certain you have the name correct?"

"Yes. Detective Brodsky called me this morning and said she was here," Cora said.

"Brodsky?" the woman said. "Hold on."

She pressed a button and spoke into her phone. "There is someone here who wants to see a Darla Day. Says you told her she was here."

She appeared to be listening to Brodsky on the other end of the phone.

"Okay," the receptionist said. She hung up and then said to Cora, "Detective Brodsky will be right out."

What was going on? Hadn't he told her that they had Darla in custody? Was she already out on bail?

Cora shivered. She didn't like the thought of Darla being at large, skulking around Indigo Gap.

When the detective came into the room, Cora surmised that something was wrong.

"What happened?" she said.

"She lawyered up," Brodsky said. "I'm still not sure who she even is. But whoever she is, she had some contacts in high places. It happens sometimes."

"You mean . . ."

"She's out," he said. "But she has instructions to stay away from your place and is not to conduct any business until further notice from the court."

That doesn't mean that she won't, Cora thought to herself.

"Is she dangerous?" Cora asked.

He smiled wryly. "Only if you get in her way, I suppose."

"What do you mean?"

"I mean that she is quite formidable."

She thought over the comments Darla had made about Jane. Jane! Was she in danger?

"What are you thinking?" the detective asked.

"Can we have a police presence at the house for the next couple of days?" Cora asked.

"We don't have the staff for that. I'm sorry," he said. "Do you think she poses a danger to you personally?"

"Not to me," Cora said. "Jane. She despises Jane."

He nodded.

"She said some horrible things about her that I had to nip in the bud," Cora said.

"I can try to drop in and out today," Brodsky said, keeping his voice low. "That's all I can promise."

"I'd appreciate that," she said. "I know it seems a bit off, but the more I think about it, the more frightened I become."

Cora thought about why the Darla Day theory didn't make much sense to her. Maybe Darla could have killed Sarah. But Josh as well? And what was her motive?

"I don't think Darla killed Josh Waters. She was busy that day catering for my retreat," Cora said.

"We'll be asking her about every minute of her day and of course, we will be talking with you to verify her schedule. But it takes very little time to kill someone and evidently Josh's murder happened right after Jude Sawyer stopped by before you did, so that leaves a narrow window of time. We believe the person who planned Josh's murder was meticulous and knew his habits," the detective said.

When the detective mentioned Jude, Cora realized

she hadn't seen him since that morning. Where was he? Off with another woman somewhere? She tried to remember if she had seen Linda today.

"What's wrong? You look confused," Brodsky said.

"You just reminded me I haven't seen Jude in a while," she said.

"Perhaps he slept in."

"If he did, let's hope he's alone."

The detective grinned. "I hear ya," he said. "Now, can I help you with anything else?"

He looked tired. She should go. She had already taken so much of his time.

"I don't think so," she said. "I have a house full of guests I should get back to. I'm sorry I missed Darla."

"I don't think you'd have gotten anywhere with her. She clammed up. She was here on a simple vandalism charge, remember. She paid the fine and was released to the custody of her lawyer."

"But you said—"

"I know what I said, but I have no evidence," he told her. "You'd be surprised at how many guilty people are walking around because there's not enough evidence to convict."

"Oh no, I wouldn't," she said. "I worked in a women's shelter, remember."

"So will you be able to hire another caterer for tonight?"

"No," she said. "But luckily I've a kitchen full of help. Speaking of which, I'd better get back."

On her brisk walk home, Cora marveled at how quiet the town was—a typical Sunday in the sleepy village of Indigo Gap. Her new home. Soon, it would feel like home, she just knew it. Soon, it would feel safe and warm, instead of confusing and like a killer might be lurking behind every bush.

But for now, as she made her way up the narrow streets, she couldn't help sensing someone watching her. She didn't like this feeling. This fear. It was something she had grown used to in Pittsburgh—until it got to be overwhelming. She didn't want to be afraid anymore. She wanted to walk down the streets without a care on her mind. Free.

Darla had been in Kildare House, had fed Cora and her guests. Cora shivered at the thought. If Darla was a killer, what had prevented her from killing the retreat guests, plus Cora, these past few days?

Calm down, she told herself. Obviously if Darla killed Sarah and Josh, she had a reason. The only strange thing was that Sarah's fingers had been cut off, which led investigators to surmise it was a crime of passion. Otherwise, it seemed like the murders were both well planned out. And for the killer to have murdered the ex-couple, both of them, made it seem they knew both people. It was definitely personal.

Now, she was going overboard, wasn't she? Statistically speaking, most murders had to do with drugs or some other kind of criminal activity. Crimes of passion were rarer. But if it was a crime of passion, what about Edgar Thorncraft? Why would he kill his girlfriend? Their disagreements about historical matters were quite public. Cora wondered about their private lives. Could Edgar be an abuser?

What about Josh Waters' second wife? Cora wouldn't know her if she tripped over her. She knew she lived in Pennsylvania with their new family. Her husband left Pennsylvania to attend to his ex-wife's estate, and he got himself killed. And now she had two children and no husband. Cora mulled over where Josh's body was— back in Pennsylvania or in North Carolina? Where would his final resting place be?

Cora walked by Sapphire Street and looked up at Kildare House, now only a few blocks away. Something ticked in her brain. Who did she know who lived on Sapphire? Darla. Darla Day lived on Sapphire Street. In that moment, Cora decided to turn right.

Chapter 56

Something was off about Darla's house. No cars were parked in the driveway. Maybe they were in the garage. But no curtains or blinds hung in the windows of the house. It was odd, as living this close to neighbors, privacy was of utmost concern.

Cora walked up to the front door and held up her hand to knock. But as she lifted her fist to the door, she heard a disturbing sound—a low growl, or possibly a moan. Shards of fear tore through her. *Calm down,* she told herself, it could just be an animal of some kind. But the noise came again—and it was definitely coming from inside the house. What was going on here?

She stood at the door, and a number of thoughts raced through her mind.

Was Darla Day the person Cora thought she was—a small-minded person who was exploiting poor Jane's bad luck?

Or was Darla herself in some sort of trouble? Did she need help?

You can't help the world, Cora heard her therapist whisper in her memory.

She started to back away from the door. The hair on the back of her neck pricked. Something was very wrong here.

As Cora turned away, the sound grew louder and something inside of her took over. She wasn't afraid anymore—someone needed her help. The door was unlocked, thankfully. She walked in, and her feet sank into plush carpet. She'd never imagined that Darla's home would be carpeted. She had pictured her a hardwood-floor kind of person. But it turned out that she was wrong about Darla—all the way wrong.

If Darla had indeed lived here, she no longer did. That much was clear.

There was no furniture—and not even any indentations in the carpet where furniture may have been. In fact, the carpet looked brand new. Cora walked farther into the living room, toward a picture window. The view outside the window was of a splay of crimson leaves on a gorgeous Japanese maple tree. She stood and took it in.

It was disturbingly quiet. Where had the noise been coming from?

She turned and moved back across the living-room floor, and something caught her eye. Just a flash. What was that? She walked across the empty room and saw a piece of jewelry lying on the carpet. A gold heart. Where had she seen that before? On Darla?

No, Darla never wore any jewelry. She was clean and crisp-looking all the time.

Cora lifted the heart and held the chain in her hand, as the heart dangled. She tried to remember where she had seen it before. Wait—maybe it did belong to Darla. Hadn't Cora seen her wearing it the first time she'd come to Kildare House?

The sound erupted from another room—what was it? Cora's heart leapt right into her mouth.

The noise came again, a little louder. It sounded like it was coming from the next room over—was it the kitchen? Without thinking, she opened the door. Her eyes took a moment to adjust to the dimmer light inside—the kitchen only had one small window. But she saw glimpses of things—a foot. A leg. A person. Her eyes traveled up the leg to the person's face, half covered in duct tape. His blue eyes were alert and his head was twitching around. He was trying to say something.

"Jude?" Cora said as she moved toward him.

Then she saw that another person was next to him. Someone smaller was crumpled in a ball, curled up next to him. Sleeping? Unconscious? Dead?

Darla Day, with her eyes closed, looked no more than eighteen years old. Cora bent over and tried to wrangle the tape off Jude's face. But she stopped when she sensed someone standing behind her.

Cora's whole body shook as she slowly turned around. She had to dig deep and stop shaking. She couldn't pass out. She couldn't throw up. A ball of fear turned into anger that moment, as she realized the person she was looking at was Ivy—or the woman she had thought was Ivy. The imposter.

"You just couldn't leave well enough alone, could you?" the imposter spat.

Cora glared at her. She could handle this woman. She must.

"Calm down, Ivy," she said, her voice controlled and calm. "What is going on here?"

"You know I'm not Ivy," the woman snarled.

"Okay," Cora said as calmly as she could. There was

a stirring behind her. Maybe it was Darla coming to. "Why don't you explain to me what's going on? Let's start by you telling me what your real name is and why you came to the retreat."

"I'm not going to tell you anything," the woman said, her voice deep and shaking. She held up something. "You've put me in a bad position. You leave me no choice."

What was she holding? Was that a gun?

"Please, don't use that gun," Cora said. "Let's talk about this."

The woman clicked the safety off. "I'm sorry, Miss Cora Crafts a Life," she said and pointed it at her.

She moved like her self-defense trainer taught her— strong, fast, and yelling loudly. She kicked the gun from the imposter's hands, and it flew through air, landing in the kitchen sink with a thud. A thud that Cora would always remember.

She then took the heel of her hand and thrust it in the woman's rib cage, prompting her to hunch over as Cora landed the final blow, her knee to the imposter's head. Hard. This final move knocked the woman out long enough to get the others untied.

Pain tore through Cora's knee, but she made her way over to Jude and Darla.

Police sirens rang out. Cora ripped the tape off Jude's and Darla's mouths and then untied their hands. They worked at untying their legs.

When she was certain that Darla and Jude were okay, Cora found the wall and sank back against it.

Chapter 57

Cora was drifting. Sounds were imprinted on her mind. The thud of the gun in the sink. The woman's groan and shriek as Cora let loose on her. The crack of her knee against the woman's head.

"Her name is Dee Waters," Detective Brodsky said to a uniformed officer standing nearby. The place was crawling with them.

Dee Waters? Why did that name sound familiar? Then she remembered—Dee was the name of the Waterses' oldest daughter. The one who became a mother when she was very young. Her parents sent her away. But she was supposed to be off somewhere in England.

"She's used a couple of different names over the years," the officer told Brodsky. "Quite the expert identity thief."

"I've got you some ice from one of the cops," Jude said, now in her view. He placed the ice bag on her knee.

She sucked in air. Her knee swelled in reaction to the sudden cold.

"What happened?" she managed to ask.

Jude sat down on the floor next to her. "I'm not sure," he said. "What I do know is that I found Dee or Ivy's phone number and called her, thinking I'd bring her to the cops."

"You did what?" Cora refrained from smacking him.

"I thought it was the least I could do after causing all this trouble. I really like you and what you're doing. I didn't mean for all this to happen. So I thought I'd make it up to you by, you know, using myself as bait to lure her to town."

Cora felt like a wet dishrag. She was so tired. Her knee was throbbing. And Jude Sawyer, the rock-star broom maker turned out to not be smart—at all. But, as his story rolled around in her mind, she realized that he had the best of intentions.

"And?"

"The plan was going well until she got this phone call this morning from some lawyer, then she almost, like, I don't know, turned into another person," he said. "The next thing I know, she pulls out this gun. She doesn't shoot me with it. But she hit me. And I woke up here. The rest is history."

"When did Darla get here?"

"I don't know," he said. "I don't even know where we are right now."

"This is Darla's house," Cora said.

"It is?" He looked around. "But there's nothing here. Are you certain?"

"I'm not certain of anything," Cora said.

"I'm certain of one thing," Brodsky said, inserting himself into their conversation. "You just don't know when to leave well enough alone. What were you doing here?"

She didn't respond.

"Never mind, I know what you were doing here," the detective continued. "I told you she wouldn't have talked with you anyway," he said. "We've got to get her out of here."

"Why? I want to press charges," Cora said. "How dare she? She owes me an explanation."

"Here's your explanation—she is planning on moving far away, going off the grid so she can start a new life. Her mother over there"—he pointed his head toward Dee Waters, aka Ivy—"is involved in one of the biggest crime syndicates in the United States. The woman you know as Darla was getting ready to start a whole new life in a new state with a new name. We think it's a good idea. When she saw her long-lost mother at the retreat, she kind of freaked out."

Cora was speechless. The reason for Darla's behavior had finally become clear. She either knew or suspected that her own mother had killed her grandmother, and then her grandfather as well. Which probably scared her half to death. How far would a daughter go to protect her wayward mother? When Darla saw that there was a scapegoat, she latched on to it. Jane was perfect, thanks to the confusion over her fingerprints and her record.

"So did Dee kill her mom and dad?" Jude said.

The detective's face was grim. "It most certainly looks that way. Plus she's a wanted woman for several crimes, especially identify theft. We are now certain that she also stole her mother's jeweled opium kit collection. Dee had Darla when she was fifteen years old and the family shunned her. They sent her away. The story is pretty typical from that point on. Typical in some ways, I should say. Darla tried hard to break free of the situation. She almost succeeded."

Cora's heart went from pounding anger to breaking in half in a second. What had happened to the Waters family? What went wrong? Was Dee born with problems—or was it the drugs she had gotten involved with as a kid? Could drug addiction spiral like this and years later lead to her killing both of her parents, not to mention placing her own daughter so much at risk that she wanted to go into hiding?

What a mess. What a confounding, heartbreaking mess.

"So why did Darla come here to Indigo Gap?" Jude asked.

"She came here to get to know her grandmother. Her mother found out, and didn't like it, obviously," Brodsky replied. "Dee has been in and out of town since she found out, evidently."

"Is that enough of a motive for murder?" Cora asked. "I mean, that she didn't want her daughter to know her grandmother?"

"That, the money, and the fact that Dee resented her parents for sending her and her new baby as far away from home as possible," Brodsky said.

"But she was going to all this trouble to lead us away from her grandmother's true killer . . . I'm confused," Jude said.

"Because the killer was her mother," Cora said. "Her *mother.*"

Cora's eyes sought the woman she knew as Darla. She was holding her mother and crying. The woman, with her addictions and her litany of criminal activities, pulled back from her daughter, brushed the hair from her face with a gentle, motherly sweep of her fingers, then cupped Darla's face in her hands. In that moment, she was nothing more or less than a mother. And, perhaps, a daughter.

Chapter 58

"The party doesn't start for several more hours. Why are you calling me?" Cora said into her phone.

"Since it appears that you're still alive, you better get your ass home before Beatrice takes over completely," Jane said. "So where are you, anyway? Is Jude with you, by any chance?"

"Yes," Cora said. "He's with me. As for the rest, you are not going to believe it." Cora then explained what had happened.

"You're right. I don't believe it," Jane said. "Darla Day's not Darla Day. She's the daughter of the Waterses' long-lost daughter, who was supposed to be in England. But, instead, she's been skulking around here posing as Ivy Renquist, stealing a priceless jeweled opium kit, and killing her parents. What's believable about that?" Jane spouted.

"Well, if you don't believe me, you can ask Jude," Cora said. "We'll both be home soon—after the medics say we're okay."

"Cora?"

"Yes?"

"Does this mean I'm officially no longer a suspect?"

"I suppose it does," Cora said. "They can probably send the fingerprint experts home."

"Thank God for that," Jane said.

"I'll see you soon," Cora said.

Later, as she and Jude walked back to Kildare House, he grabbed her by the hand. "Thanks for putting up with me this weekend," he said. "I'm so sorry for everything."

He was the charming Jude Sawyer again. But he was also still the same man who had slept with Ivy *and* Linda. Was it within twenty-four hours of one another? Cora didn't want to know. That was a mystery she'd leave unsolved.

"Apology accepted," she said and withdrew her hand from his. *As long as I don't ever have to see you again, I'll be fine,* she thought but didn't say.

"That was pretty amazing what you did back there," he said.

It was pretty amazing, Cora thought. She hadn't panicked. After the incident, she fell apart, but during it, she did fine. Even Detective Brodsky had been impressed.

Crafty girl to the rescue, he had said and winked at her.

But this was not what Cora had bargained for—at all. She wanted a peaceful small-town life. She had wanted to start fresh with her craft retreat. This felt too much like her old life, when she never knew when a disgruntled husband would come into the Sunny Street Shelter, or when a teenager would lash out. She sighed. She supposed that no matter where she lived or what she did, unpleasant incidents would occur. But perhaps there would be less now. She was deep in thought when Jude broke into it.

"Is there any way you and I can, uh, put this behind us and maybe go out? I'm very attracted to you."

She pretended not to hear him and kept walking.

"Cora?" he said, trailing after her.

"You are a beautiful, charming, drama man and I'm sure we'll run into each other again at some craft gathering. But I don't need drama in my life," she said. "No thanks."

"I guess I saw that coming," he said and laughed. "But you can't blame a guy for trying."

She was a bit surprised by his asking her out—but then again, he liked women, period. She was surprised, however, that he had yet to hit on Jane.

They shuffled along the rest of the way in silence. Kildare House stood like a beacon in the near distance. Cora wanted nothing more than a long bath and a nap. But she lacked time.

"Has it only been a few hours?" Jude asked. "I am exhausted. It feels like we've been working out all day long or something."

"Yes, it really does. I was thinking I'd like to take a nap but—"

"There you two are!" Suddenly Ruby and Beatrice were beside them. "I was just showing Bea around the neighborhood a bit."

"What happened to you?" Bea said, looking askance at Cora.

"And you?" Ruby said to Jude.

Cora's awareness switched to wondering about her condition and what the others saw when she approached them—her skirt had been torn and a button was missing from her shirt. Jude looked as if he had been hit by a truck. He was a good-looking guy and usually well put together, but now his skin was chaffed and red where the duct tape had been. And he wore an expression of utter confusion.

"You look like you've both seen a ghost," Bea said.

"Not a ghost," Cora said, and then she filled them in as they walked back to the house.

"Shocking!" Beatrice said when Cora was done.

Ruby shook her head. "That family has had its share of troubles, but I never imagined this."

"Who could?" Beatrice added.

Jude put his arm around Cora and drew her in for a friendly hug. "All I know is that this woman saved my life."

Chapter 59

When Jane spotted Jude, Beatrice, Ruby, and Cora standing at the edge of the sidewalk, she ushered them into her carriage house.

"We've got a lot of work for the party, I realize," Jane said. "But let's just take a minute here and make sure we are all on the same page."

Cora was pale and her hair mussed, as was Jude's. They both looked at Jane with weariness.

"I just want to see if I understand it all," Jane said. "I need to know the facts."

"Okay," Cora said. She looked like she might fall over any minute.

"Please sit down," Jane said to her and led her over to the red velvet couch.

"Now, did I hear you say that Jude used himself for bait?" Jane said. "He thought he could get Dee Waters to confess to stealing Sarah's opium kit collection. Is that right?"

Jude nodded and rocked back and forth on his feet, in a comforting, slow rhythm.

"Yes," Beatrice chimed in. "But Dee Waters is who you all knew as Ivy. She was using a false identity."

"And Darla?" Jane asked, opening her hands, looking for answers.

"Darla saw her criminal of a mother at the retreat. That's why she was so upset and why she tried her best to make you look guilty. She suspected her mother of killing her grandmother and was trying to protect her," Ruby said.

"Lawd," said Beatrice. "All this talk of killing mothers. I need to sit down."

She found a chair and plopped into it. Then, Ruby sat on the edge of the chair next to Beatrice.

"Are we sure that Dee stole those goods from her mother a few months back?" Jane asked.

"Yes," Jude replied. "They are searching her house now, but it's just a matter of time before they have the items in their hands. The police know she was in town at that time. She evidently travels back and forth between here and Edisto frequently. We're pretty certain that she killed both of her parents." He said this with emphasis, clearly horrified.

"Dee was upset that her mother had a relationship with Darla, who didn't want anything to do with Dee," Cora added.

"So Sarah's murder was an act of passion?" Jane asked. All the pieces were starting to fit together. It was confusing, but she was beginning to understand.

"Indeed," Cora said, swaying a bit. She looked as if she needed a nap. "When she was in town to steal the opium kits, she realized that Darla was here and knew her mother."

"What about the fingers scattered all over the house? What meaning does that have?" Jane asked.

"None that we know of," Cora said. "I mean, we just don't know."

Jane thought about that and realized she wasn't certain she actually wanted that answer.

"What about Josh?" Jane asked, almost afraid of the answer.

"He probably was putting it together," Jude said. "He probably knew what happened and she had to get rid of him. Plus, with him gone, there would be nobody around to contest her inheritance."

"Now that I think about it, her sister most likely would've been next," Ruby said in a hushed voice.

"That's a gruesome thought," Bea said. "But it's probably the truth. What's wrong with people?"

"I've asked myself that question so many times in my life," Cora said. "Sometimes, people get, I don't know, broken. And they are never able to get fixed. That's the only explanation I can come up with."

"I've known that family a long time," said Ruby. "I never knew the extent of the damage. But I think your theory is as good as any."

"What do we do now?" Jane asked. "Just go on with the party as if none of this horrible stuff has happened?"

The group sat in silence, considering. It seemed odd and insensitive to go on with a party when two of its key members had been through a traumatic event and the community of Indigo Gap had lost two of its citizens.

"We owe it to the people who paid for this retreat to

have the party," Cora said. "I'm bound and determined to throw a hell of a party."

"I'm with you," Jude said.

"It's the only thing to do," Beatrice said, with a soft firmness in her voice. "Life goes on. As it must."

Chapter 60

When Jon spotted Cora, he insisted that she nap and take her time getting ready for the party.

"Everything is under control, *mon chère*. We are family. We will take care of it all," Jon said.

Cora didn't have the wherewithal to argue. She bathed in her deep claw-foot tub, allowing the hot water to unravel her tense muscles. How had they gotten so tight? How had she not noticed? Each muscle relaxed one at a time in the hot water. Muscles she hadn't even realized existed.

After her bath, she felt a pang of guilt as she slid underneath her quilt and laid her head on the pillow. She should be mingling with her guests. But how could she? Perhaps Uncle Jon was right—she'd be better after she had a rest.

Her brain needed time to sort through everything that had happened. Luna curled up beside her and purred.

Two hours later, Luna awakened her, kneading her kitty paws on her face. The cat was hungry, no doubt.

Cora sat up, refreshed, but her knee still ached. She

was ready to close this first craft-retreat weekend. So many unplanned events had taken over. She and Jane had thought they were prepared for all possibilities. But they certainly hadn't prepared for everything that had gone down. Was it possible to plan too much? Was it possible to plan for every conceivable outcome?

She padded into the kitchenette and opened a can of cat food, Luna circling her legs and mewing.

"Okay, Luna, kitty," she said as sat the bowl on the floor for the cat.

Now to get dressed. She ambled back into her bedroom, having not given what she would wear any thought at all, and saw the doily skirt had been finished and placed on her chair, splayed out with its variety of colors, weaves, and textures.

When she had seen Josh Waters lying dead among all the bloody doilies, she had figured she'd trash the other ones that she had purchased. But now she was glad she hadn't. She ran her fingers over the skirt—someone had made the doilies; their time, talent, and energy had gone into crafting them. She pulled the skirt up over her hips and looked at herself in the mirror. She adjusted the skirt so the pink doily was in front, rather than on the side. She preferred the off-center diagonal pattern.

Where had that yellow T-shirt gone to? She sorted through the clothes still on the chair and found it. She slipped it on. Yes, perfect.

Cora twirled around and watched the colors and lace lift and move around her. She laughed.

* * *

As she walked downstairs, she spotted Jude and Cashel deep in conversation. "Hey, guys," she said. They glanced at her—then looked again.

"Wow," Cashel said. "You look amazing." He grabbed her and kissed her cheek with a little more gusto than was appropriate.

Jude cleared his throat and took his turn at hugging Cora. "Congrats, you've done a great job. I was listening in with some of the crafters. They've had such a lovely time."

Cora smiled. "That's what it's all about."

"Are those doilies?" Cashel said, reaching out and running his hands over them.

"Yes—and watch it," she said, playfully slapping his hand away.

Cora moved into the dining room, where everything had been set up. The centerpiece was dried hydrangeas and pumpkins, with lit candles. She loved it.

Trays of pies, bread, cupcakes, and cookies had been set out, and people were milling about in the room with plates brimming with chocolate goodies.

"The skirt looks incredible," Linda said as she came up beside her.

"Thank you! You know, it really does. I think I might start a new trend," Cora replied.

"I like it because it's long and flowing. It works with those doilies. But a short skirt would be cool, too," Linda said.

"I've got a ton of old doilies at home," Diane said, joining them. "I might make something with them. Maybe a vest. If I can find the time."

"You can always come back here if you need more time to craft," Cora said and smiled brightly.

"I'd love to!" Diane said. "I 'm planning to come back. I think most of us are."

"That's good to know," Cora said, as her heart lifted even more.

"You know what else is good to know?" Jane said, as she came up alongside of them. "I received a call when you were asleep. Turns out the investigators were trying hard to match my prints, but they couldn't. And since they now have a confession, I'm off the hook."

"Of course!" Cora said. "I never doubted you!"

"Thank you," Jane said. "Who knows what would've happened if you hadn't been such a pain?"

"One thing I can promise," Cora said, "I'm always going to be a pain for the people I care about, including you." Cora was filled with a sudden longing to cry— she was so filled with gratitude and emotions. So much had happened to bring them to this point.

Cora lifted her glass to take a sip, when the doorbell rang.

"I'll get it," she said, scooting out of the room, grateful for a moment to get ahold of her emotions.

When she opened the front door, she blinked in surprise. *Who is this?*

He was tall, dark, and adorable, with wavy seal-brown hair and jade-green eyes peering at her through horn-rimmed glasses. He grinned—revealing a dimple. He handed her a bouquet of yellow tea roses.

"Hi, I'm Adrian," he said. "Congratulations."

"Adrian?" Cora said. Did that breathy voice belong to her? Was that her heart thumping in her chest? Who was this man? She was positively tingling.

"Hey, Adrian," Jane said as she came up behind Cora. "So glad you could make it. Cora, this is Adrian. He works at the school. He's the new librarian."

Cora felt her lips curl into a grin and her face heat.

"Nice to meet you," she managed to say and reached out her hand to him.

"The pleasure is all mine," Adrian replied, shaking her hand.

He pushed his glasses back on his nose, such a sweet and geeky gesture, and Cora's heart thumped, making her regret her decision to change Kildare House's library into a fiber-arts room. Maybe it wasn't too late to change it back.

She caught a glance of smug satisfaction from Jane. Turned out she was right—the librarian did seem to be Cora's type. But for now, she turned her attention to her guests.

Later, everyone gathered in the dining room for a toast from Jane, including Adrian, who had not ventured far from Cora most of the evening. Cora had to concentrate to focus on her guests, but caught his eye from time to time.

Jennifer, the woman with the yarn shop, grabbed her hand. "I just want to say how wonderful this weekend has been."

"I'm so glad your daughters sent you here," Cora told her. "It's been wonderful to get to know you."

Was Cora imagining Jennifer's restful glow? Could one weekend of crafting and relaxing be enough to get her started on a healing path, away from the darkness of grief?

She continued to hold Jennifer's hand as Jane cleared her throat.

"To Cora," Jane said, "A dreamer, a doer, a good friend. Thank you for providing this space for us."

"Hear, hear!" people chanted around the room.

Cora took in the crowd—the guests lifting their glasses to her, Ruby, Cashel, Jude, her uncle and new aunt—and she felt an onslaught of warmth. She wanted to remember this moment forever.

Craft Projects

Making Your Own Herbal Beeswax Candles

This is the simple version of candle making that Ruby teaches in her cottage.

Supply List
- Rolled beeswax sheet
- Lengths of cotton wick
- Herbs
- Sharp craft knife

Directions
- To roll your own beeswax candles, start by warming the beeswax sheets until pliable. A blow-dryer works great for this purpose.
- Smooth side up, sprinkle the herbs all over the inside of the sheet.
- Tightly roll the sheet around a length of wick that has been cut slightly longer than the length of your candle. (You can cut the beeswax sheet to make smaller candles, or leave the sheet whole for taller candles.)

- If you prefer a variation, cut a diagonal from the top left-hand corner of the sheet to about halfway down the center of the right-hand side and tightly roll up the beeswax, so the candle becomes tiered as it takes shape. Experiment with different angles of the diagonal, cut to create a variety of tiered beeswax candles.

- Gently press the end of the sheet into the candle to seal it.

Making Easy Soap Balls

Making soap balls is great way to use up some of those leftover soap bits that we all seem to have lying around. You can have a jar where you collect the bits of soap instead of throwing them away. When you get a jar full, try making soap balls. You can get creative with this, if you want. Consider adding in flower petals or herbs or try layering colors.

- Collect up all of your soap scraps and divide them up into similar or complementary colors. You can mix your colors and make soaps that look like river rocks or speckled eggs.

- Using a cheese grater, shred up your soap bits into containers. If the soap has been around awhile, you may want to add a very small amount of water, essential oil, or carrier oil to moisten the mix slightly.

- Grab a small handful of the soap shreds, squeezing and rolling them into a small ball. Be sure to press until the soap ball is really hard and no longer squishy. Add another layer and continue squeezing and rolling. Keep going until the soap is the size you want it.

- If you want to cut the ball in half, you will need to use a large smooth knife or, better yet, a pastry scraper with its thin blade. Gently push the blade through the ball. You may need to do a little damage control around the edges, smoothing them back down.

- Let the balls sit for a week or two so the added moisture can evaporate and the balls can harden up.

Simple DIY Tea Cup Bird Feeder

This is one of the simplest bird feeders you can make from tea cups. If you don't have extra tea cups on hand, there's always the Goodwill and other secondhand shops. Using old tea cups to feed the birds? What could be better?

Supply List
- A tea cup and saucer
- Wild bird seed
- Super adhesive glue
- A hanger or string

Directions
- Make sure your cup and saucer are clean and dry.
- Squeeze some of the glue onto the edge of your saucer. Tip your tea cup onto its side and place on top of the glue. You will need to let it

set for about twenty-four hours before you hang it outside.

- Next all you have to do is pour in your birdseed and hang up your feeder.

Cora's Upcycled Burlap Pumpkins

This is a fun craft that you can keep as simple as you want or you can decorate it to the hilt. It's totally up to you. It's also a great way to use those leftover plastic grocery bags.

Supply List
- Burlap bags or yard burlap
- Twine
- Hot-glue gun
- Grocery bags
- Stones or beans
- Optional embellishments (ribbon, leaves, berries, etc.)

Directions
- If you don't have a burlap bag, and just have the burlap, first square up your yard of burlap (it will probably be wider that thirty-six inches). Find the center of the piece of burlap. Round the corners, creating a thirty-six-inch diameter circle.
- Cut four lengths of twine at forty-eight inches each. Lay them out symmetrically on the back side of the burlap.
- From a scrap, cut out a small two-inch circle or square of burlap. Where the twine joins in the

center, hot glue the small piece to secure all the lengths of twine. *Make sure you have something underneath the burlap because the glue will go right through to the surface beneath!!* This will be the bottom of your pumpkin.

- In order to provide weight and keep your pumpkin upright, you want to fill a ziplock bag with rocks or pinto beans.

Stuffing Assembly

- Use the natural-color bags for the outer bag so if you get a glimpse of the bag through the burlap it won't be white. (It's also a good idea to turn the bag inside out, so the store logo won't show). Place your bag of rocks or beans in first and then just stuff it full of the plastic bags. Keep stuffing until it's stuffed pretty tight. Tie the bags at the top.

- If you don't have a burlap bag, now flip your burlap circle so the twine is on the underside.

- Place filled bag on top of your burlap circle. Pull up on all sides, gathering up all the ends until the burlap circle is completely cinched up. Then, from underneath, keeping the twine lined up the way you laid it out, bring each piece of twine up on opposite sides and tie off *tightly*, creating the ribs of the pumpkin. Take another length of twine and tie around *tightly*.

- If you have a burlap bag, just stuff your stuffing inside.

- After tying off, you will have several long pieces of twine at the top. Scrunch the burlap up and

wrap the twine around to make the stem! (Hot glue the twine as you wrap to make the stem.)
- Now, just add any embellishments that you might have on hand! Embellishments could be ribbons, berries, leaves—well, whatever you want to try.

Making Your Own Decorative Broom

Here's a simple version of broom making that you can get as creative as you want with—but these fun brooms are just for decoration.

Supply List

For three broomsticks:
- Wooden dowel (one-inch diameter, thirty-six inches long)
- Tree branch (approximately thirty-six inches long)
- Bamboo branch (approximately thirty-six inches long)
- Acrylic paints (any color you like)
- Paintbrush
- Fine-grit sandpaper
- Willow twigs, bamboo, and decorative grass (for broom brushes)
- Three pieces of black interfacing fabric: two-by-ten-inch strips.
- Raffia and twine
- Hot-glue gun and hot-melt adhesive

Directions

- Paint the wooden dowel with acrylic paint; let dry. Sand with fine-grit sandpaper for a worn look.

- Choose one of the broom brush materials (willow twigs, bamboo, decorative grasses) to go with each broom handle. For each broom, lay the brush material across one length of interfacing fabric so that about two inches of brush material extends beyond the fabric. Hot glue into place; let dry.

- Wrap the interfacing end of the brush around the bottom of the broom handle (with the interfacing facing in), gluing into place as you wrap. Let dry.

- Wrap raffia or twine several times around the top of each broom brush and glue into place.

- You can get even more creative with these brooms by adding in flowers and herbs.

Cora's Peanut Butter Protein Balls

Ingredients

- 1½ cups rolled oats
- ½ cup vanilla whey protein powder (about 2 scoops)
- ½ teaspoon cinnamon
- 1 tablespoon chia seeds

- ½ cup smooth natural peanut butter (or any nut butter)*
- 3 tablespoon natural honey
- 1 teaspoon vanilla extract
- ⅓ cup raisins, chocolate chips, Craisins, or preferred add-in
- 2–4 tablespoons liquid (almond milk, milk, water, etc.)

Directions
- Add oats, protein powder, cinnamon, and chia seeds to a large bowl.
- Add in peanut butter, honey, and vanilla extract. Stir to combine.
- Add in raisins (or preferred add-in). Mixture should be slightly sticky but still crumbly.
- Slowly add in liquid one tablespoon at a time, and using hands (get dirty!), combine until it comes together in a sticky ball that holds together. If mixture is too dry, add in more liquid but not so much that it won't hold shape.
- Place in a container to set in the fridge for at least thirty minutes.
- Store in fridge until ready to eat.

Notes
* Make sure it is drippy. If not, you may need to add in extra liquid at the end.

If you enjoyed *Death Among the Doilies*
be sure not to miss Mollie Cox Bryan's
Cumberland Creek Mystery series, including

SCRAPBOOK OF THE DEAD

Halloween means spooky scrapbooks for the
Cumberland Creek Scrapbook Crop, but what's
been happening around town is truly frightening.
First a dead woman is found in the freezer at Pamela's
Pie Palace, and the next day a second woman is found
murdered by the river. Reporter Annie Chamovitz
learns the victims were sisters and is certain their
deaths are linked. Most bizarre of all, both women
were found clutching scrapbook pages.

As their Saturday night crop quickly becomes an
opportunity to puzzle out the murders, the ladies
begin to wonder if Pamela is hiding more than her
secret recipes for delicious pies—or if the crimes are
related to the startling discovery that there are gangs
in Cumberland Creek. As All Hallows Eve approaches,
the crafty croppers must cut and paste the clues to
unmask a deadly killer.

Keep reading for a special excerpt.

A Kensington mass-market paperback and e-book
on sale now!

Chapter 1

She hadn't shown up for work a few days in a row. Had she been in the sub-zero room that whole time, slowly freezing to death?

"With these immigrants, you just never know," Pamela said. "They are hard workers, but sometimes things go wrong." She wrung her hands, which were white with tension.

"What do you mean by that?" The sheriff placed his hands on his hips, as camera flashes went off. Crime scene technicians buzzed around the room.

Annie stood with her arm wrapped around Randy, who was trembling—but her recorder pointed toward the sheriff and Pamela, owner of Pamela's Pie Palace, where the body of a young woman had just been found.

"I mean sometimes they just take off, disappear. Who knows where they go or why? Just last week, one of them disappeared, never showed up for work, and I couldn't reach her," Pamela said, her voice quivering.

Randy had discovered the frozen body early this morning. He'd called the police, then Pamela, then

Annie. After that, he began to fall apart. When Annie first walked in, she had barely recognized him because he was so pale.

"Maybe they go back home? Maybe they find another job?" Pamela flung her arms out.

Annie wished she could make an educated guess—but she didn't know many of the local foreign population. Foreign to Cumberland Creek, anyway. In fact, she was surprised to hear there even *was* an immigrant population in the small town.

"She was legal, right?" the sheriff asked, leaning in toward Pamela, but Annie heard every word. A big man, Sheriff Ted Bixby sported a twisty mustache that looked like it belonged on a Spanish conquistador, not a sheriff from a small county in Virginia.

"Absolutely," Pamela replied, her jaw stiff.

Nobody should look this good at five AM, not even Pamela, Queen of Pie, wife of the wealthy Evan Kraft. She always looked like she'd stepped right out of the pages of a 1950s pinup calendar. Curvy did not begin to describe her figure. And she was not afraid to show it off.

"I need to see the victim's papers," Sheriff Bixby said more to his deputy than to Pamela. "In fact, I need to see all of them. All the papers for every damn one of them."

Annie didn't like his tone when he said the word "them." But she'd gotten used to the "white men of a certain age" attitude about some things—like foreigners. In this part of Virginia, they seemed to be ignored, treated with suspicion, or made fun of. She had bitten her tongue so many times she counted herself lucky that it didn't have a huge gash.

The sheriff faced Annie and Randy, who'd already answered a barrage of questions. "Get some rest, son." Bixby looked at him with warmth and sympathy. He was a man who knew that discovering the frozen body of a coworker in a freezer was a jolt to the system. A man with deep family roots in that part of Virginia, he had seemingly been sheriff forever.

Annie knew that Detective Adam Bryant of Cumberland Creek's police force did not care for the man. She remembered a conversation she and Bryant had had about Sheriff Bixby during one of the other cases she had covered as a freelance reporter. But this most recent crime had taken place outside of Bryant's jurisdiction, so he hadn't been called in. She thanked the universe for that. On this, her last story, she didn't want to deal with his attitude.

"Coming through," yelled someone from inside the freezer.

The body of the small, dark-haired woman came through the doorway on a gurney. One thin line of red marred her neck where her throat had been neatly slit, and a big gash glistened over the artery where she had probably bled out. A craft knife was still lodged there. Pink and white polka-dotted tape covered her mouth, left in place for the autopsy.

So neatly done. Where was all the blood?

She had taken a good look at the scene earlier, but the light shone brighter outside the metallic, dimly lit walk-in freezer and she could see the young woman in

detail. "How old did you say she was?" Annie asked
Pamela.

"Her papers say she's twenty-three," Pamela replied
with a tone leading Annie to believe that Pamela didn't
believe it. The young Mexican woman looked liked she
was sixteen, at most.

*Why would Pamela hire her if she were suspicious about her
age?* Annie felt the ping of intuition pulling at her.
Something about this was off. Way off. She needed to
talk with Randy after he calmed down, then Pamela and
the rest of the restaurant staff. It might be an even
bigger story than a murder at the local, much beloved,
Pamela's Pie Palace.

An older, dark haired woman sobbed and a young,
wet-eyed man slipped his arms around her.

Friends? Annie made a mental note to speak with
them.

"Shhh, Irina," the man said.

Irina, what a beautiful name, Annie thought amidst the
chaos.

One of the technicians held a baggie with some
colored paper and a photo inside.

"What's that?" Annie asked.

The young woman smiled politely. "Evidence." She
held it up higher.

"Really? A scrapbook page?" Randy flung his hands
up in the air. "I'm going back to the B and B. I need a
drink and bed." Never mind that it was only five AM.

Since moving back to Cumberland Creek, he had
taken a room at the new bed and breakfast in town until
he found a house to purchase.

A loud commotion erupted from around the corner.

"Randy!"

Paige and Earl, Randy's parents, rushed in.

"Oh thank God you're okay. Your daddy heard about an incident on the scanner. We were so worried."

"What happened?" Earl asked.

Randy opened his mouth, but no words came out. His face grew even paler.

"Listen, Paige, why don't you take Randy home? I don't think he should be driving," Annie said.

"That's right," the sheriff chimed in. "At least someone around here has a good head on their shoulders." He gave Annie an approving glance.

"Sheriff." Earl nodded, the appropriate manly greeting in the region. Not "hello." Not "hi there." Just a name and a nod. "My boy in trouble?"

"Oh no, no," Sheriff Bixby said. "I'll let him do the explaining on the way home." He started to walk away.

"Now, Sheriff," Pamela called to him. "I can't let you leave without a couple pies. You said we'll have to close today and I have all this pie that needs to go. Please grab one or two."

The sheriff looked liked he knew his way around pie. "Why, thank you."

Pamela had several pies already boxed up. A young man with dark skin and sullen, almost black eyes stood next to her, helping tie the boxes shut. He was the same man Annie had spotted a few moments ago holding the older woman, Irina.

Where is Irina, now? Annie eyes searched the room to no avail. The woman was gone.

"That coconut cream?" Sheriff Bixby asked, mulling over the boxes.

"It's actually pumpkin cream, a fall special," Pamela said.

Annie surveyed the scene. The sheriff and a few others gathered around the counter where Pamela doled out her treats.

"I'd just have to throw it away," she said. "You all may as well take some."

Annie turned and looked out the window at the dead body of the young woman being slid into the back of the ambulance. She glanced back at Pamela handing out boxes of pie and the sad-looking young man next to her. It had to be the oddest crime scene she'd ever witnessed.

"Annie?" Pamela said. "Do you want some pie? I have the cherry that you like so much. I also have some of my special mincemeat."

Annie knew the special mincemeat was only available for two weeks during the fall. It was one of her favorites—a delicious mix of hard-to-find local seasonal ingredients, the kind that was barely legal.

Pamela always remembered everyone's favorites.

Annie's stomach tightened. "Thanks but not today. I just couldn't."

"Well now, young lady, are you a little queasy?" the sheriff said with a patronizing tone.

Why, yes, I think I am. I just saw a frozen person with her throat slit being carried out of here on a gurney. But, on second thought, she took a deep breath. "Never mind," she said, ignoring the sheriff and speaking just to Pamela. "I'll take whatever you've got there."

The sheriff turned with his boxes of pie and started to walk out of the Pie Palace.

"Sheriff," Annie called out as she followed him. "Might I have a word?"

He turned to look at her just as he started to open the front door of the restaurant. His tan uniform stood out against the black and white tile floor and red booths.

She found the place kitschy and cute, but for some reason, this morning all the cuteness looked menacing. Murder amid the kitschiness. She didn't like it.

"What can I help you with, Ms. Chamovitz?" he asked, smiling.

Oh, this is different. Very different, indeed. A smiling law official. No Adam Bryant with his sideways, smirking grins. "What do you think happened here?"

"I don't speculate," the sheriff said. "Call my office later today. We might know something then. But it being Saturday, you never know."

"A walk-in freezer is an odd place for murder," Annie said, watching him tense.

"Well, now, who said anything about murder? It could have been an accident or suicide. As I say, Ms. Chamovitz, I don't speculate. I deal with facts."

An accidental throat slashing? Let him think I'm that gullible. "I'll call you later, then," she said, noticing the medical examiner getting ready to leave. She wanted to catch her before she left. Annie extended her hand to the sheriff. "Later, Sheriff Bixby."

He could not take her hand—his arms were full of pie boxes—but he nodded back at her, turned, and left the building.

"Ms. Jones?" Annie said as she walked over to the ME.

Ruth Jones looked up at her. She was an older, studious woman who had run into Annie frequently around town. "Yes?" Ruth dug her car keys out of a jacket pocket.

"What can you tell me about the body? About the death?"

"Not much at this point," Ruth said. "It looks like she bled to death. But I need to run some tests, of course, to be certain."

"How would someone get trapped in a freezer long enough to bleed or freeze to death?" Annie asked.

Ruth walked out of the Pie Palace carrying a big bulky bag and a pie box. Annie followed her outside into the fall morning. The sun was just beginning to rise, giving the sky a slate blue tinge. The waning moon was still visible.

"Why didn't she just open the door?" Annie wondered. "If she was in there struggling with someone who slit her throat?"

"No, she wasn't inside with someone. I don't think so, anyway. Not like what you're suggesting. There were about five hundred pounds of sugar blocking the door. She couldn't have possibly moved it. I'm sure she's less than a hundred pounds."

"But that means someone else placed the sugar in front of the door while she was in there."

"She was probably already dead when they did. But restaurants get deliveries all times of the day and night. Check with Pamela on that," Ruth said, opening her car door. "Call me later. I may have some answers for you then."

"Okay," Annie said and stepped back from the car. She had enough to file her first story on the case. But she'd need more for the complete story. A lot more.

She mentally sorted through the evidence and possibilities. She didn't know which was worse—the fact the young woman could have met her death in the freezer, crawling inside to get away from someone or that someone had killed her and then stored her dead body inside.

Connect with Us

Visit us online at
KensingtonBooks.com
to read more from your favorite authors, see books
by series, view reading group guides, and more.